# Augusta Cotton

# *Augusta Cotton*

Margaret Erhart

Z
ZOLAND BOOKS
CAMBRIDGE, MASSACHUSETTS

First edition published in 1992 by
Zoland Books, Inc.,
384 Huron Avenue, Cambridge, MA 02138

PUBLISHER'S NOTE:
This book is a work of fiction. Names, characters, places, and incidents are either the product of the author's imagination or are used fictitiously. Any resemblance to actual events or locales or persons, living or dead, is entirely coincidental.



Library of Congress Catalog Card Number 92–53830

ISBN 0-944072-21-6

First edition
Printed in the United States of America
Text design by Boskydell Studio

*Library of Congress Cataloging-in-Publication Data*

Erhart, Margaret.
Augusta Cotton / Margaret Erhart. — 1st ed.
p. cm.
ISBN 0-944072-21-6 : $19.95
I. Title.
PS3555.R426A95 1992 92-53830
813′.54—dc20 CIP

# Acknowledgments

Thanks to Dan Lewis and his computer, Laurence Enjolras, Roger Frye, a man called Dennis at the St. Aubin tree nursery, my writing friends Melanie Braverman, Sarah Randolph, Louise Rafkin and Janie Lea. The Dr. Erharts: my sister Toria and my brother Stephen. Neither one is responsible for what's written here, but when called upon they said yes, no, maybe and you're kidding, until I had enough information to make my own choices. Dr. Lucy Painter, Lew Steiger, Katina Rodis, Leslie McGrath. The Wellfleet Library. My friend and agent, Malaga Baldi. Thank you.

*It is the last dream of children,*
*to be forever untouched.*

—AUDRE LORDE

# Introduction

On the summer solstice of 1985 my brother was robbed of ten dollars and severely beaten on the head. The next day, aphasic and partially blind, he was admitted to the Hartford Hospital, where his head was opened up and blood clots removed. When his condition deteriorated he underwent a second operation to relieve the swelling in his head, which, we were told as we gathered around him—his parents and four sisters and brothers from all over the country—would probably kill him. He was given a one in ten chance to live, and virtually no chance at a normal life if he did survive. For anyone who has experienced this kind of prognosis there is what I can only describe as an immediate ringing numbness at the core of the body, an awakeness, an aliveness that refuses not to hope.

David was in bed number 1 of the intensive care unit for three weeks. Next to him a young man named Raoul, who had broken his neck, raged at the indignity of paralysis. For a week his girlfriend raged with him, then she stopped coming. As I sat with David day in and day out, Radclyffe

Hall's *The Well of Loneliness* unread in my lap, I felt deeply sorry for Raoul and his family and his girlfriend. And yet as he roared and thumped his head against the bed, and as my brother slept deeply, silently, unconsciously, his shaven head motionless on the pillow and the gasping of his respirator inhibiting my own breathing, I tried and failed to feel for everyone, every endangered body in that room, the same hopeful ringing numbness I felt for David. It must be very personal, this is what I thought.

My brother recovered completely, and since then I have experienced core hope for many other people, some of them close to me, most of them not. I simply refuse not to envision them if not alive, at least at peace. Peace, I have discovered, can be a harder road to travel than life. It must be made, unlike life, which we assume, correctly or incorrectly, is simply given—or taken, as was almost the case with my brother.

Whenever I am deeply grateful for an experience I write a book about it. And I dedicate that book to the person whose fate crossed mine with enough momentum to awaken me.

M. E.

*Truro*
*April, 1992*

For David

Augusta Cotton

# Chapter One

When we were eleven, Helen Walsh fell sick with something I'd never heard of, something that would be with her, inside of her, for the rest of her life. The name of it was lupus, "the wolf," and it attacked and retreated just like a wolf did, though in Helen's case it was more attack than retreat. Her remissions were short, and even then the spirit of the animal was present. She knew it, and so we had to know it too.

When she felt well and told me so, I was filled with equal parts of relief and dread, knowing how few were the weeks or days until the rash flared up once more and her joints burned and her tongue grew thick in her mouth so she could hardly speak or swallow. Wellness, for Helen, only meant having to become sick again too soon. How I hated that! It was a cruel year, the year of awakening, full of a sense of how dearly we paid for what we hadn't chosen.

Because I couldn't bring myself to study up on lupus that year, I learned about wolves instead, and I would bring Helen certain books and clipped articles about those animals, the ones that showed them in a good light, not as killers, but as inquisitive and even gentle creatures. "Here it shows they're vegetarians," I lied, spreading a picture book across her lap on one of my frequent after-school visits to her bed. I let the edge of the blanket fall across the bottom of the page. The picture was of a white wolf, its snout deep in the arctic wildflowers, but it was chewing on something, half hidden by the blanket, that Helen or anyone else who looked closely could see was a mangled rat or rabbit.

At times like this she said nothing, she only seemed to regard me with endless patience, as if she sympathized with me for having to try and deceive her. In the beginning of her illness I was always ready to deceive her. It was the only way I knew to make her well.

Once my propaganda took the form of a history lesson: "If not for a wolf, did you know there wouldn't have been a Roman Empire?" She liked history. She was good at it, and she could have said much more than she did. "The Romans were cruel people, Gussy. They killed anyone they didn't like, including children. If there hadn't been a Roman Empire, I don't think it would have been missed."

We were close friends. I had never had a close friend until Helen, and until me she had never had a friend at all. Her family was considered peculiar: no father, possibly a sister or brother who didn't live at home, and a mother who fascinated and frightened us. Her name was Jordan, and Helen called her that. She was extremely tall and broad-shouldered, and her body seemed to hang straight down from her shoulders like a door. Her hair was dark, streaked with gray, and she wore it loose down her back, though the first time I saw her she had it up in a twist that accentuated the great length of her neck. I was no older than six at the time, in a setting I don't remember though it must have been at our school, and her appearance impressed me so deeply that several years later, when I first heard the expression "the nape of the neck," those words brought her vividly, electrically to mind. I sensed danger and something too suggestive about them. It was a curious, slightly disturbing feeling to have involved Jordan Walsh in my thoughts, thoughts I could no longer control. I remember staring at the radio (I had been listening to a program about the Japanese kimono), unsure whether to wish "the nape of the neck" back into it or to ask for more. In the end, I simply asked for clarification; I needed more knowledge. It was not long afterwards, in the fall, just weeks before she got sick, that Helen and I began to be drawn to one another as if in answer to a prayer.

I knew her only slightly. We were schoolmates, classmates, and if her often sour expressions were any indication, we shared a dislike for sixth grade, a disappointment in the turn our lives had taken, apparently on their own, since the summer after fifth. We could not control who we were—those were the words behind the feelings; though a moment ago, or what seemed like it, we were who we were, that was all and it was enough. There weren't even any words for it. There wasn't even an "it."

Helen lived across the river, in the part of the town that was shaped like a thumb. I lived in the palm of the hand, near the base of the little finger, and my friends were the other girls who lived in the palm, or in one of the four fingers. My friends and I rode the public bus to and from school. It was twice as fast as the school bus and didn't break down as often. School was a yellow brick building near the river, on our side of it. The boys went to school across the river, in the old red building that had once held all the schoolchildren. My mother had gone to school there and remembered it as dusty and chalky inside, with not one tree around it for amusement or shade.

The name of our school, Pacific No. 9, was written in a darker colored brick over the arched entryway, and as I began to learn geography I was baffled by the minds of our great educators, who had chosen to call a school after an ocean two thousand miles away. And why not Atlantic No. 9? That seemed no more illogical. The 9 was troublesome as well, for it implied a 1 through 8 which didn't exist and never had. (The boys' school was not numbered. It was named after a former mayor of the town, Sophia Milk.) Perhaps "pacific," "peaceful" is what the founders of the school were getting at, though that hopeful adjective lay at a distance from us measurable not by miles but by years. If, at eleven, I'd had to mark serenity on a map, I couldn't have—or as an act of desperation I would have found the geographical center of China and put it there.

Our school was built on the edge of a park, which we weren't allowed to play in because our shoes would uproot the grass. Upstream from the park, three bridges stitched the thumb to the palm of the hand, and Helen walked to school over one of them, a footbridge that reminded me of the skeleton of a large dinosaur. I had never actually seen her on it, and there was a closer bridge with cars which she could have crossed on, but the footbridge was how I imagined her getting from her side of the river to ours, and that fall I asked her if this was true and she said yes. It wasn't the first exchange we'd ever had, only the most personal. If the question surprised her, she didn't show it, she just rolled her bottom lip over her top one, and there the conversation stopped.

We began that year together in a music class, where for a brief time we studied the string instruments. I noticed how

Helen liked to wrap her arms around her cello; how she took any opportunity to lift it by its waist and walk with it tucked against her, like a man and a woman walking by the river, or skating together. Sometimes she would crush the strings against her, holding the cello as if she were dancing with a partner. Or when she sat with it propped between her knees, if she wasn't playing, she liked to run the heel of her hand up and down the glossy front of it, with her fingers held slightly up off the wood, and spread. She would close her eyes at these times to make herself invisible as I watched her.

When she played, she was good. She was better than all of us who chewed our lips in concentration but could not make the right note jump from our cellos or violins. At the end of one particularly difficult hour, when we'd happened to share a music stand and I complained to her that my neck felt like a rubber carrot and I would rather walk around with a monkey on my shoulder, Helen surprised me and took the side of the violin. "If you haven't got the heart for your instrument, why is it the fault of the instrument?" I'd never heard anyone say anything like this before, and my skin tingled.

That wasn't the only time she caused this feeling in me. As the weeks passed it happened more and more often, when I watched her crossing her bridge in the afternoons, or sitting at a table of other silent girls in the lunchroom, eating a jelly sandwich she'd brought from home. I imagined sometimes she stole glances at me over the top of her black, barn-shaped lunch box, and though I never sat with her—I didn't dare to—whenever possible I sat so she could see me without turning her head. If she would only look up at me and let me catch her looking! One day I watched her in a class we didn't share. It was a gym class, and she had her back to the tall fence that surrounded the dirt lot where we all played kickball and punchball, and when we were younger, freeze tag and red rover. I was in an art class, looking down at her from a window on the second floor. I had been drawing the river and some of the buildings on the other side of it, and the footbridge that crossed it, before I spotted Helen. It seemed like a lucky coincidence, so I put her in the drawing too.

Just then Julia Swann, who was the perfect athlete of our grade, sent a red India rubber ball high into the air above Helen's head and over the fence. It arced towards me, and as it did, Helen turned and looked up at the window where I sat. She always seemed more interested in athletics than any good at them, and now she was interested in the destination of that red rubber ball and watched it carefully for the new world it might open up to her.

She saw me. I saw her see me, but then the ball crashed to the ground outside the dirt lot, onto a sidewalk or grass, and she no longer had a reason to look my way. She bent her head, more than she had to I thought, and walked over to the fence, where she did what I'd seen photographs of in a picture book about war: her fingers slipped into the chain link as if they were trying on big rings. She must have said something to a person outside the fence, and the ball came flying back over her head so again she had a chance to look up at me and this time she didn't look away. Neither of us adjusted our faces the way I was used to doing with people at school, to say something we didn't mean to say. She held her fence, and I had a piece of construction paper in front of me. I was the one who broke the spell—I simply became afraid and held up the paper, which had the beginning of a drawing of Helen in one corner of it, which of course she couldn't see.

## • 7 •

Soon after that we began to speak to each other, though it wasn't the kind of talk that would tell you who the other person liked, or what foods they liked, or even what interested them. Helen didn't say much to anyone, but when she did, I noticed, it came out sounding like a riddle or the answer to one. She wasn't a bus girl, but every Friday after we were dismissed at noon, she had to take the bus to B Street for some kind of appointment, and these afternoons were filled with our halting conversations. I had never felt so tongue-tied around anyone and filled with thoughts at the same time, thoughts that couldn't or wouldn't form themselves into sentences or words—even now I can't say them as they should have been said. For I had hit the limits of language and didn't know it, and blamed it on my own ineptitude as I retreated to a form of communication all its own, and pure, such as the animals use. I could look at Helen, or thought I could, the way I looked at her holding the fence in her gym class, and a conversation seemed sealed inside those moments; we achieved in a glance what we had lost, our old *we are what we are,* that perfect ease and comfort with one another and ourselves.

As a result, I began to notice how mundane and childish the concerns of my friends were, and often on our walks to the bus stop Helen and I would trail behind Julia the athlete, and Deirdre George, whose parents were rumored to be spies, or poor intelligent Agnes Mill with her crooked glasses, who only rode the bus on Fridays, as Helen did. I would look at the backs of these girls who were or had been my friends and wish them away forever, wish their quibbling, giggling, teasing away forever.

One Friday afternoon near the end of November, Helen and I were on our way to the bus stop, and I remember we'd almost been able to articulate some ideas that ran very deep and strong in us about the power of our own thoughts. At least we'd gotten far enough to understand that we agreed on certain things, such as this power was new since the summer, and as exhilarating as it was, it was also scary and confusing. It made us responsible for things we wanted no part in; Helen could see where it might one day make us responsible for everything. It was no wonder we felt out of control, or, as she put it, as if our selves had been cut out of us in an operation while we were asleep. The next thing to go, though neither of us said it, would clearly be our bodies. Helen's body had already started to slip, and a new one was beginning to grow. It was impossible not to notice it under her clothes.

The thought of that made me suddenly dizzy, and I took hold of her sleeve and pulled her closer to me as we walked. This was new for us, to touch, but she didn't say a word and I confessed to her that just that week I'd wished away my friends. "Now it frightens me, Helen. I wish I hadn't done it."

"Those things are hard to undo," she nodded, and just then the wind blew a cellophane wrapper from a Hostess cake against the shoulder of my coat, where it fluttered for a second and I was about to call it a butterfly, but then it flattened itself like a live bird struck and carried by the windshield of a car.

The bus came and we got on it. I flashed my pass, but she had to stand at the front and search her pockets for fifteen cents to put in the money box next to the driver. She didn't have her change ready because she didn't like buses and she still wasn't used to taking them, and together we were no good at reminding each other what the world would require of us.

I recognized the bus driver right away. He was a bald

man who sat lower in his seat than other drivers did, and he never wore his cap, so we were forced to look at a large, black birthmark shaped like India at the top of his head. The teardrop below India had landed on his forehead, above his left eye. He told Helen he couldn't keep the whole world waiting for fifteen cents. He waved her on, then his knees moved and the bus lurched forward. She grabbed for a rail, any rail, and missed and fell and hit her shoulder on the metal money box. The driver stopped the bus and told her to get back behind the white line and sit down.

She came down the aisle, pale and shaking, and sat next to me. "What white line is he talking about?" She was holding her shoulder. "You see, it's the same shoulder where you got hit with the cake wrapper. I hope this is the end of it."

"But it's your shoulder, Helen."

"The yours and mine part doesn't necessarily matter."

This was the fist time I'd seen her hurt in any way, though others were twisting their ankles or spraining their thumbs all the time—not just Julia, not just friends, but all around us the earth was covered with injuries. The bus itself had become a deer with an arrow in its side as it lurched, a shot animal stepping off the earth for the last time. This thought, this split-second connection left me so lonely I wanted to hold Helen's sleeve again, or say something. I asked her if she'd ever seen anything killed by a person.

"Yes. A lot of spiders."

"Nothing bigger than a spider?"

"I cut down a tree once."

"I've killed a fish."

"Oh. I was in the front seat when Jordan ran over a cat."

"Our cat used to bring in rabbits and some of them were dead," I said.

"A cat's not a person."

"Yes, but if they weren't dead I killed them."

"That was to save them from pain."

"We had to shoot a dog once. It went crazy."

"Never mind. It would have killed you," she said, and shifted in the seat so her knees were sticking into the aisle.

It frightened me to think how much larger our victims might have become, and how willingly I'd confessed my part in their deaths. To speak the words "I killed"; it was like the taste of blood in your mouth. It awakened memories long and quickly buried, as they'd buried the head of that dog in the same instant they shot it, threw a shovelful of dirt at its snout and warned us not to go near it. If Helen hadn't steered us away, who knows? I probably could have come up with a bear I'd killed, or seen killed. I could certainly come up with a cow.

I'd lingered behind the others to put my hand on it in the eerie, filtered twilight of the clearing behind Aunt Bella's house, where it lay, shot by a no-luck poacher who needed an easy target. It was just a calf after all, and I couldn't help but think, *Like me, like me.* I touched the leg because I didn't trust the head's backwards angle, the two eyes as if behind windows and impossibly long-lashed. I didn't trust the belly, which was bloated and seemed diseased, and the leg offered itself—all four of them did; they stuck straight up in the air with no bend or give to them at all. Was that what made us alive, the bend? the give? It felt wooden, and not part of anyone or anything's body. Keeping my back to the eyes, I made myself move on, move up the leg until some understanding of flesh came to me through my fingers, there where the leg joined the body. I held my breath against the smell and counted five. There was no warmth, yet under the stiffness, a softness. I yanked my hand away and ran to catch up, trying to tell myself I hadn't liked it but it had been necessary.

I let the window of the bus distract me. It was cold and hard that day, I could feel it through my coat as I leaned against it. This was my favorite part of the ride, where the route turned away from the river and its sycamore trees, to a world of streets named alphabetically beginning with Z. Zoroaster Street, nicknamed Zorro by those of us who, young and small, had needed the meaning of every block to be within our reach. Zoroaster was slippery, ungraspable, but Zorro! Even his mask hid nothing from us, until we were older and began to imagine him without it.

We named the river too, many times over. We sat, a small stone-throwing gang, on its bank one day when we were seven or eight, and as each girl tossed her rock she called out a word, and the word, attached to the rock, sank into the river as her gift to it. It seemed an impressively spiritual act for such young people, though the words fell apart almost immediately, became irreverent and allowed us to say and giggle over and bury all the indelicate language we were just beginning to attract. Precocious Deirdre, child of the CIA and a year older than the rest of us, started us off with "intercourse." Ashley Hobb, who eavesdropped on her older sister Gloria, tossed a puzzling one, "Kotex," into the water a few feet from the bank. I remember Helen was with us that day, looking miserable, and she waited to throw her rock until right before I did, after the more frightening girls had laughed all they wanted and moved away. She was a serious person, with a thin face and a head too large for her body, but already long-legged. Her hair was brown and medium length, and on a day of rain or high humidity it became wavy. She looked at her rock, then she looked at the river, then she looked at me, then at her rock again, so it was the rock she spoke to. "I have a mother named Jordan, and that's what I'd like to call this river, but there's already a Jordan River, Gussy, so what do I do now?"

I was surprised to be made part of her decision, and in the end we both tossed a rock and called the name "Harriet" after it, which was my mother's name, so twice it became the river Harriet. *Our stones are still sunk there,* I thought, and turned away from Redjay Street, for the next one would be Pine, and it always disturbed me that *q* had been skipped over. It was like a tooth missing.

Inside the bus we were forced farther back in our seats as the hill rose from under us and we slowly labored up it. I loved to look through the back window at this time, and always hoped the bus might give up and hang there, right at the top, and please me with an endless view. On the side of the river where Helen lived the buildings were lower and poorer, and they looked blank and white at this time of day, with the sun directly on them, the river curling in front of them like a slow, blinding snake. There was the tall smoke-stack of the factory, and the factory itself, a mass of silver, blinding windows, and not far from it was her house. "Look!" I touched Helen's leg, and pointed with my head, backwards, but she wouldn't have any part of it. She said she felt carsick facing that direction.

And who didn't? And who doesn't, daring a long look over the shoulder to behold the inscrutable past? But to see, you have to be willing to look, and that day I was. Which was why, at the crest of the hill, the word "rapture" came to me, my private understanding of it, as around us the light and sympathetic traffic flashed sunlight in mirrors and glass. In my mind I caught sight of a younger Helen in Miss Blue Teal's music class—she was a Harriet too, Miss Harriet Blue Teal; it seemed like a made-up name. The rest of us were singing a fourth-grade song about a fox and grapes, but not Helen. Her mouth opened and closed without a sound, as if a door had swung shut in her throat, and she pointed out the window at our river. There, gliding by like an iron on a silk pant leg, just beyond the braids and blue tunics of our friends lined up at the dirt lot fence, was a submarine. Impossible in our little river, but we must have needed a submarine that day, and that's what we called it. Not one of us had ever seen a real submarine before, though they often showed up in the sea on television. But television, where everything was black and white or gray, hadn't prepared us for this: this submarine was a bright, baby blue! How odd it was to see it out where it didn't belong, in sunlight, in air, in our river, with its little crew of sailors standing in a fenced-in area on the top side, waving their arms and hats at our schoolmates, who looked just like them—except the fence around the dirt lot was higher, and the girls had no hats to wave, and shorter arms.

"All boats are shes," Harriet Blue Teal informed us, "as are tropical storms." She stood on her toes, her face rapturously melted against the window, and her lips looked suddenly thicker; the tip of her tongue showed between them. Even as the submarine passed before us, I glanced at her, and her eyes were half shut, dreaming or drowsy, while the rest of her body lengthened and quivered as if she were squeezing something between her knees. For the rest of the hour she was unable to return to the world of music, to the trouble of school, and this alarmed me, though it delighted everyone else. I'd glimpsed her emboldened for a moment, but by what? She was our shy teacher who rarely spoke or lifted her head in class, yet with the passing of a submarine she had shown me a posture—but more than that—a depth I recognized as adult.

Surrounded by my hooting, cheering, waving friends, I wished it had never surfaced and had instead cut its clean way up the river unseen. If Harriet Blue Teal were two people, if I would someday be, I didn't want to know it yet; I didn't want to see it, that look on her face as she gazed through the only pane in the window not fogged by the breath of her students. I was not too young, at nine, to recognize rapture, but not old enough to be anything but afraid of it. For the rest of the week I avoided the windows of every classroom and determined to get a hall pass for the bathroom if the submarine should appear again, as it had to, to get back to where it came from and where it belonged. I hated it. But it must have traveled at night, or possibly it was headed upriver on its last voyage, to be scuttled, because no one saw it again; and my own feelings about it were absorbed by the larger, simpler state of being who I was, *we are who we are*. Soon enough, it was forgotten.

Until this view from the top of the hill, when for the second time a loneliness rushed in on me and I wanted to pull Helen into a conversation, but she was no longer beside me. The bus was filling up, which always happened between Pine and Dorothy, those thirteen crowded blocks of the alphabet. More people got on than got off, and now a woman with a package and a reddish pinpricked nose wanted Helen's seat, then the minute she moved on, a man did. "There's elderly people, honey. You don't keep a seat empty when there's elderly." But I'd already planted my arm, and I didn't move it.

I looked around for Helen and saw her sitting across the aisle, two rows behind, next to a woman who didn't look like someone she would know. She was glamorous but not pretty, with puffy hair of a tired blond color, and enough makeup to indicate she might be an actress. Even her neck was made up, down to the collar of her fur coat. The fur was dull, and thin across the shoulders, as if whatever animal it was had never been fed properly. She was picking things out of a carton of Chinese food, sorting through the food with her fingers and pulling out what looked like tiny shrimp. She wasn't eating them; they just came out of the carton and went back in. They were shiny because they were greasy and wet, but in the fingers of that woman they could have been artificial gems.

Helen said something to her, and the woman cocked her head to the side like a bird on a roof listening to an airplane. Her hand stayed inside the carton and didn't move; then someone in the aisle blocked my view.

The bus was moving in little jerks, through traffic, passing the drugstore on Mozart Street, where a window sign advertised Dr. Scholl's foot pads, and behind that were the loofah sponges, lined up like stones on a tidy beach. I'd once bought a tortoiseshell comb in that drugstore, though now it embarrassed me to go in there; it was too dangerous. The two aisles were full of suggestive boxes and bottles with confusing labels that never really told you what you were looking at, or worse, what you'd already touched. Everything that started with a "c" or a "v" I was suspicious of; I blushed at the words "ooze" and "lubricant." And the naked foot in the window made my skin crawl in an ugly way. Even the smell inside the store I now associated with all things out of my control: "c" and "v" words, yes, but any word with a hard sound in the middle of it, or a soft "oo" sound, or with too many syllables or too few. Nothing was safe, nothing was beyond my judgment, nothing was incapable of hurting or embarrassing me. Everything was tied to rapture. Every evening there was rapture in the unembarrassed cries of the neighborhood women calling in their cats. Every morning and afternoon that rapture hung above me in the bus: "Heartbreak of Psoriasis" posters; advertisements for Preparation H in which the word "hemorrhoid" was enough to cause a small disturbance that I wouldn't recover from until the doors broke open and I pushed my way off the bus and into the neutral glare and safety of the street. Even the doors sighing open, or springing open with a jolt as they did on the older buses; these, too, were the sounds, the dogged, relentless motions of rapture.

Now the Mozart Street drugstore, which I usually turned my head not to see, swept through me—it felt like the store itself passed into my body from front to back. As it did, a woman up front shouted, "No! Oh God, no! We're not human!" I could see her. She held a radio to her ear, a small transistor radio. The bus rolled off the street to the curb. A noisy, flapping sound was coming from under our feet, and inside a few people were screaming.

Helen found me then and reminded me how to sit with my head between my knees, something we'd learned from school air raid drills. Our sides were touching and our faces hung down, almost touching. I told her, "It's a flat tire, that's all."

"It's more than that. Otherwise he'd be letting people off."

"Maybe the doors are jammed."

"It's the cake wrapper again, Gussy. It's that damn cake wrapper."

The woman with the radio turned it up so the bus was filled with loud static. I raised my head, and in the narrow break between two people I saw Helen's friend, the actress, close the lid on the Chinese food. It was like seeing her in a doorway, and as I watched there came that depth again, the warning of an adult world in the slow way she licked her fingers and wiped them on her hair. Then everyone in the aisles began to move at the same time, some with their hands in the air as if they were being poked with a gun, and some with faces so still they could have been a drawing or a photograph. Their shoes were loud on the floor of the bus because now the screaming had stopped, all the shouting and radio noise had stopped, and whatever had stopped it had been unusual and important news that made strangers rush at one another with their arms up and their faces showing nothing but how badly they wanted not to be afraid.

I had missed it. I had been busy watching that woman. It had come across the radio and Helen had heard it, and now as the loud crying and screaming started up again she dragged my head down next to hers, which was still between her knees. Below the seat it was quieter and she could tell me, "The president, Gussy, Kennedy's been shot."

We learned on a bus what some people learned in the street, or at home in bed, or in a chair, or at school standing up, bending over, pulling their arms back to throw something, or their legs to kick something, or their lips to laugh out loud. I smiled at the news and Helen reassured me that this was what people often did, they smiled. My cheeks ached, my whole face hurt from it, but it stuck there even after I covered it with my hand.

It was impossible, after that, to ride the bus past Mozart Street without feeling a shot go through me, and a confused sense that whatever the root of rapture was, the root of murder was the same. It lay there in the drugstore, whose shadow deepened and lengthened against the sidewalk every time I rode by and didn't look away; and more and more often I didn't look away. It was inside me when I ran from a calf in a clearing, the first time I'd been carried somewhere I didn't mean to go, by touch. In Harriet Blue Teal's face I saw it, on her lips; and in the fingers and murderous hair of that actress. I could find it in my own parents if I looked, or in Jordan Walsh; and someday Helen and I would live entirely in that world too, wouldn't we? Or was it possible to cut around it, to become old children together?

I had a sense of the globe for the first time in my life. It was round, not pear-shaped, and though people died daily and were born as we woke or as we ate, we didn't welcome them or wish them off because we couldn't feel them anymore. Only a very few could we feel, and more often we could only feel ourselves. But sometimes, as on the bus, a death, a birth, even an idea, an accident or an illness, broke us open; it widened us, as the wide view from space widened the astronauts, and without knowing it or trying to, they wrote notes for the earth to hear in a language more beautiful than any they'd ever used before, full of contentment and praise.

# Chapter Two

Before the winter vacation, on the day the sixth grade was scheduled to sit through a movie called *Precious Life,* Helen Walsh stayed home with the flu and didn't return to school until January. On that December day I envied her. I sat with an empty seat on either side of me in the school auditorium, which also served as the lunchroom, wishing I were anywhere in the world but there. I felt as hollow as that room felt hollow, for there was no one to trust, we were changing by the minute. Our only constant was our need not to luxuriate in a self we might own for a day or for an hour, because by tomorrow—especially if we loved it—it would surely be gone.

The twins, Rachel and Annabel Jones, sat down the row from me. They were a homely pair, surprisingly mannish for young girls. They were bent over a thin pamphlet called "Welcome to Womanhood!" Annabel was turning the pages as fast as she could, but Rachel kept laying a hand on her wrist to stop her. "Will you *look* at that!" she whispered. "That's never going to happen to me. I'm never going to do that."

"You will," said Annabel cruelly.

"Annabel, no! Will *you*?"

"Of course. Everybody does."

I hated her for that. My own copy of "Welcome to Womanhood!" had burned a hole in my pocket all week as I carried it around unopened, hoping somehow to absorb its information through my clothes and skin. For we were told we'd be tested on it. We laughed in disbelief! To be asked to fill a page with what had only been whispered illicitly among us—or once, on that rare occasion, been spoken aloud as we tossed our rocks into the concealing waters of the river Harriet? Impossible!

Just then somebody flicked off the lights, and behind me I heard the rickety projector start up, beginning to unwind its lethal message. But *Precious Life* was so old and frail that hardly a minute went by without a breakdown, and if you hadn't guessed the truth about reproduction you never could have learned it from that movie. What I remember most clearly is two tall, sweating glasses of milk, odd hairstyles and appliances, and the soft, humorous swearing of our young science teacher, Mrs. Strand, who was acting as projectionist that day. Not far into it she was relieved of her job, as the father cried, "Let's talk!" and the mother and teenage daughter sat down after clearing the table, and the teenage son spread his prodigious hands on the table and coughed. There the film suddenly became twisted up in itself, and in one great moment all the embarrassed, coughing teenagers of the world joined the one on the screen, multiplying themselves a hundred blurry times in spirit, in image, until with a fizzle and a pop the film simply melted. There appeared what looked like a giant cigarette burn, followed by a bad smell and a blast of white light from the projector. Everyone hooted and laughed—except for a few of us who were silent, troubled by having seen how easily the life of a family, precious or not, could come to an end.

"You're in a funk," observed my father, parting dumplings to scoop the chicken neck from the stew.

"We're studying reproduction," I said. "I hate reproduction."

"You wait," he laughed. "You may find it useful." He fished with a spoon and couldn't find the neck anywhere. "Where is the darn thing? You're sure it's in here, Harriet?"

"God help me I should buy a headless chicken! It clings to the bottom, Julian. I know it for a fact." But when he found it, clinging, and served it to my mother, she begged him, "Take it. You don't want it? Go on, take it!"

He shook his head. I could hardly bear to look or hear as she sucked it greedily, stopping only to clean her teeth of the meat with her tongue.

She had once been a nervy, robust woman—"plenty of verve," she said of others like her, and "plenty of good looks"; a "young" thirty-eight when she married. But something had yoked her spirit, which year by year diminished her physical beauty until she sat before us as she did now, thin and pinched, taking her one weekly pleasure in the neck of a chicken, which she couldn't enjoy until she'd first flung it at her loved ones. "Take it from me!" she seemed to beg, "damn me for my appetite! Go on, Augusta, try it! Don't say you don't like till you try!" She thrust her plate at me or held the neck in her trembling hand and passed it in front of my nose as if the smell alone must move me to reach out and grab it. I was never tempted. Neither was my father. She said this was the mincing gentile in us both, and without her we would find a cat to throw it to.

Now, as I watched, she sucked and swallowed, almost smiling around the bone as she teased the meat from it. How seldom I saw my mother's old, vibrant self aroused! But always the neck aroused it, like a thin, bony bridge she crossed to enter the spirit and body of the Harriet she'd once been. Her voice often raised, she used to roar in the silence of our house: "So, what? You're not proud to be a Jew?" I was eight or nine at the time, and assigned to fit the history of my family onto five blue lines. My mother cocked her eye at me. "Your grandfather built every bridge in this town, and he was a Jew. Tell them you're a Jew! Write for the teacher you're a Jew and an American. There!" She stabbed the page with her finger, leaving an inky smudge.

"It's got to be longer, Mama. It's got to go from here to here. And we're supposed to be one thing." I made this up. "Not a lot of things."

"Two's a lot? A Jew and an American? Who's one thing? Five lines for one thing! Give the pencil." And she wrote:

> Augusta Cotton of Flat and Second Street whose parents are Dr.
> Julian and Mrs. Harriet Cotton is one thing, a Jewish
> American [she erased American] North American girl whose
> grandfather built the three bridges in front of your nose,
> and whose other grandfather sold mink coats made from minks
> he shot himself in Canada.

"It's too long," I said. The last five words hung down on a sixth line.

"Easy. We'll fix that." She put a period after "minks." She laughed. "Go tell your father his father shot himself in Canada!"

◆ 23 ◆

I showed the page to Julian, who reminded me that though everything on it was true, what wasn't on it kept it from truly representing me. "In other words"—he raised his head to scrutinize the assignment through the bifocals he wore low on his nose—"you've omitted the one half for the sake of the other. You're Jewish, Gustopher, but you're equally Protestant French. That's not conveyed by the term North American, I'm afraid."

"But I'm too many things, Papa!"

"Never mind. It's better than being too few." He turned his attention to the page again. "To say someone sold mink coats made from minks is redundant, and when you erase, as you've done on the line below it, you needn't press so hard. It looks like you've spilled pink oatmeal."

His only other comment was that to tell a teacher what was or wasn't in front of her nose might not be the best way to endear myself to her. He suggested I change the wording to "the three bridges here in town," or simply "our three bridges."

"Dull," sniffed Harriet, eavesdropping. "Dry as a book."

"My dear," he said, "I don't think it's always wise to be too colorful."

"So let her be as colorful as what she's made of. She's a person of nice blood and flesh. That's not colorful?"

But he closed his ears to her and would not argue, and I took this to mean they got along. If you love someone you look at the floor is what I understood from my father. And from my mother: For love you make yourself a slave.

For years she worked as my father's secretary and never drew a salary. His practice was well-established by the time I was born, but she continued to work and earn nothing, leaving me in the care of a neighbor for most of the day, or when I was older leaving me to play alone or entertain myself with friends. On most days my parents returned in the late afternoon, and if I was home I would pull a chair in front of the door and wait for them, hoping to notice a pleasant heat they gave off as they entered the house together, or a pleasant odor that lingered in their clothes, something to indicate what their world away from me offered, and why they chose it instead of my company. But the clue was never there. They came in grumbling, tired, smelling of carbon paper and ether, and it was a rare evening when they crossed the threshold at the same time, and never did I see them touch or so much as brush shoulders. In the warm weather my father would hang behind my mother to inspect his columbine, narcissus, phlox, foxglove, rubyslipper, impatiens, his great bushes of peonies, beds of roses and soft, trumpeting daylilies, his crab apple, muskapple, gentian, and creeping Charlie; in the winter he'd find something small to repair.

Once I heard her call him stingy, and he hushed her with a look that echoed from the four walls. Once she hissed at him, "It's for you I'm not a stay-at-home!" and he responded tersely: "Harriet, it would drive you mad." Little by little, year by year, she lost her voice, her nerve, her chosen, willful self. Even her hair thinned—it had always been thick, abundant and dark like mine, but spliced with gray. Her arms grew thin and weak looking. Even her ankles lost their strong, blocky character as if they'd been whittled away, and her body seemed to wave and wobble on them; I was afraid someday they would snap like a flag.

One hot night in the summer between fifth grade and sixth, my father and I were playing a game of old maid at the table, putting off our evening chore of washing and drying the dishes. We had the windows open, and a breeze from Flat Street was playing woman-in-the-curtains, bulging and billowing the flimsy material until one arm of white organdy came to rest on Julian's shoulder. We laughed as it moved off again, brushing the side of his face.

Just then my mother came into our tiny, narrow kitchen wearing an emerald green satin dress covered with a layer of black lace. The dress was not tight fitting or revealing, but the lace made it dangerous, to my eyes more daring and sexy. She was not a poser, but she almost posed in the doorway. As she approached the table her voice was careful, but firm and clear as it used to be. She looked directly at my father. She said she'd bought the dress but would return it if he didn't like it. "It costs, but I think we can afford it, Julian." The breeze pushed at her hair and at the skirt of her dress. Her face seemed so beautiful to me. Everything about that dress made her beautiful and expectant, and he didn't like it, and she cried and went out of the kitchen and we never saw it again.

In memory it always came to me as a green flame, her spirit. Since that day there had been something so missing from the house, at times I found myself upturning objects in the bedroom they shared—a roll of stamps on the dresser, a mezuzah—or searching her small, square jewelry box that held nothing but a pair of scallop-shaped earrings and a pin that I said I LIKE IKE. Or I lay across the bed they both slept in and wondered what it would be like to be him, to be her. Soon after that night in the kitchen she stopped working for my father and he hired a secretary, a woman named Mrs. Gott, whose plainness my mother approved of. Harriet and I looked for ways to become close, as other daughters and mothers who stayed at home were close, but it was an experiment that failed after only a few weeks, and, restless, she became the bookkeeper for the Woolworth's store, and later for the drugstore on Mozart Street, and the fire department.

My father was seven years younger than my mother (a humiliation I seemed to suffer alone). He had a long, almost comically long face, capped by a widow's peak and dark hair rushing everywhere. I was so unused to thinking of him as anyone but my father, I remember the extreme discomfort I felt one day when it occurred to me that the newborns once coughing, sputtering and crying naked in his hands had all grown up to be my friends. He was their doctor. He had held them. He had stuck a finger in to clean the green goo from their air passages. He had searched the perfection of their tiny, naked bodies, meticulously counting fingers and toes and heartbeats—even orifices! I shivered, and worried aloud to Harriet, who only scolded me for setting a cat among the pigeons.

"I don't even know what that means!" I protested.

"It means thank God you're a child, and children aren't punished for their thoughts."

Aren't they? I wondered. I was sure they were.

Julian used to bring me small presents from work—tongue depressors, empty boxes with my surname printed in large block letters under the words "Johnson & Johnson," whose sound I loved; and, best of all, surgical gloves the color of swiss cheese and chalky inside. These I liked to inflate or fill with water and play with.

One day I found myself too old for these tokens and unable to tell him so. Instead, I held a glove at arm's length, as if it were my own hand and repulsive to me. "They're too thin," I complained.

"No thinner than they've ever been."

"They leak and blow up in my face."

"If they were thicker we wouldn't be able to feel as much."

"What do you need to feel so much for?"

"Think a minute."

I counted to ten. "A minute's up."

He sighed loudly. "There are times when it's a profession of limited visibility, Gussy. That's when we learn to rely on our other senses, and touch is one of the most important ones."

I don't remember that he ever addressed me as a child, my father, and he encouraged the same frankness in me, but that day there was something newly disturbing about him wearing these flimsy things in public, or worse, carrying them home to me, and I could say nothing; I could only stand and scowl. For I was haunted and confused by an object that looked like them. That afternoon I'd stooped to pick it up off the sidewalk, but Harriet had yanked my arm and whispered, "Leave it! the filthy thing." Others had given us a wide berth.

Julian kept his hands impeccably clean; they shone with cleanliness. Once I was sure I saw the page of a book reflected in his palm. He was fastidious about his nails, which he trimmed so often they were never tipped with a crescent moon (a pleasant hiding place for germs, he explained). He could cut the nails of one hand himself, but not the other, and once or twice weekly, after we'd done and dried the dishes, he and Harriet would sit at the kitchen table with their sides touching—the only time I ever saw my parents touch—his hand in hers, and without calling it by name she would give him a manicure. Bending over him, squinting with her good eye, she would take time to find fault, but more kindly than usual, not in her chafing way. "Your pinkie's gone to pot, Julian. Look! Here's a hanging man, here and here!" "Hanging man" was my mother's expression for hangnail, and at these sessions she took them on like personal enemies. And though he never offered it to her, sometimes she would take and start to trim the nails on his other hand, the hand he could manage himself. "Weapons!" she would mutter, "Bayonets!" expertly rounding a square edge, or poking the scissors tips into his soft flesh to get at another hanging man. I was sure these moments were full of messages between them, intimate signs and signals from which I was excluded. If he stirred in his chair, or if she did, what did it mean? Or if a wordless sound came from him, was it a "hmmph" of satisfaction or dismay? Were they happy together? Did I please them? Were we a family? It seemed that only they were a family. They welcomed me into their evenings, but seldom into their lives. Two were a family, three were a bother, and though I might be called in to replace, I could not join.

One day, at the end of the summer before sixth grade, Harriet called me into the kitchen. "Come do for your father," she said, for her arthritic fingers ached and swelled like those gloves I'd inflated, until they no longer fit the scissors. I was given her chair at the table, but I couldn't sit close to my father or hold his hand—not with my mother coaching from behind, yet not without her. This was the summer of the green dress, and I was feeling uneasy, and it seemed unnecessary that we should all struggle so when there was an implement, I'd seen it hanging near the counter of the Woolworth's store where my mother worked, and it was made for just such a situation. The next day I went out and bought it and carried it home, and after supper that night I produced it.

"She would bribe us with gifts. This means what, Augusta?"

Julian picked it up. "It's a nail clipper." He turned it in his hand as if it were the wheel I'd invented and laid before him.

"Why's she spending her money on a nail clipper when we've got a perfectly good scissors?"

"Have you ever seen one before?" I asked.

"Sure, sure." Backhanded, she batted a strand of hair from her face.

"Well, they sell them in your store."

"And this is meant to impress me?"

"What's this for, Gustopher?"

Their obtuseness pressed me into a silence, troubled and deep. I only shrugged and left the kitchen, which had never, until that moment, felt so much their territory and theirs together, with no scrap of me in it. I waited out the week, expecting every evening to be called into service for my father, but not a word was said. He did for himself after that, and no longer in front of me, but bent over a wastebasket in the bedroom, where, with the door ajar, I might see his back and hear the deep metallic click of the clippers, which was never a happy sound. Once as I moved past, alert in all my useful senses, I thought the sawing sound of a nail file came to me, but I couldn't be sure.

In December we traveled to the city where my father's distant relatives lived. They were fussy, hunched-over people who didn't like children, so every time we visited them I walked myself to the Lands and People Museum, carrying a paper bag with a sandwich and a hard-boiled egg in it, and there I spent a few hours with crustaceans, or waited in line to see the dinosaur skeleton that Helen's footbridge reminded me of. I liked the museum. The air in it was heavier than any air I'd ever felt. It felt like water to me, and we who moved through it had the bodies of crayfish or crabs, or sea horses if we were gangly boys with jutting chins and jerky gaits, or barnacles if we were babies. Once, the elaborately swirled hair of one woman, southern by her accent, looked exactly like a shell called frilled dogwinkle.

Whenever I walked up the twenty-six steps to the museum and tugged on the high handles of its tall wooden doors, and joined a line that twice doubled back on itself before it ended in the great hall of the dinosaurs, I felt a sense of place and purpose, a proud burning in my head, like a fever, and a warmth down the front of my shirt as if I'd spilled a hot drink. I didn't have the words, but the sense was that I'd *volunteered* myself to history—it hadn't simply snatched me up. Here the steps were wide and the doors were warped and the line doubled back because history was generous and one-sided and repeated itself. When I wandered through Mollusks and Crustaceans, moving slowly, trailing a slow crowd, as if all of us walked with a rock tied to our ankles or a shell on our backs, I was happier and more content than anywhere in the world. It pleased me to do nothing but smell the cold faces and the warmth of an open coat, or to watch people fanning themselves with museum maps folded into shapes as odd and numerous as the shells of the oceans. The rooms felt deep and wide and shoreless, full of variety and noise and life. I saw a man faint once. I saw a whole family sway like a plant in front of a tank of live lobsters. I saw a young boy with idiot mittens on a long, itchy string around his neck, who kept flipping them back over his shoulder as if he were throwing away his own hands.

I was always glad to escape to the museum. In fact, it troubled me to think that one of these years, perhaps when I was twenty or thirty, I would no longer be considered a child by this cranky couple, and instead of running off, I would have to spend my time in one of their hard guest chairs, listening to them yawn and complain. But for the moment I was free, or relatively so. I took a new way to the museum to celebrate my freedom, and every street, every narrow, unknown alley offered itself to me with delicious promise. The sidewalks brought a salty-sweet taste to my mouth that at first I thought was my own sweat, but it was a cool day and I wasn't sweating. On one block of brown, two-story houses, each with a row of stone front steps and a place beside the steps for a little garden in the summer, I paid particular attention; the buildings and the street itself seemed to call for that. In the middle of the block, something winked at me from the gutter, and as soon as I saw what it was I had to pick it up and hold it, letting my hand sink under its small but familiar weight.

It was a large, gray cat's-eye marble, exactly the size and weight, though not the shape, of my mother's glass eye. Her good eye was green, but her glass one was a pale gray that drew people to it, which annoyed her. She felt it was like a lie on her face, and people were such easy fools, just shortsighted enough not to guess a fake when they saw it—for wouldn't they have turned from her if they'd known? She refused to take pleasure from their attention in any way, but neither would she consider replacing her "piece," as she called it, with a better match, or a more modern one.

"What would I do with a third eye? Two eyes are good enough for every other human being, including you, Julian."

My father had done his research, and he could approach her with facts, but facts were never a way to Harriet's heart—which governed her mind, however well she denied it. "They make them absolutely featherweight now," he would instruct her, "and of every color of the rainbow."

"Terrific. Get me a pink one. A woman should look pretty in pink. Or they'd take me for a rat and ignore me. Ha!"

"You look pretty in green, Mother," I wanted to say, but I kept the memory of that brilliant dress to myself.

Every morning she washed it in sterile water, leaning over the bathroom sink to do so, and as a child I thought this was part of every mother's routine, to take her eye in her hand at dawn and dip it in the sink, careful not to let it roll and shatter. She was eleven or twelve when the eye came out, poked by a neighbor boy using a stick for a gun and shooting accidentally at close range. The day she told me this was the same day I saw the open socket for the first time (for usually, instinctively, she squeezed it shut), and I suppose she felt revealed to me already. It looked like the open mouth of a baby, and it didn't move me in any way. It certainly didn't frighten me. I only became afraid after she put her eye back in and we sat together, for some reason not leaving the bathroom, she on the narrow edge of the bathtub and me on the closed lid of the toilet, while she described the accident. She told it quickly, leaving too much up to my imagination. I was only four or five at the time, and until that moment I'd supposed that when I got older I'd have a removable eye too. I had no real idea she couldn't see out of it; I hadn't given it that much thought. At the end of the story I was trembling, as if a small wind had come up between us, and she took me against her knees and held me vaguely, wordlessly. I couldn't tell her that I shivered for that neighbor boy. I wouldn't have traded any part of my life to be him.

Midblock, in a strange city's unfamiliar street, I considered this, rolling the marble between my fingers, then pressing it between my palms. It felt perfect, as her oddly shaped eye had felt smooth and perfect. For as soon as I knew it couldn't see, I often asked to hold it, and she gave it up to me while she wriggled into her girdle or smoothed on her stockings, or she let me hold it underwater in the sink—where it wasn't weightless! It surprised me. It had a solid and slightly sinking feeling that I liked, which became equal to my mother for me. And with my feet planted in the gutter, *that* was what I yearned for: her solid, small weight, not in me or on me, but near me again.

I dropped the marble and went on, needing all of a sudden to walk quickly and blindly through that neighborhood that had moments ago offered only its abundance but now felt like an open closet of rattling bones. I was raw to pain, as if wind or rain had passed right through me, though it was a dry, still day, weatherless and close to noon. I had remembered too much, that was it. I had stood and recalled certain facts, facts I lived in, as inside my own skin, and now as I passed from block to block I was sloughing these facts from me, lifting Harriet off me, and my pain measured my progress away from her and Julian towards whatever would have me next.

# Chapter Three

It had seemed like a simple question. "Where were you born, Helen? You weren't born here, were you?"

"No. In another, smaller place. I forget the name of it."

"Were you born by a midwife? I was."

She looked at me suspiciously. "I guess I'm not sure what that is. It's a woman who isn't your mother, who's your father's wife, isn't it?"

"Oh no! She's nobody's wife. That's her profession. She pulls out babies, usually in a small town."

There was a silence from my friend, then she asked, "Does your mother have a profession?"

"She's a bookkeeper."

"Does your father?"

"Yes, I thought you knew. If you'd been born here you'd know. He's a doctor."

"Why didn't he pull you out?"

"It's something called the Hypocritical Oath. It means doctors don't do the same things to their family that they do to other people."

"Isn't he your doctor?"

"He's not supposed to be." I was quiet a minute, waiting for the thought to explode: "Helen, we might have been born by the same midwife!"

She rolled her bottom lip over her top one and I asked, "What's your father?" She only looked at me, and suddenly I remembered why we'd never talked about families before. I was seared with my mistake, but I couldn't say a word to change it, and I looked at a stone on the ground as if it might absorb the question.

"He worked in the factory. He worked assembly, and then he was promoted to friction mold operator. On the outside he was learning how to fly a plane, we think."

It was the beginning of January, but it felt more like March or October. We were walking by the river. I was taking her to her bridge that day, and here the sycamores grew closely, their branches clasped above our heads and their roots spilling lavishly over the bank. At the beginning of that brief conversation I had felt the sunlight falling in triangles all over our clothes, as if we were walking in the tops of the trees themselves. Now I felt depleted, buoyed up for a moment by the mention of that airplane, but falling steadily, slowly, like the slow, determined leaves of the sycamore. The last five or six must have waited all autumn long for Helen and me to pass beneath them, and now they all came down together and touched the ground and ran along it like goose feet without the geese.

Helen knew my thoughts, for as we said good-bye she touched me under the elbow as if to raise me up. Then she spread her hand in the air and closed it, which was her way to wave.

She had been sick all vacation with one flu after another, but now that we were back in school again she seemed her old self. Something else had changed, though, something that made me ball my hand into a fist and hit it against my thigh and whisper, "I knew it!" For there in the corner of the lunchroom, at the table of girls who ate a lunch they'd brought from home, and ate without talking, without even seeming to recognize one another though every day it was the same group, sat Helen, and next to her was an empty seat, and next to that sat Connie Browne—Constance, as she wanted to be called; Constance Browne with an "e." She was leaning into Helen, and I couldn't tell if Helen was leaning back, but they had their heads close together like two people looking at the same crumb on the table, and every now and then the crumb would remind them where they were and what they were meant to be doing, and they'd pick at their sandwiches. Suddenly I saw Helen pull the crust off hers all in one piece, as if she were unwinding a string, and push it over to Constance.

This girl had fluffy, light, almost white hair and a troubled face that Helen said came from having three older sisters, Prudence, Patience and Hope, in that order. "It isn't easy being the youngest in a family of—"

"Puritans!" I spat out.

"Oh, no, Gussy. The parents had a sense of humor with names, that's all. They had a hard time making babies, Constance says."

This was the first time I'd ever heard Helen talk about making babies, and I didn't like it. "And you know what about making babies?" I accused her, stunned by the voice in my mouth, which was Harriet's.

She chose to ignore or forgive—or placate, and as soon as it seemed we were again sharing a joke about the Browne family I said, "Come on. Let's call her Constant Frowne—with an 'e'! Or Constantly Blue, Helen."

"I like to call her what she likes to be called."

"Is that so! I never knew there was a goody-two-shoes in you until now."

In every remark I made I could feel myself skidding down a greasy hill towards a black lake which no one had ever been to the bottom of, all depth and chill and darkness thick as night. I shivered. Every day in the lunchroom the food turned cold on my plate and I longed to sit with Helen. I never had, because there was something exciting but forbidden about that table of silent people, all of them girls like her from the other side of the river, and some of them sisters or cousins or neighbors to one another. "Do they talk at home?" I once asked her.

"How do I know?"

"Well, do you talk at home, Helen?"

"Yes, if there's something to talk about. Some people talk too much at home, so they come to school to be quiet."

Agnes Mill sat at this table of girls. She usually sat next to Helen, who sat on the aisle, and on the other side of Agnes sat Constance and her three sisters. That was one side of the table. Every day it was the same: Helen, Agnes, Constance, Hope, Patience, Prudence. If someone was absent, you knew it because her chair was empty. This was different from the rest of the lunchroom, where an empty chair between two people told everyone else that a fight had gone on or was about to. It was as loud as a declaration of war.

Agnes had been absent for a week with the German measles and was still absent, but one day her chair wasn't empty, and I strained my neck to see if Constance had moved closer to Helen or if Helen had moved in next to Constance. There was a gap on the aisle, a gap that felt so full of things, so full of angry shouts and dumb smiles pasted on, and claws and arrows and teeth and rocks, so full of everything besides Helen, I almost imagined for a split second that it was full of Helen too, and not a gap at all, and it didn't mean what I knew it meant, which was *I have had a friend and now I don't.* But the next second everything was clear to me, and I was able to think and say to myself, I have loved someone who doesn't love me, which means I won't love her anymore. Then, with a great noise, my tray tilted up and my hot lunch spilled into my lap, creamed chicken, rice, peas and cocoa; and while some girls saw this and laughed, others came forward and offered me their napkins. I quickly looked for Helen to see what she would do. Her head had come away from Connie Browne's, and her eyes were open wide as if she pitied me.

After that we still walked together sometimes, and talked together, though more than once Connie raced up behind us in the sycamore woods and without asking if it was a private conversation, stuck herself like flypaper to Helen's shoulder.

"You love that girl," I accused Helen one day. "I see Agnes is sitting on the aisle now." Agnes had gotten over her German measles, but instead of going back to the old seating arrangement, she and Helen had traded places so Helen and Constance could still sit together and touch heads like little lovebirds.

She shrugged. "Agnes likes the aisle. She needs to spread out when she eats." This was true. Agnes carried her lunch in a big brown paper bag which she called a sack. When she started to eat she pulled everything out of the sack, flattened the sack and put everything she'd pulled out on top of it, as if it were a tablecloth. Then she ate everything, the sandwich, the orange, the three or four graham crackers. She never mixed things, but got all the way through one food before she started on the next.

"You know that's not the reason."

Helen didn't say anything.

"I made a mistake. I thought I'd know you for a long time, Helen. I thought I could see right into the future and there you were, right in the middle of my future. But that's not true anymore, is it?" I looked right at her and made her look at me. "Do you think that's true anymore?" We had come to the point in our walk where she crossed over the river and I went straight ahead.

"Sometimes I can see the future too," she said, "or I think I can, and you're not in it. Nobody is. I'm sorry."

A big tear fell out of my eye and landed on my cheek. She shifted her shoulders away from mine, which meant she was about to cross her bridge.

"See that tree back there?" she said.

I looked. "There're fifty trees back there."

"Well, pick one of them. That tree means everything to me." She marched away and I watched her, clasping my book bag so hard against my chest I could feel the corners of the books jabbing my ribs, and it felt good.

In our yard was a bush we called pearly everlasting, whether that was its true name or not. Before I met Helen, I used to sit out under this bush almost every warm day, even on the warm spring days when a thin skin of snow might still cover the ground or, if not, a soft patch of mud that quickly soaked through my school uniform until I felt as stiff as a piece of tin. Under the bush I would send things to people; anyone I knew who needed anything, I would send it to them. To my father's patient, a woman I'd never met who'd given birth to a baby with a huge head and what my father described to my mother as a horn growing from the forehead, I sent a normal baby, an angel. To my old, cranky relatives in the city, I sent a plague of mice. What people needed was not always what they wanted, I understood, and I did my best to keep from being too sympathetic or too spiteful; I tried to act the way I knew God must, without becoming too little or too much involved.

My packages didn't always arrive, however. I must have sent Harriet her emerald green dress at least a hundred times. And whenever I began to doubt my own power to spread gifts or plagues to loved ones or strangers, I did something else under the bush: I buried something that meant a lot to me. Once it was a glass ring, another time it was a letter soaked in perfume from the first girl I thought to be my friend, years and years ago. I buried a tiny wooden train under the bush, and the stuffed leg of a favorite doll, the only doll I'd ever had; and the ticket stub from a ballet. The summer before sixth grade, on the day I turned eleven, I dug the deepest hole I'd ever dug and laid a hatchet in it. I'd found the hatchet in a pile of rubble across the river, near the boys' school, in a part of town I'd been forbidden, until my eleventh birthday, to explore.

Julian was convinced the moles were tearing up the ground around his pearly everlasting, and he ringed it with little poison traps. This was around the time I met Helen and gave up sitting out under the bush, and the power of thoughts became something quite different from what it had been. My thoughts now held power over me instead of giving me power over other people, and if I so much as turned my head or blinked my eye, in they would rush, bringing me nothing but turmoil and unhappiness.

Once again in January I started sitting out under the bush. The days were a deep yellow and full of all kinds of small winter birds, and the birds flocked to the bush, which was woolly and gray, so it was impossible to see where the birds ended and the bush began. How could it be so warm in January? How could we be so lucky to have the fall stretch past Christmas and into the new year? Or just to have two feet and hands and one smallish head with no horn growing from it—this seemed like impossible good fortune, and I wondered how it had ever come to be. I realized that if Helen were with me we could make a whole conversation out of these questions, a conversation of perhaps a few important words. Whenever I thought of her having such a conversation with her new friend, Connie Browne, I couldn't help but cry out, "What a waste!" I imagined them both at that very moment, holding hands on their side of the river, or skipping along, or awkwardly touching heads as they walked. Sometimes I had their heads crashing together, which started a fight, but mostly they were the same little lovebirds who ate together at school, though they didn't eat much and Helen especially was growing thinner and thinner, as well as taller and with new little bumps for breasts. All of this worried me.

One day under my bush, after I hadn't said one word to Helen for at least a week, I started to cry and cried until my eyes felt dry and brittle. I wanted to take them out, as Harriet did hers, and wet them under the faucet. Suddenly I remembered she had been just my age at the time of her accident, and this thought spun me around and onto my feet, and I started shooing the birds out of the bush, shouting and flapping my blue tunic at them. They rose up in a messy ball and rolled away to the next yard, where they floated above a bare cherry tree before dividing and landing on the roof of that house. I kicked the ground as if a spring were unwinding in each leg, and my chest was full of a pressure I'd only felt once before, when in gym class a larger girl had stumbled and brought me down under her, like a cushion to soften her landing in a game of running bases. I needed to bury something again—this thought flashed into my mind—something as heavy and important as the hatchet. And it couldn't belong to me, I realized, it had to belong to Helen. But to bury something of Helen's I had to get something from her, and to get something from her I had to go to her house, which meant I had to leave quickly and cross the river and be back before my parents got home. To be safe I wrote a note saying I'd gone back to school for play rehearsal, and I signed it with the word "love," which so puzzled me these days. It felt like a sore in my mouth.

From where we lived on Flat Street, I ran all the way to the river, dodging Harriet outside the Woolworth's store on her way home from work. She was like a blind woman at this time of day, making her way directly into the sun, stepping through columns of tilted light and the long shadows cast by buildings, like someone stepping through a falling forest of amber trees. I saw her first and ducked behind a parked car. Yet I could have stood directly in front of her and still she wouldn't have noticed, for as she passed she wasn't walking with her usual public impatience, she was stumbling ahead, as if through difficult terrain, clutching her papers and account books to her with one arm, and the other hand draped across her eyes as if to rest or protect them. She was wearing a white cotton blouse and a green skirt under an open coat, and a pair of gray, flat shoes that I remembered I used to hate—how they had embarrassed me! As I looked after her down the street, that seemed like a long time ago, when I was a different person.

At the bottom of the hill I crossed the river on Helen's footbridge, and suddenly I wanted to bring her something, some token of peace that would satisfy us both. She would see that I felt deeply for her, and I would join myself to her life again in some small way. I had no idea what she'd make of my visit, or my request for something meaningful of hers that I might cart away and bury, but if I brought her something of value, maybe that would seem to her a fair exchange.

Her street was shady, shadier than mine, which in January meant that the shadows of the tree limbs crisscrossed darkly in the late afternoon, and the sight of this made me wish I'd left my house wearing more than a scarf and a sweater. Her street ran steeply uphill from the river, so the doorways were at an angle, and the doors, I was certain, had all been especially cut; only one door fit one house. The houses were much more colorful than where I lived. The house next to Helen's was pink, and the house next to that was blue. Her house was at the top of the street, and it was yellow, and beside it, finishing off the street then turning the corner, was a purple wall.

On top of the wall lay a pencil, an unusual pencil that I recognized right away because I used to have one just like it, and it was the only thing that had ever disappeared from my desk at school, and it had disappeared just that week. It had a picture of Millard Fillmore on it and a few words about what kind of person he'd been, and the year he was born and the year he'd died, though this pencil had been sharpened all the way down through the person he'd been, through his death and birth, and soon the side of his face would be gone. I suddenly felt weak and shaky just thinking about it, and I sat down on the wall. Instead I thought about how Millard Fillmore had looked new, the thirteenth pencil in a long, flat box of thirty-five pencils, one for each president. Now the box would hold thirty-six, I remembered. They would have to make a new box as often as someone was assassinated.

The pencils had been a gift from Julian on my eleventh birthday, and they came with an apology:

> To my only Gustopher, in the hope that you may have inherited something from your old, old father besides his rotten memory for historical fact. These will help you soak in dates and numbers through your skin while you scribble your real passions and what you're really good at.
>
> Kisses and hugs,
> your Papa

Harriet read the card aloud over my shoulder, then in silence she shoved her package at me across the table, where the three of us sat eating doll-sized portions of ice cream and angel food cake. She insisted I save the ribbon. "For good prospects in love, Augusta."

"We can't accuse your mother of not pushing it, can we?" laughed Julian.

"So, she needs to be pushed. Who doesn't need to be pushed?" She turned to me. "Such a serious man, your father."

"It needn't be unwelcome news to you, but she's only eleven, Harriet."

"And you at eleven were elsewhere in your," she whispered the word, "desires?"

"What do I do with it, Mother?" The ribbon dangled from the tips of my fingers.

"I'll tell you what you do with it," said Julian.

"Don't listen to him!" she hissed.

"You boil it up and make a strong tea out of it. You drink the tea, turn three times in a circle and shout the name of the one you love."

"Enough!" Her hand came down hard on the table so

our three little dishes chattered and the spoon fell out of mine and onto the kitchen floor. Her eyes were wet. If I'd known that I never would have looked at them. She looked at me, and whatever she saw in my face at that moment, she spoke to it. "It's not the eyes that cry, my precious, it's the tear ducts." She drew a deep breath. "Of which I have two perfectly good ones. Now the gift. Open your gift." She shooed an invisible fly in the air.

It was a jar of clover honey. The jar was glass and shaped like a bear, and if you took the bear's head off, inside you found the honey. I threw my arms around my mother's neck so suddenly that neither of us had time to think, then just as suddenly I sat down again and we all occupied ourselves with another piece of sweet, cottony, angel food cake. Julian tore his apart with a dexterous maneuver of two forks, while Harriet and I ripped with our fingers and filled our mouths quickly, and I would have given anything to have that moment extend forever, full of the sweet taste and with no room for argument or talk.

It was a familiar voice, though not Helen's, that returned me to the wall where I sat, rolling the Millard Fillmore pencil between my two palms and shivering—for by now all the shadows had melted into one, and the sun was only visible as a faintly blue color in the corner of the sky, just above where my house might be.

"Helen tells me your father's a doctor," said Jordan, "and I wonder if he's the kind of doctor who can peel a grapefruit so the skin comes off in one long corkscrew. That's something I've always admired."

She stood at the end of the wall, holding the biggest grapefruit I'd ever seen. She had Helen's face, I noticed. Somewhere inside her face was Helen's face. She was wearing a gray skirt and gray knee socks, and instead of a shirt, a yellow sweater that buttoned. In that light, the sweater and the grapefruit and the house all looked the same color. The skirt hung squarely on her, and the sweater didn't quite meet it at the top, and when I felt I'd looked too long at her face, I looked there, at the gap.

"We haven't met for a long time, have we?" The hand that wasn't holding the grapefruit came towards me, and I guessed I was supposed to shake it and I did. "She's inside," said Jordan, "sick again. We both spotted you and Helen thought you might have brought her homework. She sent me out to shanghai you."

I was confused. "But she was in school today. You don't pick up homework unless somebody's been absent."

"Ah," Jordan nodded. "How true. She must have had something else in mind. Are you cold, Augusta? You must be cold. I'm cold. Though sitting on a purple wall keeps you warmer. People do studies about these things and they say purple and red inspire warmth, blue and yellow inspire—" She broke off. "Now what's the opposite of warmth? It's not cold, exactly. Cold's too cold."

"Cool," I suggested. "Coolth." We both laughed, and in a minute we were standing in the kitchen, where as soon as that luxury of warm air swept over me I began to shiver in earnest.

"We need to wrap you very tightly and warmly in blankets."

"Is she here?" Helen called from another part of the house. "She's here, isn't she!" There was a swishing along what sounded like a long hall, and Helen appeared wearing a sheet.

"I thought you were hot," said Jordan.

"Now I'm cold."

"Back in bed."

Helen didn't move. She leaned against the kitchen door, blinking like an animal come out of its hole. "Turn the light off, Jordan. The sky is doing a beautiful thing." And it was. There were shades of gray out there I'd never seen before. As she pointed out, every color in the world has gray in it, and in gray you can find every color, and at a certain time every morning and evening, if you understand this and look in the right direction, and especially if there are clouds, you can have your own show.

"I want to know who taught you that," said Jordan.

"Wallace did."

"Your father knew the sky better than anyone, didn't he?"

We were all quiet for a minute, then Helen said, "If that was a question, you know the answer."

Jordan looked at her. "You're barefoot. You're bare legged. It's after dark in January in a drafty house. You were sick all December. You came home sick today. Your friend Augusta's here, and if I don't put my foot down you're going to hop around with her and say you're not hungry for supper, and wake up tomorrow with aches and a rash again, and a fever; and this time when Dr. Beveridge says," Jordan lowered her voice, "'Has she been overdoing it, Mrs. Walsh?' I'm going to say, 'Helen knows. Ask Helen.' My question to you, young lady, and this *is* a question, is whether you'd like me to save you some embarrassment in front of the doctor by taking Augusta home, or whether you'd rather enjoy yourself now and pay for it later?"

Helen looked at the floor, then I did too. I said, "I don't think there'll be much hopping around, Mrs. Walsh."

"Call me Jordan. I like my name."

"There won't be any hopping around"—I set my mind to the next word—"Jordan. There won't be any not being hungry. You see, Helen has someone else she does all that with now, and I just came to—" I shrugged. "I just came to bring her something, I don't know what, and say hello and good-bye, and well, you know, see if she was alive and—" Here I stopped. "I miss you, Helen."

"Pfff." She made a sound like a tire going flat. "I miss you too, Gussy. If I'm sick tomorrow—I know I'll be sick tomorrow—come see me." And away she swished, down the hall. I heard a door close, then open again, and she called out, "Your pencil's on top of the wall."

She was sick the next day, and for a week after that. She had an ugly rash on her face, and a fever, and her hands ached so much she kept them wrapped in hot, steaming towels. Jordan wrapped them for her, and she changed the towels every hour. When I came over in the afternoon with her homework, I got to change them.

The first afternoon I told Jordan, "I've never had the German measles, but I don't mind catching them." I was afraid if I didn't say this she'd make me stand in the doorway.

She didn't say anything for a long time, she just looked at me. "It doesn't matter, Augusta. You don't have to worry about catching German measles. Now go in and see Helen. I'm sure she's had enough of me for one day. Take the kettle in with you, there's a basin by her bed. Get her to show you how to change her towels."

There were books piled up everywhere in Helen's room. It was a plain room with plain white walls and a bed, a soft chair, a hard chair, a desk and a dresser for furniture. Some of the piles of books reached as high up as the bed or the seat of the hard chair before they toppled over. I would visit one day and a pile would be organized and standing, and the next day it would cover the floor. "Why don't you put them somewhere?" I was hopping and holding my foot after a large volume called *Steam* fell from the desk and landed on it. "They are somewhere" came the answer, and how could I argue?

We hardly ever talked about school or people, I just sat on her bed and she read aloud to me as I changed her towels, and I turned the pages for her. She was always reading several books at once. Two of her favorites were *Lives of the Saints* and the *World Atlas*. She knew the color of every country on earth, and which ones had the best names of cities and towns, and sometimes if she read the names of these cities and towns—and lakes were also good for interesting names—I could sit on her bed and imagine I was listening to the greatest story in the highest language. If I rubbed my arm on her prickly blanket, I was right there in the grasslands of Bechuanaland, Africa. Or we were both in Peru, South America, paddling a boat on Lake Titicaca as I tipped the kettle and the water splashed into the basin.

The saints were less interesting to me, though Helen loved them. She preferred the lesser known to the greats, and her particular favorite was a seven-year-old, Saint Dominic del Val, who was kidnapped and nailed to a wall. "What did he do wrong?" I wondered, as she read to me about his horrible death.

"Wrong? He didn't do anything wrong, Gussy. He was only a little boy. He was a second-grader, think of it that way. He lit the candles in the church and they killed him for that."

"I guess I don't understand saints. Do you think they had certain powers? Can people today be saints?"

"I think people can always be saints, but it was easier a long time ago."

"How come?"

"Because saints are a little mysterious, and there were more mysteries then; at least mysteries were more popular." She thought a moment. "Like this, Gussy. I knew if I took your pencil you'd follow it over here, and you did."

"That's not—"

"Yes it is."

"You're not a saint, Helen. A saint wouldn't have gotten us in all this trouble to begin with. A saint wouldn't look twice at that Connie Browne. She's too queer. Sandals and socks all winter long—she looks like she's from another country."

"She is."

"Or another planet. Or from under the sea, with that pale hair of hers. I heard she shakes hands with her parents, and her sandwiches always have sardines in them, and her sister Prudence is a nymphomaniac, and Hope's a kleptomaniac, and I don't know about Patience except everyone says she has different what do you call it?—hormones—and she shoots baskets all day long, and I've seen this, Helen. She can sit on her braids."

"What's a nymphomaniac?"

I lied. "I think it's someone who likes dead bodies."

"No, that's a necrophiliac."

"Well then it's something worse."

"Constance was born in England," said Helen. "When someone is born in England and everyone else is born right here, it makes them interesting, don't you think? It makes them interesting and a little mysterious, so the people who don't like mysteries aren't going to like them."

"You weren't born here, Helen."

"And who likes me?" she nodded, "besides you?"

"I guess Constance does."

"I like Constance for liking me, and I like her for being born in England the way you like me for not living on Flat Street."

"I'd love it if you lived on Flat Street! Come live on Flat Street!"

"No, you wouldn't." She shook her head, and there the conversation ended. She looked down at the covers at that moment and I did too, and I saw that the T-shirt she wore for pajamas had worked its way up her ribs, and the covers had worked their way down, and there lay her bare stomach, and below her bare stomach a patch of hair that should have been on her head. Only it was too dark for her head. She brought the covers up and talked about something else for a minute, I don't remember what.

Near the middle of her illness Helen gave me a saint, Saint Hilaria, who'd been shot through the chin with an arrow. Helen had renamed her Saint Hole-in-the-head. "I'll take her," I said, "but I don't like the way she died at all."

"Oh, but Gussy, you can't have Saint Augusta." She made a face. "She was poisoned."

"What's the matter with that?"

"By her *father*."

I shivered. "How about Saint Helen?"

"There were nine, and they all died quietly in their sleep, and they're all mine."

A few days later she was better. Her rash, which had spread out from the middle of her face like the two wings of a butterfly, now looked like the butterfly had landed on the bridge of her nose. Her hands were getting better, though I still liked to wrap them when I came to visit. I looked forward to wrapping them. I liked carrying the kettle in, and the steam that rose out of the basin by Helen's bed, I liked that. I liked Helen's hands all bound up like boxing gloves. She waved them around like a boxer, especially after her fever went down and her strength was back.

She was restless. Jordan poked her head in to say she was going out, and Helen said, "You always go out. Why don't you stay in?"

"I've been in all day, Helen, now I'm going out."

"What do you do out there?"

"The same thing you do in here. I talk to somebody my own age and wait for someone not to be sick anymore."

"Someone who?"

"You."

"Oh," said Helen, "I thought you went out to smoke. After you go out you always smell of smoke. I've seen you pull up in that square car, and when you get out, all the smoke comes out with you. It looks like there's a fire in there."

Jordan laughed. "The other somebody smokes."

"Well, I don't like it. Tell them not to. Just stay in."

She didn't just stay in, though for a long moment she looked at Helen, who had started punching the air. "Somebody's feeling their oats," she said, and pulled her head back through the door and closed it.

The last afternoon I came to see her, Helen's hands weren't wrapped and she lay in bed with one hand covering her eyes. "Harriet does that," I told her. "Why do you do that?"

"Why do I do what?"

"Your hand across your eyes."

"Don't you ever do it?"

I thought, then shook my head.

"You don't ever do it, Gussy?"

"I'm telling you, no."

"That, I can hear." She took her hand away and opened

her eyes. "If I was blind, and your friend, we'd both have a lot to get used to. You'd see more, but I'd taste and smell and hear and feel more. Would you rather be me?" She leaned forward, then dropped back onto her pillow. "Or would you rather be who you are?"

I looked at her in wild confusion. I'd never been asked such a question before. "You," I whispered.

She just laughed.

We tore ourselves in two that winter, looking for the person inside us who was us, and that day, at that moment, I believed myself to be more truly Helen than Augusta, so Helen ridiculed us both by doubting me. But the next day at school she stuck close and I was proud of her again. She'd gained some notoriety because of her constant illness. My old friends, girls who'd never spoken one word to Helen Walsh, now poked her gently and asked her every kind of question in earnest, questions that had never occurred to me. Had she been able to eat? What had she eaten? Who was her doctor? Why not Dr. Cotton? Agnes, whose recent experience with German measles had turned her into a kind of medical zealot, insisted on hearing all of Helen's symptoms, then shook her head sadly and, quick as a cat, grabbed Helen's wrist. She seemed to know exactly how to take a pulse, though not how to read one, and was only able to prove to us that our friend was alive.

Helen, I thought, did beautifully through all this. She reminded me of a tame and patient horse, and each girl, each one of us, was a hand that stroked her in a different place and in a different way, but more for us than for her. What she had, we had never felt before. There was something about her. I couldn't have said what it was—none of us could have, though I suspect by then she knew. I was afraid for her that day, among all the other things I felt. I was afraid she wasn't up to our attentions, she would fail us—no, she would fail *them,* and this was an important distinction.

Julia Swann stopped us in the hall. "Helen! How's it going?"

"Hello." Helen cleared her throat. "I'm going to class."

"No, *how*. *How*'s it going?"

"Oh, I thought you said *where*. That's why I said to class."

Julia was known for her impatience, which always seeped out through her feet. The motion was one of walking in place, and she was doing that now.

"We've got to go, Helen."

"She doesn't belong to you, Gussy. Let her answer the question." She turned to Helen again. "How are you? How's it going?"

Helen flashed a smile and made a thumbs-up sign, and without a word we were on our way.

"Who taught you how to do that?"

"What?"

"With the thumb."

"Oh. Wallace."

We all acted as if she'd been gone for years. I even took her hand sometimes to lead her through the halls, which were simple and all laid out in an organized pattern, and of course she knew them as well as I did and couldn't have forgotten them in a week. But I wanted that hand with me, and I was beginning to know in the vaguest of ways that what I wanted with Helen, she usually wanted back. If she didn't, she would tell me, in a gesture more often than a word, which is how I guessed Connie Browne was heading right for us before I ever saw that girl—because Helen gave a little tug and dropped my hand.

They were plainly not in love; at least Helen wasn't. I

thought they spoke like two people meeting on the street corner, when one person is sincerely glad to see the other but the other is struggling inside with the first person's happiness because, to them, this meeting is unimportant. I said, and it was meant to be friendly, "Where do you *get* sandals like that?"

"Britain," said Constance so fast it was barely a syllable. Her voice had never sounded English to me. It reminded me of the time a man came to our school to play cutlery, which meant he sat on the stage in the auditorium and made high, clear, almost aching noises come out of forks.

I don't remember what they said to each other, Constance and Helen, but I remember leaving that encounter with a troubled feeling inside me. I decided it was the same troubled feeling Constance carried on her face. I took Helen's hand again. We walked a few more steps and Miss Piscina, who taught Latin, poked her head out the door of a classroom with a strange greeting: "Dante! Beatrice! *Nonne erratis in hoc inferno.*" Our puzzled looks must have reminded her we were only sixth-graders, and she explained, "It means 'You two look lost in hell.' Now, scoot! The bell's about to ring. Welcome back, Helen."

"Her name in Italian means swimming pool," Helen whispered as we ducked into the stairwell.

Our social studies class was on the second floor. Helen stopped on the step above me. She was shaking my hand like a thermometer. "Let's not go."

"We can't just sit on the stairs."

"Why can't we?"

"*I* know." We climbed one more flight to the top of the school, and in front of a red metal door we held our breath, listening.

"I can hear the dog," said Helen.

"What dog?"

"St. John's big dog."

"How do you know she has a dog? I never heard of any dog."

"That, Gussy. What's that?"

"I think it's a radiator banging."

"She has a dog, but it's not a dog she brings to school."

"Then what we're hearing couldn't be the dog."

It was a heavy door, and we both pulled on it until, halfway open, it sighed and rushed at us and we sprang in out of the way. The entire third floor of the school was a gymnasium. It had a brown cork floor and cork walls, and set high up in the walls were the windows that let in the same angular light all winter long, thick columns of light like huge, amber tree trunks. It was a forest thick and twisted—the room was a jungle, noisy and complicated in its sights and smells, in all its sensations. Even the cork underfoot gave in an unusual way for the floor of a school, and brought to mind deep lanes of springy lichen, or logs rotting and becoming that thing I only later had a name for and laughed when I heard it: peat.

Half the gym was taken up with equipment: a balance beam, a set of parallel bars, a trampoline no larger than a lady's sun hat (we called it the young tramp, from the days when "young" and "small" were interchangeable) and a dozen ropes and rings, which swung from the ceiling and defied all but the strongest arms. Though if you caught your rhythm, the rings gave you a chance to travel—down and back from one to the next without having to touch the floor. I did it once by imagining I was a very colorful parrot, and on my way I flew close above a conference of white monkeys, rubbing and scratching and chattering in the trees.

No one but Julia, Rachel and Annabel Jones, and, I'd heard, Patience Browne, made it to the top of the ropes, which were stiff and burned your hands and were rumored to lead you out onto the roof through a trapdoor in the ceiling. Whether I believed this or not, I wasn't certain I ever wanted to leave the foliage of the jungle. I liked the way the ground steamed and the air thickened around us when we played capture the flag or battlefield, or learned to circle-dance or high-jump or broad-jump or just plain race each other and wrestle like beasts or wild people across the jungle floor. I liked the way girls changed here, how we lost our composure, all but a timid few, and became charged with an animal velocity I'd noticed in some boys at a distance—for they brought it out in public, "into the light of day," as Harriet put it. She found it as indecent to watch a sports match or an informal street game as I found it enjoyable.

"Pah! They make a sweaty war out there and we have to watch it!" she complained. But if we were on a bus somewhere, off on an errand, at the sight of a game of stickball she'd jab at the window and push herself out of her seat before she knew it, unable to sit still while her life ranged so close, at the very edge of that physical energy and pleasure.

Whenever I had nowhere else to go at school, I came up here to the gym. Even empty, it was resonant, and it was here I learned that sounds have their ghosts as much as sights do. In fact there was a ghost for every sense, and in the gym they flocked to me in no kind of frightening way, but with persistence, like agile reptiles or rodents scurrying across the backs of my hands and up my arms; I could feel the small weight of them against my lips and in my ears, or a slight drumming on my scalp. If I was alone and closed my eyes and leaned against the cork wall, pretending it was a wild jungle tree, I could surely hear Helen's cello, rich, deep and now abandoned by her because she'd been too sick to play it, and in music class we were no longer studying the strings, but our own voices.

"I can't believe we have it all to ourselves!" she cried. "Let's kick a ball." She started hunting for a ball to kick and came back with a rubber football.

"That won't work."

"Help me look then."

We found a red India rubber ball in one corner of the gym. It had gone flat so it didn't roll, it skidded, and soon she got tired of it and I was tired of it before we began. "Let's lie in the sun," I said. The sun made long rectangles on the floor, exactly the size of our bodies. We each lay down in our own rectangle. It was like being in a boat on the river.

"Except my feet stick out the end of the boat," said Helen. She got up and lay down next to me, measuring my boat. "I'd fit in your boat, though." I rolled my head to the side and she did too, at the same moment, so our faces were only a few inches apart, and I got good and ready to take a long, quiet look at her.

But then a ghost came and lay down between us. It wasn't a sight, it was a feeling. I knew it from somewhere. I knew it from those times when I stood right next to Julian or Harriet in a store, or at home drying the dishes—when our bodies almost touched, which is always when I missed them the most. I said, "Helen," but not a sound came out of me. I tried again, "Helen," and this time I heard someone pushing their way through a dry thicket, and her arm came up over the shoulder of the ghost and dropped, light as paper, onto my hair. It didn't frighten me, but I was startled and she felt it and lifted her hand away.

"Please leave it on me," I tried to say, but my lips wouldn't open and her hand didn't come back, and instead of Helen or ghost or jungle or river, I saw the word "close." I saw it in two ways, its two meanings, and they both rushed at me like the same solid door, and written on the door in my own flat writing were the words "The way in is the way out."

"I just got a message from God," I told her. She had gotten up and gone back to her spot in the sun. My spot had moved ahead a few inches, like any boat on a river, so everything below my ankles felt cool, and then cold. When the cold hit halfway up my shins I heard Helen roll over. "I had a strange thought too," she said.

"What was it?"

"People don't usually marry who they love."

I don't remember what we did with the rest of that hour, except scoot along the floor to keep up with the traveling sun. Later, when I came back for my afternoon gym class, I didn't run and shove as usual for an early place in line at the balance beam (which seemed the safest and happiest of all the apparatus). Instead, I stood and stared at the ribbon of floor, our old river, which had just this morning contained Helen and me—though our boats were gone. The sun had moved all the way around the gym and at that moment illumined a small group of girls, turning their long hair white as veils.

"You look any harder you're going to set fire to the floor!" yelled Miss St. John. She was the oldest teacher in the school, with a mysteriously plump face while the rest of her was thin and wiry. She wore kilts, and white crew socks rolled down to a fat tube above her ankles, and her hair was metallic gray but cut short like a little girl's. "Get moving!" She blew her whistle at me and I wondered, *Where to?*

*Why?* and *What if I don't?* As old and tired as these thoughts might have been to anyone else, to me they were new and explosive, and for the first time in my life I had a full sense that I was being prepared for something, made keen for something, something that would blow up soon and change me. Not in the same way I had changed since the summer, which was me at the mercy of what I from time to time called God—though others used the word "hormones." This new change would be the difference between being snow on the road and being the road itself.

I was hopeful. I was cheerful through and through for the first time in weeks. I was ready to hear anything and decide yes to it, because I was certain as I'd never been before that I would just as often, when I felt like it, say no.

"Can you lift your own weight, Gussy?" I turned around and there was Agnes, earnest as ever, with her glasses sitting lopsided on her nose. She looked like she'd had a fright, and even if it was easy to tease that girl, it was almost impossible to scare her. Her father was the undertaker, which made us different and alike in some ways.

"What happened to you?" I asked, though I was impatient to spill my news to someone, anyone: We are what we *choose*! "Yes, I guess I can lift my own weight. On strong days I can. Why?"

"Good." She grabbed my elbow and led me towards the ropes. "Good," she said again, as if that might explain everything, and in case I hadn't heard it the first time. The gym echoed with shouts and high, thin shrieks, joined every now and then by a long, mean note from St. John's whistle, but over by the ropes a lovely calm seemed to envelop us. I don't believe Agnes felt it, but for me it lasted a full few minutes, the whole time we talked, and it reminded me of the good parts of my life with Helen in it.

"The weirdest thing happened. The ropes," said Agnes, lowering her voice and moving her head like an owl, though there was no one within ten yards of us, "the ropes just gave me this thump-thump feeling. You know, like a tiny earthquake. I got halfway up—I've never been halfway up before—and there it was, this feeling, *right down here*!" She pointed with both hands to the hem of her tunic, which was short because she'd grown recently.

"Is this the rope?"

She nodded and stood up stiff and straight right next to it, though she was careful not to touch it or let it touch her.

"If you climbed it now do you think it would happen again?"

She sucked in her breath. "I don't want it to happen again. I want you to climb it and see if it happens to you."

"It's happened to me before, Agnes."

"Then it's the rope!"

"It's not the rope." I shook my head. "It's never happened to me at school. You'd like it better, I think, if it didn't happen at school."

Her hands were balled into tight fists, and a tear surprised me and slipped out from behind one of her lenses. "How can I *help* where it happens if I don't know where it came from?"

"Where it came from," I said, as kindly as I knew how, "is from the new person you are, the new Agnes."

"I *loved* the old Agnes. I loved the *old* Agnes. A lot of people did."

"Well, they'll like the new Agnes."

"What if they don't?"

I didn't have the answer to that so I said, "You wonder all the same things I wonder."

"What if they don't, Gussy?"

"Okay. We'll live."

Agnes thought about her next question for a long time. "This feeling. Other people who get this feeling, do they like it?"

"Oh yes!" I swept my arm around, feeling grand all of a sudden. "Some of these girls make a big thing about the physical sensations. They love the way it feels. When they feel a certain way, they call it love and say they're in it. Haven't you heard them? They talk about it all the time."

She stared at me and didn't say a word, and I thought if I didn't keep talking she'd either fall down flat or float up. So I said, "Julia Swann says her knees give out when she's in love. She says they get shot through with something hot. They feel like they've been boiled and turned runny."

"That's it," Agnes whispered.

"Deirdre can feel hot things shooting up her front."

"Like someone making soup inside you. I know! It came right before the tiny earthquake!"

"If the love feeling goes away and you want it back again, you can think about certain people."

"Ashley keeps a picture of those men inside her desk. Is that to get the feeling back again?"

"The Beatles," I nodded.

"If you don't want the feeling, can you get rid of it?"

"You can stay off the ropes," I said, because I could see that, more than anything else in the world, Agnes wanted a useful answer, even if it wasn't quite the truth. After that she told me two sudden, true things about herself that people only tell you when you've given them something they don't know how to thank you for, such as a simple answer or some peace of mind. She told me that she planned to be a doctor, and that her father often walked around with just a towel on. I was about to say the wrong thing, "Agnes, a towel's a towel," which would have ruined our understanding, when I caught sight of something across the gym. "Look at that," I said. "What's the matter with Ashley?"

Ashley had come late to class. Her mouth looked like it was bleeding, and her eyes were bruised. She hung against the wall of the gym; then, as the room went quiet, she must have thought we would come at her. She thrust her palms out to stop us, at least to stop our turning heads, though it would have been easier to stop the slow, stubborn lengthening of our bones, or the circulation of our blood, or the awakening of nerves and sensibilities—and frailties—that seized us daily in a most painful and clandestine way. We stared and she stared back. A long minute went by. There was no need to shout (we could hear each other breathe or sweat or think), but Miss St. John shouted, "Go take it off, Hobb!"

Ashley lowered her arms. "I can't take it off."

*"Now!"*

"You need special stuff to take it off. You need cold cream and cotton."

"That's not true," Agnes whispered. "Any kind of grease will take it off. Even chicken fat will." I knew how she knew all she knew about makeup, and it gave me every reason not to doubt her.

By the time the bell rang, Ashley had rubbed her face raw in the bathroom, though there were still patches of something that looked like moss around her eyes. After that, there was always moss around her eyes, or lipstick on her teeth, or what Agnes called "undertaker's pink" in her cheeks. Agnes, the new Agnes, had become a kind of oracle for girls like Ashley, though Ashley herself steered clear and her face showed it. I heard her complain, "All she's ever worked on is dead people!"

"That's more people than no people," said Deirdre, who wore makeup now too, but it looked harmless and pretty on her because Agnes had given her two full hours of instruction and gone with her to buy supplies.

I guessed this was also part of love, the sudden world of blush and shadow that had engulfed my friends, or at least a few of the people I used to know. It was part of drawing the love feeling to you. I said as much to Helen, who only shrugged. "If you can't be yourself, you pretend you're someone else, that's all. I do it, too."

"Who?" I wanted to know. "Who do you pretend you are?"

"It's more what," she answered, "and I pretend I'm well."

I had to wait until the weather turned cold at the beginning of February before I had any really friendly feelings towards that word "love." The more I heard it, the less I knew what it meant. Helen had said it once, that day in the gym. It had come at the end of a sentence, and it sat like a bright star over the rest of the day, long into the dark afternoon. But since then, nothing; not one ounce of light. Though I must have believed it was out there still, stuck at the bottom of a cloud but *willing* to visit, because one day I called it by name, wondering aloud to my friend whether we were born under the wrong star of love.

"Where do you get that?"

Ashley had accused me of it in a belligerent moment in the bathroom, but now I said nothing.

"Not wrong," Helen insisted. "I know what you mean but I wish you wouldn't call it that."

"Call it what, then? What would you call it?"

"Awkward. That's all it feels like, Gussy." She tucked her chin deeper into the collar of her jacket to keep out the sudden blizzard we were walking home through.

The morning had been warm and bright, but now the snow was so thick we couldn't see the length of our arms when we held them out in front of us. Our wrists were there, but our bare hands were vague and purplish, which was the color of shadow in a storm, Helen said (she was much more sensitive to color than I). We had set off from school in a small band, but now all the girls who crossed the river had fallen ahead or behind, and my old friends never cut through these woods; they walked in the street, where we could hear the last bus or two still running. "If you don't go now you'll be walking all the way home," Helen warned me, but I stayed on beside her and we said nothing and saw nothing until we lost the path, or it became crowded with sycamores.

"Stand still," I told her. "I think the trees are coming at us."

"No they aren't. Of course they aren't. There wouldn't be any reason for it." She put her arm around my shoulder and turned me and pressed me to her, the way she used to hold her cello. My cheek was on the cold zipper of her jacket, and I could feel where a tuft of stuffing leaked out a hole in her jacket. She said, "We'll need everything, Gussy. Every big thought, we'll need it." After that she released me and we walked towards the only noise we could hear anymore, the river, and I said to myself: *Augusta Cotton, I start here at this moment.*

I felt I'd been living only in my thumbs, and something had come along to awaken me to my eight good fingers, and now all of a sudden the world was mine to *grasp*. "Helen!"

I called to her. She had stopped slightly ahead of me where she'd found the riverbank. "Helen!" But I couldn't think of one other word to say, and we stood looking into the water, which was the same faint purple color our hands had been just minutes ago and yards away.

# Chapter Four

That was a leap year. Never had a month moved so haltingly forward, nor stretched so endlessly ahead, until by the end of it I felt I'd lived inside every hour. Helen was sick often, and finally her doctor, a man called Dr. Beveridge, sent her away somewhere for a day of tests, and after she returned she was given a name for the problem inside her. That was the first time I heard the word "lupus."

What a word can do to a life was something I had little knowledge of, unless it was the word "love" or "rapture." Helen had simply said, from her bed, as I arrived with a small bundle of her homework, "They think I have lupus, Gussy," and her books felt no heavier in my arms. Nothing cold passed through me. I asked, "What's that exactly?" But she only shook her head on the pillow. "We're not sure."

"I can find out from Julian."

"No, don't!" she cried. She rose up on one elbow and I rushed to her, letting history and geography slide from my arms as I dropped down onto the foot of her bed. "It's not for anyone else to know!" she whispered. "Swear to me!"

My right hand shot up and the other one rested on the lump of her knee. "I swear it."

It was the first oath I ever made to anyone, and the only one I ever meant to keep. But at supper that night I had a hard job swallowing, as if whatever I'd sworn had struggled up from the deep place I thought I'd put it and now asked to be spoken. Until it was, I couldn't eat. I laid my napkin over my plate, stood up and headed straight for the sink.

"What are you, sick?" asked Harriet. I shook my head. "There's perfectly good food under there. Julian, stop her!"

He stuck his arm out like a turnstile to catch me, but I dodged him, dumped my whole meal upside down in the soapy water and fled to my room, where I gave anyone a minute or two to come and collect me. When no one did, I climbed off my bed and walked back to the kitchen. Harriet had just raised the lid off a pot of baked apples, and the smell of clove and cinnamon was the loudest thing in that room.

"Helen's sick," I said. I said it twice, softly. "Helen's sick. They think she's got lupus."

Harriet scooped an apple into a dish. "You're not in good favor, Augusta."

"Who's this?" asked Julian. "Who's sick?"

"Here. Go and pass this to your father."

"Helen," I said.

"Helen who?" asked Harriet.

"Helen Walsh."

"Is she a friend of yours?" asked Julian.

"They think she's got lupus."

He put his spoon down and looked at me. "Lupus erythematosus?"

I shrugged. "How do I know? I don't know everything, Julian."

"Shush! What kind of name is that to call your father!"

"It's what you call him."

"God help us, Augusta, at your age you should turn a smarty-pants. Listen to her, Julian. She learns too much from her friends."

"I don't. I only have one friend."

"This Helen," said Harriet.

"Don't call her 'this Helen'!"

"I wouldn't be too hard on her, Harriet." Julian hadn't begun to eat his baked apple, but now he folded his napkin and tucked it under his dish the way he always did at the end of a meal. "She may be quite a sick girl, your friend. I don't think this town's had a case of lupus in all the years I've practiced medicine—I know I've never seen one. It doesn't crop up among your age, in general, which is what worries me."

"Can people die of lupus?" I asked. "Is it a mortal illness?" It was a conversation I'd had once before with him. The feeling of it was familiar, though the actual when and where escaped me.

"Yes and no," he said. "You die of the complications brought on by the disease. A kidney goes, or there can be mental debilitation over a long period of time. It's what we call an autoimmune disease. The body forms antibodies to itself. It doesn't happen quickly, Gussy. Some patients have long periods of remission—"

"How long?"

"Months or years. But others—"

"Others aren't so lucky," I said, just to be the one to say it. "I know."

"Too much you know," said Harriet. She didn't say it

unkindly. "Try and know less. If I could give one gift to a daughter, it would be this: To be still and stupid like me."

"You're not stupid, Mother. I don't think you're stupid."

"Aren't I? Never mind, Augusta, I've been told I'm not clever." She turned her eyes towards Julian and whispered loudly to me, "She'll be fine, your friend!" and her mouth made every word large and distinct, and believable.

"Harriet, there's no point—"

"'There's no point, there's no point.' You M.D.s, you're gloombags, all of you! The worst gloombag in the world is that Sal Beveridge. Break your knee, he'll cut your leg off. It's happened, believe me."

"It hasn't happened. Don't spread rumors."

"Oh, Julian, he weighs like a stone!"

"It hardly seems fair to discredit a man's diagnostic abilities just because he's not naturally cheerful. I dislike him intensely, but I don't yet have a reason to distrust him, nor do you."

"That's her doctor," I said. "That's Helen's doctor."

"Of course it's her doctor," said Harriet. "Your friend's from across the river, isn't she? It's Cotton on this side, Beveridge on that. Don't ask me why, it always has been. Now sit, Augusta. Eat something." She waved me into a chair and I half-expected my old plate back again—meat loaf, cabbage and a boiled potato somehow resurrected from the sink. Instead she brought me two baked apples floating in cream.

"One's yours, Mother."

"Shh, go on, I don't want it."

"Have something. Keep us company."

She poured herself half a glass of milk, and I thought I knew the reason her hand shook so I said, "Helen says it's not contagious. It's not contagious, is it, Papa?"

He took a long time to answer, a few long seconds, then his answer was a disconcerting question. "Are you close to this child?"

"Close?"

"Have you had close contact with her in the past several weeks? Do you play with her?"

I looked from him to Harriet. "I don't know if I play with her."

"Of course she doesn't play with her," said Harriet crossly. "Children play. They're not children."

"But we're not adults either!"

"That hardly matters." Julian shook his head. "What matters it that your friend is almost surely right, Gussy. Her disease isn't contagious, as far as we know. We suspect it may pass through families"—Wallace? I wondered—"but friends, we have no evidence for. It's highly unlikely. I would say it's not possible."

Be sure! I wanted to shout at him. Look inside me and see! For I remembered the "Open widely!" of my childhood—a sudden light weight on my tongue, and the beam of a slender flashlight stinging my eyes. I had once thought my father sure of everything, of every word and inexplicable movement. How he could spot flu or fever by squinting down my throat, I couldn't imagine. Or see inside my lungs! He'd done that as well. It seemed impossible now that something might be living *unnoticed* inside me, something of Helen's, Helen's lupus. "If it *is* in me," I asked, trying to keep my voice steady, "is there any way of finding it and getting it out of me?"

"Me, me, me!" Harriet spun around at the sink. "Stop worrying about yourself, Augusta, you don't have it. If you want to worry, worry about that poor girl, your friend!"

And as she turned again into the steam (I could almost feel it curl her hair back), I was suddenly and bitterly ashamed.

I spent a good deal of February by myself, with Helen flat on her back for most of it, sleeping or exhausted by her new medicine, which puffed her up like a seal. Whenever I went to see her, I always stood for a minute or two in the hall outside her room, listening to a shade flap (she liked the shade lowered and the window cracked open), and getting used to who would be lying there in the bed. "It's Helen," I would whisper to myself, and I'd bring into my mind a picture of my friend without those pillowy cheeks. If she was asleep when I went in, I'd leave her homework on the floor and stand right by her bed and look at her. She usually slept with one leg on top of the sheet and the other leg under, and always with her arms up over her head like a person giving up in a gunfight.

There were days when I couldn't go to her, when the distance between the school yard and Helen's house seemed to have grown overnight; when her footbridge arched away into another country altogether, a country I couldn't pass into or through, though I could see it from the second-floor window where I sat in art class drawing Annabel Jones. That poor girl. Fruit and bottles I could do, but I was no good at people, and at the end she cried, "That isn't me! That's Rachel! *My* head is squarish." I said nothing. I'd tried to flatter Annabel by softening her edges. It hadn't been the truth and now we all knew it.

Her rendering of me was no more successful. I thought it moody and too melancholy, and I accused her of knitting my brows together just to show off with her pencil. "How do you know what you look like, Gussy?" She stabbed the paper for emphasis. "That's what you look like when you look across the river. It's the boys' school, isn't it?" she whispered, and her face lit up so I knew I'd disappoint her twice in the same hour.

How much easier if it had been the boys' school! I would have leapt the river with my classmates instead of sitting on the bank until dark, kicking pebbles into the water with my heels and wondering what pulled me to her, to Helen, and at the same time kept me from crossing any one of those bridges. Often, lifted and carried by those bridges, and by the histories that unfolded inside me at the sight of them, my eyes would skim along the bank on her side until, beyond the edge of the places where people lived, a hill rose up, a steep rise. This was where the Corinth Sanatorium had once stood like a fortress protecting the town—though Harriet still called it the leper colony and described a circle of three unimpressive stone-block buildings weathered a mean gray. Two of the buildings had been taken apart piece by piece and hauled off to improve a county road. The third, also stripped down to its foundation and hauled away, was visible in the north and east walls of the factory, and on one of our earliest architectural excursions, when I was still small enough to be piggybacked around the town, Julian had pointed out the line where the old block met the modern brick as if to say, Learn to be *useful,* Gussy. You'll endure.

He had an eye for structure, and had loved Harriet's engineer father, whose bridges were built in service to the sanatorium, replacing the old ferry across the river. It impressed my father, and he impressed me with the fact that every eastbound patient had to cross the river in order to shake free of their disease, or take it on so fully it finally killed them, and wasn't that a weight for a bridge to bear! He and I used to walk around the ruins of Corinth (Harriet refused to join us) and share a picnic in what might have been the operating room, then with surprising insouciance stretch out for naps. I remember not one nightmare from that time, not even a troubled dream, only a rest so complete, so resplendent I always woke happily after twenty minutes and sat and listened to my father snore.

I felt I owned Corinth. I had never been afraid of it. Julian had always been willing to match my exacting questions with explanations, so from a very young age I knew more about sanatoriums and tuberculosis than most adults. I welcomed the knowledge and wanted more, and perhaps for this reason the disease lodged in me. It chose me. It offered itself to my lungs as an honored guest and they didn't refuse. I remember nothing of that illness except that I was just old enough to read, and I read through dozens of picture books with large print and happily missed school for several weeks. If I coughed once or had a moment of pain, it made little impression. Yet how well I knew that, without the isoniazid cures of the day, my favorite pile of rubble would have been a working sanatorium and my bed would have been across the river! Rather than frighten me, this thrilled me, and from that time on I felt at home up there on the hill. I belonged among the patients of Corinth. I had fallen sick, as they had, and if I believed as Harriet did that a ghost is more opaque for each mortal illness its body once survived, some of us should have been quite visible to each other. Though one day I questioned Julian about the mortal part of it. This was shortly after my eighth birthday, and we were climbing slowly up to the sanatorium, swinging the picnic basket between us. Bright red wildflowers covered the hill, and I knew to expect to see them pushing up through every crack in the foundation—they needed only a hair's breadth.

"I wasn't about to die of tuberculosis, Papa."

"Is that a question?"

I considered, then said yes.

"Anyone can die of anything at any time, Gustopher, but certain people are more ripe and ready for it than others."

"You mean it could have killed me?"

"I mean it would have had to work very hard to, but yes." He was quiet a moment. "Do you know what the Supreme Court is?"

I thought I did so I nodded.

"The term 'mortal illness' is something like a pathological Supreme Court, and until recently tuberculosis sat on that court, and now it doesn't."

"What sits where it sat?" I asked, not certain whether I was on the track or off it.

"Oh," Julian laughed, not a happy laugh. "Countless others, I'm afraid." He mentioned diabetes. He mentioned cancer, though he called it carcinoma and I had to ask what that was. Rabies was on the list, as well as multiple sclerosis.

"What's multiple sclerosis?"

"You remember it, you just don't know you remember it. It killed my sister, your aunt Kate."

I tried at that moment to come up with a picture of Kate, of her body, of her presence at least, but all I saw were the hollow arms of her crutches, a white porcelain bedpan and a closet of canes. "I remember her," I lied.

"No you don't. You remember what killed her."

Illness ought to be as straightforward as architecture, Julian had once told me, and he said without saying, My life would be easier if this were true.

After that conversation I lovingly wandered our ruins, imagining myself enclosed by walls that weren't there, lying on long-gone beds and allowing a row of twigs to become the tables at which we patients ate our small, bland meals. I found Kate drowsing in the sun against what had once been a south-facing wall, and I joined her—or so I thought. But the next moment it was Julian, patting the ground beside him for me to come and sit closer. Something occurred to me.

"She was just like you, Papa, wasn't she? She was your twin."

He only pointed to the hazy plain below us, where the river ran away for good. "I'm afraid we won't have this fine weather for long," he said, and I puzzled over that because it was barely August, and of all our months August was the most brilliant and reliable.

Later we walked together and he pointed up high in the invisible walls and described the windows of the sanatorium. They were narrow and lightless, each roughly the size of a box of flowers. This was something I'd never imagined as I stepped from room to ruined room, wrapped in feverish daylight. I tried to contradict Julian, but he insisted.

"Then it was like a prison," I said, "or a church." I'd never been in a church, but from the outside they all looked like the lack of air might kill you. "Why is it always dark in the places they punish people?"

"What? Like prisons and churches?"

I nodded, and he laughed with his mouth wide open and his white teeth showing, a laugh I heard only when we were alone together.

"People didn't come here to get punished, Papa, they came here to get well."

He did something then that he'd never done before. I was facing him and he put his hands on my head and gripped it hard. "There are two things you must never confuse or forget: People are often punished for being sick, but being sick isn't a form of punishment, it's simply a fair trial. Let that sink in for a good long time."

I gave it a minute or two, and when it still didn't make sense I went back to a safe place where the ground wouldn't rock, a simple question: "Who could get well without windows?"

He said nothing, and there was a trembling under my feet again. Then he said, "Your aunt Kate's house had dozens of windows. There were eight in her bedroom alone."

I remembered. They ran from ceiling to floor and I stood in them, willing all that sun into me like a plant begging to be grown. I was struck with the sudden thought: *I* had darkened Kate's bed and killed her! Perhaps it was an audible thought, because Julian said, "You brought her nothing but joy, Gussy." After that we sat down on a heap of bricks and ate the rest of our lunch.

That was the last visit we ever made to the place together, I'm not sure why. I soon found other places to explore, like the old bus barn on my side of the river, and even if I didn't feel at home there as I had at the sanatorium, it would do. It was littered with old car parts, which opened up a whole imaginary world of mobility to me. All that rusted potential, swifts and swallows sawing the air, and here and there on the dirt floor, the bones and leather wings of a dead bat. If I'd known Helen then and we'd sainted each other, she would have been Saint Helen of Silence, and I, Saint Augusta of Inanimate Objects. For when I tired of starred windshields, or a hubcap holding a solitary shaft of light, dark as oil, and when the lace of corroded mufflers no longer held my attention, it wasn't human company I sought and found, it was the pearly everlasting bush in my own, still yard. I sat under it for a year until the February

Helen got sick, when some fate or mystery lit a match and I had to give it up.

I had come home from school, and for no reason at all I stopped beside the bush and brushed a small circle of snow from the top of it, using my coat sleeve. It was a dark afternoon, with a sky as flat gray as the side of a Greyhound bus, and I looked down into the darkness of the pearly everlasting as if years ago I'd left something inside it, something that had grown quietly and now asked to be collected—my first thought was that, whatever it was in there, it had surely added to my life.

Just then a bird flew out of the bush as fast as a bullet, and it shot between me and the winter sky. Another one followed it, then several more. The last one came out with a squawk of alarm and a sound that might have been its wings catching and tearing on the branches. They won't come back again, I decided. Not tonight. I know them.

I went into the house. I made myself a bread and butter sandwich and ate it standing up in the kitchen. I sat at the kitchen table and looked through an old *National Geographic*. Finally I went to get my homework. As I passed the window that faced the yard and Flat Street, I looked out and saw my bush on fire.

I'd heard of "acts of God," though it never occurred to me that God could find a person at home and walk right in and take something precious from them. For a long time I couldn't move, and then when I could I filled a pot with water and walked out and flung it at the spot where only an hour before there'd been a bush with birds in it, my pearly everlasting.

"Hoodlums" was Harriet's reaction. (Anyone roaming the block who didn't belong there was a hoodlum.) It was after dark when she and Julian came home, and I led them out and lit up the stump with a flashlight. "They did this very same thing to the Carl Swann family on I Street."

"But he's the fire chief," I said.

"I can't help it, Augusta. Ruth Ann Swann snooped around for an hour on hands and knees and finally came up with the corner of an old kerosene rag hitched on a twig."

"I hardly call that evidence," said Julian. He turned to me. "You're certain you saw no one, Gussy? No strange behavior of any kind?"

"Nothing, Papa. It just burned down."

He took the flashlight from me and swooshed it over the ground and turned it off. "When I was a boy I set a door on fire once with a magnifying glass. It wasn't like that, was it?"

I shook my head in the dark, and all I could think to say was, "I'm not you, Julian. I loved that bush."

The next afternoon I went to see Helen, but she was feverish and kept complaining of a noise I couldn't hear. "It's something bumping the window," she said.

"There's nothing bumping the window."

"Yes," she insisted, "there it goes again."

I saw her flinch, as if whatever it was had entered the room and barely missed her as it flew around. We established that it flew around, and that it hadn't found its way inside yet but it might at any moment. To prevent this I got up and closed the window.

"What are you doing?"

"I'm keeping whatever-it-is out."

"It's already in!" she cried.

"It couldn't be. A second ago you said it was out."

"Well now it's in. You can see it's in!" She swatted at something above her head.

"I can't see anything, Helen."

"You're looking in the wrong place. Look where I'm looking."

Instead I set my eyes on my friend, who was tossing back and forth in the bed. Her hair was damp, and drops of sweat had come out on her forehead. "Did you know I had tuberculosis once? I could have died of it," I told her.

"Don't say anything you don't mean, Gussy." She kicked the sheets off her and onto the floor and lay still. "Jordan says that's what killed Wallace the first time. TB."

"How many times did he die, Helen?"

She held up two fingers.

"What killed him the second time?"

"I think we did."

Without another word she fell asleep. It was the kind of sleep that wraps you like a coat, where each breath buttons another button. Not a sleep you fall down into, with your own weight and gravity on your side, so for a minute or two you're as still as a stump in a wildfire. Not that. This sleep was of the rising up kind. It came and collected Helen and was meant to last. I sat through the first of it—about twenty minutes—reading a good book, *The Yearling,* and checking her breathing from time to time. It was like watching a table breathe, that's how still she was.

I closed the book and could have said anything or nothing then, it made no difference to her, but I chose the words "thank you" and said them right out loud, because we'd done nothing but argue that month and to have her close and quiet now seemed well worth thanking somebody for. Maybe the medicine made her argue, but more likely she hated to have me whole, living, breathing and walking on two feet towards her, when she could barely raise her head off the pillow to take juice or soup through a straw. We argued about the smallest things. We argued so she could keep up with me—and keep me with her. More than once, at the end of the afternoon when I stood up to say good-bye, she caught hold of the hem of my blue school tunic and wouldn't let go; and though the arm that held me was weak and light as air, I couldn't have moved if her bed was on fire, unless she moved with me.

I thought the bad moods of my friend were all my doing I didn't connect them to her long, idle hours alone in her room, often alone in that house. Jordan Walsh was seldom there when I arrived, and never there when I left, and in one of our few conversations that wasn't an argument, I discovered why.

"What does she do in the afternoons?"

"Now she has a job."

"She should be with you!"

"Well she can't be. She has to have a job. This"—Helen swept her hand down her T-shirt and across the light blanket that covered her—"isn't exactly something we asked for." She lowered her voice. "I think it's breaking the bank."

I was speechless for a minute or two, so thoroughly unused to thinking in terms of what it cost to be ill, for I was treated free by my father the few times I cut myself or ran a fever, and the tuberculosis was too long ago to remember. Finally I said, "What is it, her job?" But the queer look on Helen's face told me *no,* and we finished up that afternoon arguing about Asia Minor, which I made the mistake of calling a place.

"Oh no, it's not a place, Gussy."

I felt like saying, "Miss Know-it-all, what is it then?" But I raised my eyebrows instead, and that asked the question for me.

"It was a place," said Helen, "but so was the Roman Empire and that's not a place anymore, either. Look it up in the *World Atlas* if you don't believe me." She pointed to the book that was never far from her, but I had no intention of leaving my chair.

"If something was a place, then it's still a place," I said. "Maybe its name changes, but once there's something, there can't be nothing all of a sudden. It's got to go somewhere, and wherever it goes that's where it is."

I finished off this thought in a great deal of mental confusion, knowing I was in above my head and hoping the plunge was necessary. Helen laughed at me. Often it was the kindest thing she could do. The few times it wasn't, we both knew it and felt it, and I wasn't likely to visit her for a day or two—though it gave me no peace to stay away. I had tried to find a friend in any one of my old school friends—Agnes, Julia, Deirdre, Ashley, the Jones twins, even Connie Browne—but it was too late, for the talk always came around to Helen, and when it did I had to clamp my tongue between my teeth and lie for her, nodding Yes! She's much better! and, while I turned away with my hands shredding paper in my pockets, they basked in the false good news.

I don't believe a child's meant to know the loneliness I knew; I was lucky and didn't know it for long. It's a different thing in the hands of a child than it is when an older person gets hold of it. Jordan Walsh was the first one to put this thought in my head, and she knew loneliness from back to front and inside out I discovered. I met her one day in the middle of the footbridge that crossed the river, the same footbridge that had in its own way introduced me to Helen. Before we could open our mouths to speak, the factory whistle blew five o'clock, a superstitious hour for me. I thought it was a good sign at the time.

I was coming from her side and she from mine. "I just saw Helen," I explained. It was almost dark. I had stayed longer than usual.

"Of course you did, Augusta. How is she?"

I was hit with a sudden shock and confusion that made me say, "You know she has lupus, don't you?"

"Yes, thank you. I knew that. I think I've known that for a long time. I mean, it's been a familiar face, hasn't it? Now the face has a name."

I said I guessed it had, and we both stamped our feet in the cold. Jordan said, "Helen steers for you, Augusta. It may not feel like it, but she never loses sight of you, not for one minute. Do you realize that?"

I didn't know what I realized, but I doubted Helen steered for anything these days. She found hope impractical. It was too airy for her. She needed something as solid and honest as *what had been,* and in the middle of that bridge I told Jordan so. I described our adventure of the week before, when feeling well, or at least impatient to be up out of her bed and in motion, Helen had tossed her covers aside and, using my arm to lean against, she'd led me out of her room. Jordan's room was next to Helen's, and next to that was a room I'd never once set foot inside. It was there we were headed. She kicked the door—"Stubborn!"—and told me to turn the knob at the same time, and after a few tries we forced it open.

It was a large room, twice the size of Helen's, and its near emptiness gave the air a heavy feeling that reminded me of the Lands and People Museum. The only furniture was a narrow bed against one wall, with a bare pillow at one end of it and a tall stack of sheets and blankets at the other. A couple of the whitest light bulbs I'd ever seen lay on the pillow, like a pair of white doves. Under the bed I noticed a single long, brown shoe. It was as long as both my feet together, and the length and solitude of it spoiled the sudden lightheartedness I'd been given by those light bulbs. I shivered, and asked Helen about it, but she only scowled and said, "Someone with a big foot would need a big shoe, wouldn't they?"

"Someone with one big foot would have two," I shot back. "Who lives here?"

Her eyes searched the room, which had so little in it I didn't know what she expected to find. But the emptiness itself seemed to satisfy her, and she answered, "I hope nobody does soon."

Just then a cloud shifted and the sun dropped in a solid square from the room's only window, illuminating a strange object on the floor. It looked like a small seamstress's dummy with a pair of leather goggles slung about the neck. "What's that?" I wondered.

Helen had her back to me, waiting to go. She didn't even look up. "Aviator's goggles. They were Wallace's."

"No, *that*. Turn around."

"Oh. Jordan used to make our clothes."

"But it's only a child's size, Helen."

She glared at me. "Well we were children!"

The "we" made it a curious answer. She never talked about a sibling, but now I remembered it was the other mystery in her life—eclipsed by Wallace. "Who's 'we'?" I asked, but she had her face set in a familiar way, with her bottom lip rolled over her top one, and I knew she'd say nothing. Before we left I dragged the dummy to the window and propped her up so she could see what she could see, and

Helen named her after a couple of trapped insects that groggily crisscrossed the glass: Saint Bees.

Now I said to Jordan, "Today she asked me to take her into that room again, but it was different. The bed was made. Saint Bees was gone. Helen got angry. There was a chair, and a shelf for books, and a dresser, and there were some framed pictures on the wall. They were photographs," I remembered, "all of the same lady. She was dressed up like a queen."

"She is a queen." Jordan smiled. "She's the queen of England. Was that shoe still under the bed?"

Before I could answer a pair of jets passed, flying in formation, followed by a dark pack of ten or fifteen more. Their sound trailed them, which was odd. The only other time I'd seen such a thing the sound had rushed ahead to warn us.

"I find them sinister!" Jordan shouted over the noise.

"I think they're beautiful!" I shouted back.

Their wing lights kept them in sight for a long time, though the sky itself was the same drab color they were. When they finally disappeared, they disappeared over the old ruins of the sanatorium, and Jordan nodded. "You watch. They come and go through a crack in the sky."

"Wallace did that, didn't he?"

She didn't answer. Her head was tilted up, looking at the hill, where it was too late to distinguish the rubble of Corinth unless you knew it and could imagine it.

"He flew planes, didn't he?"

"That was one of the things he said he did."

"I had TB too," I said. It was the only thing in the world I could think of that meant something to both of us—besides Helen, and besides the recent jets.

We said good-bye. I put my hand out awkwardly to

shake hers, but she put hers on top of my head, and from there it slipped down to my shoulder. I thought about her that night, and all the next day, which was a Saturday. I'd never been to Helen's house on a Saturday. I was kept from it by the sight of my own mother, who wrapped herself in her robe until four or five in the afternoon, going barefoot—or worse, treading on the backs of her slippers. On that day we walked around in twilight, for as often as Julian yanked up one venetian blind I lowered it again. "Mother's not dressed yet!"

"Gussy, it's a Saturday."

"Why can't she dress? You dress. Other people dress." But of this last I wasn't so sure, and the thought of surprising Jordan Walsh at home, undressed, smelling faintly sour, as a room does when someone has slept in it too long, made me blush with embarrassment. I had only to ask Helen to find out it wasn't so, and that Saturday when I went to visit her I mustered the courage.

"Oh no." My friend firmly shook her head. "If anyone doesn't dress around our house it's Joan."

"Who's Joan?"

"She doesn't live here."

"But who is she, Helen?"

"Sometimes she comes to take a bath and I see her in the hall with a towel on, but the towel's wrapped around her head."

"Maybe she shampoos her hair in the bath," I suggested, suddenly so caught up in the toilette of this stranger I forgot to wonder any longer who she was and why she bathed in Helen's house.

"We call it a hairwash," Helen scowled.

"What's the difference? It's the same thing."

"My mother used to give my father a hairwash every morning."

"Who, Jordan?" I'd never heard her called anyone's mother before.

"They both liked clean hair. When we lived at the lake, before we moved here, the sink wasn't big enough, so she'd say, 'Wal, sit on the bed,' and he'd sit on the bed and tip his head into a basin."

"This basin was on the floor?"

"No, the basin was up on a chair. She'd rub his head all over with a bar of soap. It was brown soap."

"That's laundry soap."

"Maybe it was laundry soap. When she was done with the soap she'd pour water from the kettle on his hair until the basin almost ran over. Then he'd sit up and shave from the basin. Or when he was sick, we shaved him. He taught Jordan and she taught us."

I was astonished at that particular talent hidden in Helen. To shave a father! She'd crossed a line I'd up until then considered uncrossable. I remembered I'd once refused to cut Julian's nails—a demeaning request, no art to that at all. And Harriet's eye, I'd held that in my hand, but she was a mother, female like me. I had an idea. It involved Helen, and I helped her into the bathroom, where we stood with the sink between us, awkwardly avoiding the mirror. "You look fine," I reassured her.

"No, I look fat."

"I like you in a plain white T-shirt."

"It's not plain white," she said, and turned so I could see the back of it, which was covered with the faces of the astronauts. "It's the cosmonauts," she corrected me. "Joan made it for me. It's the Russians."

"It can't be. They look like our people. Anyway, they

don't send Russians up there, the Russians send monkeys."

She would have won that argument if we'd pursued it, but we were less inclined to argue when she was out of bed and in motion. We had a job ahead of us. While I searched the bathroom for the tool we needed, she leaned over the sink, working the hot and cold taps until she had the right mixture.

"I can't find it, Helen."

"Look around the bathtub."

"I did."

"Did you look under it?"

"Oh. Ours doesn't have an under." I got down on all fours. I'd never seen claw-and-ball feet before, nor the rounded underbelly of a bathtub, and perhaps because I was Julian's daughter, I gasped in admiration and surprise. Helen wondered what I saw, then became impatient when I started naming objects. I finally found what I was looking for, all the way at the back, and pulled it out.

"It's rusty," I said.

"Well, it's been there for a while."

"Doesn't she use it?"

"Not if she can help it." Helen examined it. "Only the blade's rusty. That's easy, we've got a new blade." She took out the old blade, put in a new one and twisted the razor shut. I was amazed at her ease with this equipment and told her so.

"Girls have to shave too," she said. "You'll shave, Gussy. You have dark hair and a lot of it, and when you wear stockings it will scratch your legs."

"I don't think so," I frowned, uncomfortable with these predictions.

"I know somebody our age who shaves. Deirdre George."

"She's not. She's a year older."

"There's someone I know with a mustache, and she shaves it."

I was horrified by this, or perhaps by my friend's sudden animation. "Who?" I had to know. "Who?"

"Miss Piscina."

"I don't believe you. I've never seen it."

"Because she shaves it, that's why. Jordan's seen it. She's a friend of Jordan's."

I felt too exasperated to say another word. The color had faded from this adventure. But there was Helen soaking a washcloth in the sink, squeezing the water through it, and suddenly everything seemed calm again. She made me sit down on the toilet seat. She patted my cheek with the washcloth. "Is it too hot? It ought to be hot but not uncomfortable."

"It's hot. It feels good."

"Then tip your head back."

"Is this how you did it to Wallace?"

She didn't answer. She opened the washcloth and laid it over my face, and the steam filled my nose so it hurt to breathe. She took it off, soaked it and did the same thing again.

"How do you know how long to do it?"

"You wait for the right color pink. Bring your head up."

"I thought you had to use special soap."

"You can."

"Julian puts it on with a brush."

"It's better with a brush, but we don't have a brush. If the beard is tough, you have to do certain things to soften it or you'll cut the person. Hold still."

"If—"

"Don't move! Don't say anything."

She started to draw the razor down one cheek, then

moved it across my lip with short, downward strokes. Under my chin she reversed the motion. Every few strokes she rinsed the razor under the tap and shook the water off it, something I'd seen Julian do. "What about the sideburns?" she wondered.

"What are you going to do to them?"

"Even them up."

"Oh, I'm not sure, Helen!" I was thrown into a panic for a second or two, torn by my own vanity and the pleasure it would give her to change my appearance.

"For heaven's sake, Gussy, who will know?"

She had finished one and was lining up the blade to do the other, when the bathroom door flew open. A woman not much taller than me, somewhere between Helen's height and mine, with curly auburn hair that fanned out across her shoulders, hurried into the bathroom. She was wearing a long robe that bunched on the floor. It was a small bathroom, and the door, as it opened, knocked Helen's arm. Though I could feel nothing, nothing throbbed or trickled, I imagined I'd been cut by the razor, cut on the temple where the blue vein runs through. I started to raise my hand to my head when a cry from the woman stopped me. "Oh, I am cha*grined*. Helen, I'm so sorry. I'm interrupting something." She backed out as suddenly as she'd arrived.

"She has a southern accent," I said.

Helen nodded. "She's from the South." She opened the door and called out into the hallway, "Is Jordan home yet?"

"No, honey, I'm here by myself. What are you all doing in there? Is everything all right?"

"I think I'm bleeding," I whispered.

My friend looked at me and shook her head. "It's fine!" she called back. "Don't tell Jordan."

"Don't tell Jordan what?" But Helen couldn't think of what to say. "Don't you worry," came the voice. "I won't tell Jordan. Cross my heart."

I practically carried Helen back to her bed, where she collapsed against the pillows. We heard Joan running her bath, and I asked, "Are you sure she doesn't live with you?" I remembered the room next to Jordan's that showed all the recent signs of being occupied.

"She can't. She smokes too many cigarettes."

"Do you like her?"

"She's Jordan's friend."

"Where's Jordan now?"

"I'm right here."

Jordan stood in the doorway with one arm up, touching the top of the doorframe. She hadn't seemed so tall to me outside on the footbridge, and I had a moment of believing this wasn't the same person who'd filled my thoughts. "Sit down, Augusta. Go on, sit down." She motioned me back onto Helen's bed, for I'd jumped to my feet in surprise and without thinking. "I understand you're feeling much better, Helen."

"She told you."

"Nobody told me anything. I've just been in the bathroom."

"But Joan's in there," I said.

"Joan's the least of what's in there," said Jordan. "The basin's full of water. The toilet seat's wet. There's soap everywhere and you've found my razor."

"Is there a problem?" asked Helen.

"You, are the problem. I don't know anyone who can be so conveniently well or not well as you manage to be, Helen Walsh. Any more of this, my girl, and you're going back to school. That's a promise."

My friend and I both cried out at once, as if someone had issued a ban on talking or thinking or reading, or sitting quietly and saying nothing, but sitting side by side at least. I said I thought school would be quite honestly dangerous for Helen at this point. "You're unhappy there, Augusta," was Jordan's reply, "and she's unhappy here. It's not a foolish thing I'm suggesting. It's not a punishment. If her health is better, why shouldn't you both be unhappy in the same place? At least you'd be together, you'd have each other, and who knows? Company often creates happiness."

"Or more unhappiness," said Helen sullenly. "You're trying to get rid of me, it's obvious. When's he coming?"

I watched Jordan's arm drop, hitting her thigh without a sound. "He's coming tomorrow," she said quietly. "Joan and I will pick him up."

"I'll come with you."

"I'd hoped you'd be in school, Helen."

"On a Sunday?" I said, trying to find my place in the conversation. "We don't go to school on Sunday, Jordan."

"Is it only Sunday?" she asked. I nodded. "Then I've left out Sunday. We don't collect him until Monday. Joan's promised the car and I'll skip a day of work. Helen, look. It's a long drive, the trip will be tiring, we'll leave very early and probably get home at six or seven, in time for supper. You're welcome to come, you know that, but it didn't occur to me you'd want to, and frankly, the emotion of it might not be the best thing in the world for you or for him. Though oddly enough I worry less about him."

"Who?" I said.

"If he was lying here in front of you, you'd worry about him," said Helen. "You don't know him. You haven't seen him in five years."

"That's not true. I saw him a week ago, and once in November, and we both saw him in March."

"A few days a year, I don't count."

"A few days a year is a few days a year, Helen. I will not have you saying they don't count. They're all we can manage, and all he can manage—"

"If that's true," Helen interrupted, "then I don't see why you think he can live here. Anyway, I didn't say *they* don't count, Jordan, I said *I* don't count them. For me they were nothing, they were just a long car ride. I hated to see him in that place because he hated being there. They were teaching him how to knit! Gussy, they were teaching my brother how to *knit*! I couldn't stand that."

"Harry likes to knit, Helen. Don't say he hated the place."

"That, I can't stand."

"Before the accident he liked to cook. You didn't mind him cooking."

"I never cared for his food," she said, and turned her face into her pillow.

I sat with her after Jordan left, and when she still wouldn't say anything or move—"Nod if you want me here, Helen. You don't want me here? Raise your finger if you want me here"—I said good-bye, I'd see her soon. I really believed this, though some part of me must have known it wasn't true, because as I left I reached for something to take with me, something to remind me of my friend. I took *The Yearling*.

Jordan was standing in the kitchen wearing a raincoat. The coat was buttoned, and the buttons were the color of oil when the light hits it. They were large and not quite round.

"Where's he coming from?" I asked.

"I was outside putting the trash in the bin. Look what the weather's done!" She shook some ice out of her hair.

"No, where's *he* coming from? The brother?"

"Please, Augusta, don't call him the brother. He has a name. His name is Harry. Hasn't Helen ever told you about Harry?"

"She's told me about Wallace," I offered, "one or two things. She'll talk about his hair."

"His hair!" Jordan smiled. "She's a deeply practical child when she wants to be—when she needs to be. She didn't say anything about her own hair, did she?" I shook my head. "She may lose it. I don't say this to worry you, but it doesn't seem fair not to prepare you. She doesn't know it yet and I wouldn't tell her, but with high doses of cortisone it's a possibility. Though it's equally possible nothing will happen, or it can go the other way and she'll have hair everywhere."

"What!" I whispered. "Bearded!"

"No no. Just more hair."

"Because I know someone, a lady with a mustache," I said, forgetting who the source of this information had been. The afternoon suddenly weighed on me and I had to tell Jordan I was certain that too little hair was better than too much. "Anyway," I added, "I was once on a drug that was strong enough to cure a mortal illness, and nothing happened to my, you know." I rubbed my chin and cheeks.

"What on earth was the illness?"

"I had TB, I told you."

Yesterday's footbridge, which had seemed so solidly beneath my feet, started to buckle and sway like a mad dog I'd once described to Helen. I was not about to forgive Jordan for forgetting one word of our conversation, though she quickly said, "TB! How awful for you!"

I shrugged. "Wasn't Wallace on isoniazid?"

"Isoniazid? No, I don't think so. What Wallace had—" She looked at me almost apologetically. "Well, in the old days it was arsenic."

I said I didn't follow that, and she said we might as well sit down. There was a certain kind of silence in the room—like emptiness with teeth, which was something Helen had come up with to describe the moment before she put her bow to her cello. We sat at the table in front of the window. Jordan still had her coat done up to the collar. For some reason it seemed important to me to touch the curtain, to have hold of it in case she talked. It wasn't as thin as our curtain at home, and I was about to guess chintz and say the word, a word I liked, a word I'd learned from Harriet, when I noticed how late it was. The window was dark gray, and some constant thing rapped the glass—a spray of pebbles? Was someone locked out? I thought wildly of Joan wearing only her towel and laughed to myself, then knew it had to be hail.

"Joan says I lack courage at the crucial moments," said Jordan.

"I don't think Joan knows everything."

"You won't like him for this, Augusta." She spread her hands on the table. They were large hands, like the feet of an ostrich, both pink and pale. "But try not to hate him for it, we've done that already. He had something called syphilis and didn't know it, not for a long time, not for months. I never caught it. He recovered. What the children knew of it was only what they could see, and that, oddly enough, wasn't where the pain lay. It's a horrid disease. It looks a lot like Helen's lupus, the same rash, the swelling, the aches and fevers. But the pain is elsewhere." She put one of those large hands on the top button of her raincoat. "Up here."

"Syphilis? Jordan, that can't be the same thing as TB. Helen told me he had TB."

"TB? Oh, dear God!" She laughed. "Dear, dear Helen. No, it's nothing like TB, Augusta, you're absolutely right. It's sometimes called by two letters, that's what confused her. It's a venereal disease. VD. That's what she was thinking of."

"Oh. Well, how do you get it? How bad is it?"

"Some people die from it."

"How do you get it?"

"You get it—" She stopped and looked at me. "You can get it from having sex with someone who has it. Sometimes you're born with it."

"Wallace was—?"

"Not born with it. He got it from— He worked at the plant, at the factory here in town, and he got it from a woman at the factory."

"He couldn't have!" I cried, for the impossibility of it suddenly struck me, and I only wondered why it hadn't occurred to Jordan. "He was sick before you lived here. I thought he was sick when you lived at the lake."

"That's right. We lived at the lake but Wallace drove all the way into town to work. He stayed in town for the five workdays, and then he drove back to the lake to spend the weekends with us."

"He didn't live with you and you weren't divorced?"

Her lips twitched and she shook her head. "No, we weren't divorced. We just didn't spend every day together. I liked it out at the lake, and Helen and Harry did too. They loved the lake."

I was about to say I loved a place once too, that I loved the sanatorium and the whole hill it was on, and for a while my place had been more important than any person. Instead I said, "Too bad it's easier to come back to a place than a person."

Jordan nodded and pushed herself out of her chair, and I did the same. Then she surprised me. She bent her knees and put her arms all the way around me, pulling me close. It lasted only a few seconds, not long enough for me to remember to relax, then she let me go.

"Doesn't anybody ever hug you, Gussy?" Gussy! The name in her mouth, and the soft way she said it. It was anything but diminutive, and it tied me to her the way that embrace had not. "We ought to run you home soon."

"You can put me on a bus."

"No, Joan will take you in the car."

"She's here?"

As if summoned, we heard a door open and slam shut, and quick footsteps approaching. Joan appeared wearing a yellow sweater that belonged to one of my dearest memories of Jordan. She had on a pair of black stretch pants with a strap that went under each foot. She wore white socks without shoes, and the black strap went over the socks.

"Don't slam the door, Jazie, the whole house shakes."

"It's the fault of the door. I cannot shut that door gently and have it stay shut. If it were me, Jordan, I'd let it stay open." She seemed to see me for the first time, though I was standing right next to Jordan. "Well, look at me, stocking footed in front of our guest! I know you must be the famous Augusta Cotton. How do you do. I'm the famous Joan. We caught a glimpse of each other in the bathroom. My goodness!" Her hands came together as if she was praying. "You certainly have done something unusual to your hair. I would say you were missing a sideburn."

I only glared at her. "That's not your sweater. You don't

go into somebody's house and take their sweater. Maybe they do that where you live, in the South, but here we don't. Does Jordan go into your house and take your things? No, she doesn't."

My face burned. I carried my coat to the kitchen door and put it on there, facing away from the room.

"I'll take you," said Jordan.

Joan made a shushing noise. "Honey, you know you don't drive."

"It's a short way. I'll take her."

"Look out there! It's thick as milk!" It was true, the hail had turned to a wet snow. "You'll never make it down the hill, and if you make it down you'll never make it back again."

"I'll walk from the bottom."

"You may walk from the ditch."

Jordan lifted her finger at me. "Wait, Augusta. Wait here. Promise me?"

They argued in the hallway, doing little to cover their voices. "To involve a child, Jordan, I just won't allow it. What kind of serious talk were you having, to put you both in such a fiery state? Two powder kegs. And that explosion about the sweater, I've never—"

"Shh! Wallace came up."

"Wallace came up?"

"The syphilis came up. His thing with Audrey Alexander."

"How on earth? Oh, Jordie!"

"We were calm until now."

"You can't have been! I don't see how you can speak about it without getting ugly."

"That child doesn't need my judgment in her world."

Before the wrong one returned to take me home, I took

myself. I jammed Helen's copy of *The Yearling* in my pocket, and it slapped my leg all the way down to the river. I didn't bother to think what Jordan saw when she saw that place by the door that no longer held me. She called Harriet—the phone was ringing as I touched our house—and was told I was safely somewhere at least.

As for Joan, I'd already chosen to harden my heart against her. I wasn't bright or tragic about it. I was eleven and a half, impulsive and in love with my own faulty logic. Perhaps I needed to learn the lesson that to sever ties with one means to lose them all. Like whacking an arm or leg from the body, with fatal consequences; and Joan was no less a limb of that body than I was. She was Jordan's good friend, as I was Helen's. What shocked and surprised me—and ashamed me, so I told no one—was that the place I wished to occupy in Jordan Walsh's heart, the place I, at that age, had assumed open to me, that place beyond good friendship, sometimes called love, was taken, filled, not available. Joan had it. I knew this the moment I saw her appear in Jordan's sweater, wearing that particular yellow memory of mine into a state so brittle and thin I questioned everything, and closed my heart, and thought I could single out one to exclude while the other remained. I was dead wrong about that, and the only consolation was that the one to point out my wrong reasoning was the one I'd reasoned wrongly for. Jordan literally caught me by the collar as I was leaving school on the Thursday after the Saturday I'd last seen Helen. I hadn't crossed the river all that week, and she scolded me severely.

"We would mind it less if you were punishing only yourself, Augusta, but we miss you as much as you miss us. This week was like a slap in the face to Helen." She read my thoughts and nodded. "Yes, it hurt me too."

We walked to the bridge together, and I half-expected a blizzard to enfold us, or one of us to speak about the trees, or a Hostess cake wrapper to fly against her coat or mine—all things from my life with Helen. But it was nothing like that, and I was relieved. I walked lightly, my feet flashing three times for Jordan's every single step.

"Come and meet Harry," she offered.

"I can't today, I'm getting glasses."

"Does Helen know that?"

"Probably not."

"She's always wanted glasses."

We had entered the sycamore wood when I suddenly wondered, "What about your job? Jordan, why aren't you at your job?"

"I've got Harry at home, that's one reason, and Helen's being impossible, really as difficult as she knows how to be. I can't go off to work anymore when they're my work. That's what I've just told my job."

"What about money?"

"We'll have to see about money."

"Can't you tell Joan to work? You could have some of her money."

"You *are* tyrannical," she laughed. "The trouble is, Joan works already and I have some of her money."

"What does she do?"

"She drives a taxi."

"Really?"

"What I need is someone to stay home with my two embattled children."

"Well, tell her not to work. Tell her to stay home."

"Is that what happens at your house? Your mother tells your father to stay home, and he stays home?"

"Usually it's the other way around. Sure, it happens often, all the time," I lied.

"I have trouble believing that, but even if I did, do you think our house is like your house in every way?"

I said nothing, which seemed better than lying twice. Finally I said, "I asked Helen where you worked and she wouldn't tell me."

"That's because Helen hates to think of herself as the reason I slave away, but I don't, I didn't slave away. I had an easy job and I liked the company. I loved the company. The company and I are old friends. We once took a train across Canada together. We go way back."

"Who's the company?"

"Jean Fox. Jean Wolfe, your art teacher. She was Fox before she became Mrs. Wolfe, and as if that wasn't enough, her nickname was always Weasel!"

"It rhymes with easel," I said, "maybe that's why."

"It could be. What a thought! It certainly could be."

Jordan was filled with a sudden, puzzling excitement, and I had to ask, "Is that really the company?" As hard as I tried to shrink Canada, it still seemed too vast a country to cross by train with Mrs. Wolfe.

"Yes, that's who I worked for," said Jordan. "I worked at your school, up in the art room. After all of you went home, I helped Jean tidy up and sweep the floor and get ready for the next day's classes. You girls never wash out your brushes well enough, and they get gummy and ruined." She stopped and turned to me. "If you started using more color and less line in your drawings, Augusta, I think you'd find people just as interesting as fruit bowls."

"You've seen them!" I cried. "Oh, Jordan!" I shielded my face with my hands in embarrassment.

"No, you mustn't hide. They're good work. The squareness of that girl's head is marvelous."

We started talking again, and with each step my confidence seeped back into my body, until in the middle of the sycamore wood, with the footbridge not yet in sight, I knew what a talented artist I could be, and chattered easily about many things, beginning with the relative squareness of Annabel Jones's head. "She didn't think it was square enough!" I laughed.

"Then she's an optimist."

"Wouldn't that make her a pessimist?"

We juggled those words for a moment or two, and as we did I remembered another word I'd wondered about, a word I'd found scribbled inside the front cover of *The Yearling*. The inscription read, *For HW, Love JZ. NOT a potboiler! A damn good story and friend!* Now I asked Jordan, "What's a potboiler?"

"Gosh, a potboiler?"

I nodded, then saw in the corner of my eye the footbridge. It seemed to approach us and darken our conversation. There was a bench close by, by the river, and I said, "Let's sit down on that."

"I don't know what to tell you. A potboiler. What exactly is a potboiler? Honestly, Augusta," she laughed, "you're sounding more and more like Helen every day."

"The old Helen, you mean."

"No, I don't think I meant the old Helen, or the new Helen. I meant the Helen we know, both of us, the Helen who refuses to stay in bed, who refuses to say boo to her brother unless it's to torment him, who won't let the doctor near her—he came twice this week and we're back to the hot towels."

"The hot towels!"

"That's the Helen I mean," said Jordan. "The Helen who's always been with us and always will."

"Always might not be for very long!" I cried, feeling suddenly impatient with the crawling pace of our conversation, and its little importance, and the nearness of the bridge, and the humor and happiness—the satisfaction of the afternoon, while my friend's lupus raced from blood to muscle to bone like a swift horse.

Jordan looked at me as she never had before, with a solemnity that seemed to leave her speechless. I knew she would try to explain something. I knew we'd traveled a long way and would not go back. "Look at me," she said, and I did. "I think I understand life—all our lives—as being wider and deeper than they ever are long. Don't, Augusta, please don't worry about long. Deep and wide, yes. Like this river. I'm all for that." And she leaned forward as if to seal a privacy between us.

# Chapter Five

"That," said Julian, "is another issue altogether, and one you'll have to bring up with your mother. If she feels your friend is—"

"Unsafe! Papa, she said it, 'unsafe'!"

"Unsafe then. If she feels she's unsafe, it must be for other than medical reasons. There's just not a shred of evidence that lupus is contagious, and she knows that as well as I do."

While Julian washed and I dried the dishes, I tried to think of Helen as someone dangerous, someone whom Harriet had good reason to forbid me to see. It had happened suddenly, on the way home from the optician's. I had possession of my first pair of glasses, for reading only, but unlike other girls who boasted of the event, and wore their glasses ceaselessly for weeks, until their eyes wobbled and their noses ached, I hid them in my pocket and even then felt vulnerable and degraded. Except for Jordan Walsh I had told no one, and planned to keep the secret as long as I could.

Harriet, however, seemed to need to march the streets in celebration, inflicting her joy on perfect strangers or dim acquaintances, so reassured was she that life would take me too. It would sweep me up and carry me along; I would grow and change—and decay. I sat in the hard chair of the optician and felt my mother's pleasure so increase, an actual rise in temperature in that chill, dark room, an office smelling bitterly of ammonia and an occasional streak of spearmint whenever the old optician snapped his gum. For Harriet it happened there, my leap, my passage out of a world she'd never understood and into one she had no trouble imagining, where people who had once been children lost bits of themselves, and with aches and pains repeated their days until, in the end, they softened and succumbed.

I was only happy to be rid of that room. The old man's hands trembled, and an old, pounding radiator spat steam. We'd read about Hades, and here was Hades, dark and damp, lined from floor to ceiling with display cases of every kind of glasses frame imaginable, each with its own blank look and a cumulative gaze so unwavering I felt myself thrown in among the Lost Souls. Outside the world of mythology, I knew little enough about death to let those frames remind me of the vacant eyes of the calf I'd once come across in a clearing—and given in to, and raced away from.

Now I burst out onto the street and waited there for Harriet, who had stopped a woman entering the building. They spoke intently about farsightedness, astigmatism, every possible defect of the eye, the way other mothers gossiped with pride about a daughter's farewell to the world of undershirts. Most of my friends, I knew, had fallen from that graceful world. I wondered why we had to celebrate these flaws.

She caught up to me and I whispered, "Do you need to announce it, Mother?"

"Why not?" We crossed the street. "We'll just stop by and show Mrs. Greene, the druggist's wife."

"We won't! We hardly know her!"

"Augusta, we're right here. Be proud!" She pushed me in ahead of her, her hand glued to my back like a gun.

There was Mrs. Greene, dispensing something to someone. She stood behind the counter, a bony, erect woman wearing a tan blouse pinned at the collar with her only piece of jewelry, a dog's-eye brooch. It was the size of a dog's eye, and it was milky gray, a blind eye. We had laughed and pointed at it as children, but as I saw it now with the growing pressure of Harriet's hand on my back, I knew it to be the cause of all the unhappiness I'd ever felt inside that store, an unhappiness that formed like a mist inside the colored bottles in the window, and tainted the two aisles, and I felt sorry for this woman who had to wear it as an ornament.

"Show her!" Harriet nudged me, and called out, "Hullo, Mrs. Greene!"

I brought the glasses from my pocket in their hard, brown case and endured the scrutiny of that brooch (which occurred exactly at my eye level), and suffered the compliments of the druggist's wife, though she directed them not to me but to my mother. I heard the words "owlish" and "inexpensive," for they were plain black frames that might have made me look intelligent; then as quickly as I dared I took the glasses off again and moved fretfully along the counter, gazing at antacids—which turned suddenly to laxatives! Beyond that, at last, I found a rack of Life Savers.

I put a nickel down and rolled the hard, rum-flavored candy on my tongue. Yet how impossible it seemed, to enjoy those minutes standing in the rubber- and sulfur- and salt-smelling drugstore.

On the way home I dragged a step or two behind Harriet, whose zest for presenting my new self to the world had worn off. She was cranky. Supper would be late. "Don't dawdle, Augusta, you do it to annoy me. Walk beside me, not like a dog I kicked."

"That lady's pin, her brooch. What did it remind you of?"

"It reminded me of what it is," she snapped. "A simple question gets a simple answer."

We walked in silence for a block. "Does she know about your eye?"

"Who? Which eye? I've got two."

"The one that isn't there."

"So the whole world needs to know? I don't tell everybody everything. I tell Mrs. Greene what's Mrs. Greene's business."

"I'm not her business, Mother." My hand went to my pocket, where I squeezed the glasses case, to crush it and what was inside it if I could.

Harriet seldom flew at me, and never in public, but now she caught my arm and shook us both to a standstill on the corner of I Street. "All the time now I'm living with a little Mrs. Wise Guy. You can believe me, Augusta, it's not attractive." She started to release me but remembered something and gripped me harder. "She's unsafe."

"Who is?"

"I never said this about anyone your age before, but that girl is sick and she's unsafe. And her mother who calls me after dark in a snowstorm and asks if you're home, home in your own house where you're supposed to be, not out crossing the town by yourself, she's a mother who deserves what she gets for her own child, I hate to say it, but she can darn well leave me mine!"

A car slowed at the corner and honked, and Harriet's hands flew up in the air, a guilty gesture disguised as a greeting. "Wave!" she ordered. My own hand floated up. The car continued down I Street, and I asked, "Who was that?"

"How should I know? Someone who knows us."

In silence we swung off Second Street into the piercing quiet of Flat Street, and for the first time I looked and noticed how the first few days of March had changed the neighbor's cherry tree; how it flooded out darkly against the dark sky, instead of holding back, holding in, as it had all winter long. It was bare and bright and dark all at once. Was this possible? I had never felt the feeling of "hopeful" before from anything in nature, and now it stunned me, and I put my hand out towards it, though it was far away in the next yard.

Harriet had her hand on the gate. I waited for her to go through into our yard. "Make me happy," she said, "don't see her again." I shook my head. "Why? You have other friends, Augusta. If you don't you ought to. Don't make me forbid it." When she was gone I swung on the gate like a child and waited for Julian to come home.

It was well after dark when he stumbled in, laughing under the redolent weight of a fifty-pound bag. "Hot manure," he explained, shrugging it off his shoulder and into the garden, where the bag split and lay steaming in the pale light of the house.

"It looks like something else," I said, walking backwards, unable to take my eyes from it. We went inside, and my mind still played with it, until by suppertime I couldn't have said what it was, a bag of manure or a freshly killed body in our yard.

Julian gave it another name. "It's called payment in kind, Gussy. When a family or an individual can't pay money, they pay in goods or services. It assures poor people the medical care they're entitled to, especially if for some reason they have inadequate insurance. It's an old, old tradition."

"Archaic," said Harriet. She stood at the stove, salting a pot of noodles. "You make it sound like every other doctor in the world does this, Julian, brings home a bag of, excuse me, shit, in exchange for a week of his time."

"Hardly a week, Harriet."

"What then, an hour? Even better." She laughed bitterly. "One bag an hour we'll be buried in the stuff, you wait. That child's not out of the woods yet, not by a long shot, and you know it." She turned to me. "He hates to hear it. He's stubborn. He closes his ears to the truth."

We ate without a word. Finally Harriet stood up and left her plate in the sink. "Next time, see if you can squeeze a chicken out of them, something useful," she said, and reeled around suddenly as if one of us had tugged a string. "Get her to tell you what she did today." She nodded at me. "Ask your daughter what she did today. Tell him, Augusta."

"Harriet, privately," he soothed her. "When you go." She went, and we sat for several minutes saying nothing.

"Okay," I shrugged. "I got glasses."

"I know. She told me."

"They make me feel dizzy."

"That will go away. Bifocals are worse." He took his place in front of the sink. "Wash or dry, Gussy?"

"I don't care. Dry. It doesn't matter."

I watched him roll his sleeves above his elbows, taking forever as he always did. I wondered if it was the simplicity of the act itself he relished, or the chore ahead he dreaded. "Do you look like that when you deliver a baby?"

"Like what?" he laughed. "Wearing your mother's apron?"

"I'd like to see that sometime, Papa. Birth." We were quiet a minute, then I asked, "Why can't you be Helen's doctor?"

He looked at me. "What would any of us gain by that?"

"They don't have any money."

"How would they pay?"

"I thought they wouldn't pay. I thought"—and here I had to stop and wait for my steady voice to come back to me—"I thought they could pay in kind. Jordan could work in the garden or something, or I could work for her."

"Jordan?"

"That's Helen's mother."

He frowned and added a roll to each sleeve, though one was too high and tight on his arm already and it seemed to cause him actual pain. "It's not possible, Gussy."

"Why?"

"For a dozen reasons."

"Name one."

"She's already under a doctor's care."

"But you don't like him."

"I'm afraid that's irrelevant in this business. If anything, it makes it more difficult to take a patient from him."

"What if he gave her to you?"

"He wouldn't. For everything else he isn't, Sal Beveridge is territorial to a fault. That's his side of the river"—Julian nodded vaguely in Helen's direction—"and the width of a river can be useful to two human beings who have nothing in common but the tools they use and the town they live in."

"You're both doctors!"

"With all people, especially with doctors, it's not just what we do but how we do it. You know that."

I did know that, but I knew something else too, and let myself say it. "She's not getting better, Papa. I don't care how. Helen doesn't care how. She cares what, and she's not getting better. Anyway," I said softly, for there was nothing left to argue, I was sure I was right, "you already have one patient from his side of the river. It's whoever gave you that horse manure."

Harriet stuck her head in to tell us she was going to bed. "You go too, Augusta."

"It's early, Mother. Look, we haven't even started the dishes."

"Slowpokes!" She lowered her voice. "He'll talk to you. Why? He never talks to me, only to contradict."

"That's not true—" Julian stopped himself, but she'd already won her point and turned her back on us.

"We love you , Mother," I called after her. "I love you." If not for me she wouldn't have a friend in the world, I thought. She's like Helen.

"How old a person is she?"

"Harriet? I don't know. Around fifty."

"Fifty!" Helen shook her head in disbelief. "Jordan's only thirty-seven, and she seems old. Fifty!"

"Joan's how old?"

"If you listen to her, thirty-three."

"She's not thirty-three," I scowled. "I bet she lies about her age."

My friend nodded. She rolled onto her side and held her arm out to me, and I wrapped her hand in a hot towel.

"Why do you think we lie, Gussy? Why does she lie? Why does anyone lie?"

"Maybe we've tried telling the truth," I said. It wasn't enough, but it was all I could offer.

"Jordan says Wallace lied. He lied in little ways about almost everything. She says he probably wasn't learning how to fly a plane, he was spending his money on something else. Someone else is what she said."

"She told you that?"

"No. She told Joan with the bathwater running and I heard it."

"Well, pretend you didn't hear it. It wasn't meant for you."

Neither of us was satisfied, and we looked at different corners of the ceiling for a while. I started to kick my heel against the bed until she told me, "Don't."

"Okay. Can I say something?" The sheets rustled, but she didn't say no. "Helen? Is there someone named Audrey Alexander?"

She looked at me in blank surprise.

"Jordan said her name. She and Joan were arguing in the hallway."

"You know her. You've met her."

"What do you mean I've met her? Who is she? I haven't met her. I've barely even heard of her."

"Yes, you met her on a bus. The day Kennedy—"

"Not the actress!" I cried. "You sat next to her. She had a fur coat on and she was eating Chinese food out of a carton."

"How do I know what she was eating? Anyway, she's not an actress, Gussy. When Wallace lived in town she used to do his laundry. That's what Jordan told us. She's a laundress."

"A laundress?"

"We went to her house once, and it was covered with laundry. It wasn't really a house, it was a room. It looked like a jail if you want to know the truth. The sink and the toilet were right next to the bed, and there was a—"

"Helen, I thought she worked at the factory."

"Well, she didn't." She glared at me and added, "There was a bathtub you sat on."

"Oh." Then I wondered, "How do you sit on a bathtub?"

"It had a board over it. That's where Harry and I sat, and I don't know where Jordan sat unless it was on the bed." She thought a minute. "No, that's where Mrs. Alexander sat."

"Maybe they both sat on the bed."

"They wouldn't have."

"Someone sat on the toilet then."

"Oh Gussy, no!"

"Maybe Jordan stood up."

Helen seemed to like that. "Yes, she stood up. She kept her coat on."

"I've seen that," I said. "I've seen her keep her coat on."

"There was nowhere to put your coat if you didn't want to put it on the bed or the bathtub."

"Or on the floor," I offered. "Was it a linoleum floor?"

She nodded.

"Oh, good. I love linoleum."

"You wouldn't if you lived with it. At our house at the lake everything was linoleum, even the roof. Even the blankets, even the lake when it froze, that's what Wallace used to say. Jordan says it's just something you live with if you're poor."

"Mrs. Alexander was poor?"

"She was so poor we saw a rat in her house."

"I've seen a rat."

"You haven't!"

"Sure. Plenty of times. They live under the boys' school and up at the sanatorium. Nature's full of them."

"This rat," Helen whispered, "was as big as a dog!"

"No." I refused to believe it. "Maybe the size of a cat. Maybe a cat the size of a kitten."

"I'm telling you, Gussy!" She held her hands two feet apart, not giving an inch. "It crawled in through the broken window and onto the bathtub and right across Harry's leg!"

"I would have jumped up and screamed!"

"Mrs. Alexander did that."

"Well, what did you do?"

"I watched Harry. He caught it. He put his hand right around its neck. It was opening and closing its mouth like it was trying to say words."

"Helen, it was choking!"

"Then he pretended he was the rat speaking. He said things like, 'Hello, my name is John, my name is Oh Boy,' and he barked like a dog. Jordan told him to put it down, but the rat started singing a song. Harry only knows one song, 'Some Enchanted Evening,' because Jordan doesn't sing and Wallace tried to teach us songs, but with Harry only that one stuck. The rat sang a little, then it started to sort of gallop, the way a dog does when it's dreaming. You've seen that. That's when Jordan grabbed some linen off the floor and—"

"Some what?"

"Linen. It means sheets."

"I know what it means."

"She wrapped her hands in the sheets and got the rat

away from Harry and threw it out the window. She tried to throw it out the window, but there were bars on it, so she had to stuff it through the bars, sheet and all."

I turned away in disgust, wondering many things; wondering how far that rat had fallen and whether it had landed in an alley or a busy street; wondering if it had lived, or whether it had died singing. I didn't know the song "Some Enchanted Evening," but the name of it made me think of a warm place where people lived in families, a clean place where night meant that delicious roughness of sheets, of linen, and a stack of covers trapping you in a pleasant way. I said to Helen, "Why did you go there? Why couldn't Wallace pick up his own laundry?"

"We didn't pick up his laundry."

"I thought she was a laundress! You said she was a laundress and when Wallace lived in town she did his laundry."

"He was dead, Gussy. There wasn't any Wallace. We went to pick up an ant farm. It was Mrs. Alexander's, and she gave it to Harry. She said if you cut him off at the knee and made him fatter and gave him a smaller head he looked just like her own son."

I didn't know what to say so I got up and stood by the window. I needed to see something out there that had nothing to do with Helen; a leaf or an animal that kept no secrets from me, that couldn't surprise me or hurt me. There were crocuses coming out right below the window ledge, and a few feet away a fat brown bird walked across the ground, listening for worms. I could see last year's garden, still full of what looked like paper cabbages, some of them pale green and others a deep purple, possibly in the brussels sprout family. Julian would know.

"What did she give you, Helen? Did she give you anything?"

"No. A roll of peppermints."

I opened the window and leaned way out so I could look up and see the gutters, and after the gutters the sky. "I think gutters are my favorite part of a house."

"I like the fire escape."

"We don't have a fire escape."

"We don't either."

"Helen, there's a cloud up there in the shape of a person's hand!"

"It's always there."

"It's not."

"Is it more like a fist, and it's missing a finger?"

"Yes!"

"It's always there."

The next morning was a Saturday, the first Saturday in March. I woke early to the sound of Julian's shovel hitting a rock in the garden and couldn't help but feel the excitement set loose in the world by a ringing tool. I opened the window and called out, "Where's Mother, Papa?"

"Hello! You awake, sleepyhead?"

"Where is she?"

"She's not feeling well. She's in bed."

"Oh. Well I'm going somewhere. I'll be back sometime, if she asks." I started to draw my head back through the window.

"Gussy! Augusta Cotton!" I was used to his bouts of severity and pretended not to hear. This one, like the rest, lasted only seconds, the length of my name said twice, then he raised the shovel and took another swipe at the dark earth, and this time the blade sank deeply and cleanly and he was satisfied.

I dressed quickly. In the kitchen I took a hard roll from the cupboard and spread jam on it, and skipped so happily away from Flat Street it occurred to me how often I felt a prisoner there. I breathed deeply and shook my head, and flew downhill towards the river with the first unruly energy of spring. I loved that season. It meant the world to me. Whole days of what felt like dog's breath on your skin, and the trees coming out with leaves whose shapes you'd forgotten: the ginkgo armed with tiny shovels, the goose feet of the sycamore, the sassafras tree wearing mittens, as well as the boring oaks and elms. And the fruit trees, our neighbor's cherry, a plum tree in Julia Swann's yard on I Street. I loved the secret life of those trees, their blossoms. I liked to climb up and lie along their redolent branches at sundown after the bees went home, just lie and breathe and think of nothing; or spy on Julia eating pancakes for supper between her parents, Carl and Ruth Ann, and after dark skinny down the trunk and wander home to Flat Street. Often there were kids on the block playing hopscotch by flashlight, or playing flashlight tag in somebody's yard. Or on the warm nights, closer to summer, the cry *All-y all-y in come free!* flew from one end of town to the other, skimming the streets of the alphabet from Accidental to Zoroaster, as screen doors banged open and fathers and mothers and older sisters stepped out under the stars to put an end to a game of kick the can. I never joined in, but sat in front of an open window doing fractions, or tracing Marco Polo's route to China, while my parents read or played cards at the folding table and we listened to the kind of music they liked on the radio. Though one night, as I watched half the neighborhood erupt from under our front steps after a game of sardines, I wondered what it might be like to sit close and cramped in a dark, quiet place for what seemed like forever, waiting for friends to find me.

There were mysteries in spring. Sometimes the wind woke me up in the middle of the night speaking whole sentences. Or the crocuses shot up out of nowhere and broke your heart with their sudden, waxen beauty, yet smelled of old ashtrays. Or the river doubled in size and left a gleaming skin of minnows writhing on its banks, a sight so sad and lonesome, and, when the sun hit it, so glorious, I confused death with beauty for the hundredth time that week. I had a sense that death was when that thing called the universe leaned close and could teach us the most. But what was the universe anyway? In my own mind it was suns and stars and hundreds upon hundreds of tiny, tilting planets, all of them alive but not in the same way people or animals are, and all of them thrashing in space for only one good reason: to instruct us. It was highly impersonal, the universe. It never brought us anything directly, no knowledge, no love, no feeling of any kind. Instead it threw people in our way with such persistence, we learned from them.

Almost by accident Helen and I had spoken of the universe. One afternoon I confessed to her that I heard voices in the night, probably only the wind, but what if it were more than the wind? "It was your parents," she answered matter-of-factly. "The voices at night are your parents."

"My parents?"

"Isn't their room next to yours?"

"Yes, but so what?"

"Don't you ever hear them talking through the wall?"

I had once. I'd woken from a dream about a man who walked through mirrors backwards holding a hat, and I'd heard them arguing. It was the first time I'd ever heard them talk in bed, and it was hard to believe they were my parents and not two people I didn't know, arguing in a motel. That was years ago.

"No," I told her. "No, it wasn't that." She wanted to know what the voices said, but I was embarrassed.

"Gussy, come on."

"Okay. It's always the same thing. They ask, 'Who made you?' then they say, 'God made you,' then they ask, 'Why did God make you?' and that's all."

"I don't think it's the wind," said Helen.

"What else would it be?"

"Nuns."

I stared at her. "Nuns?"

"When we lived at the lake I went to a school with nuns and they always said things like that. Wallace told us to ignore them, but Jordan said, 'Be careful what you believe.' Or sometimes she said, 'Believe in Helen. Believe in Harry.' If I had children I think I'd want them to believe in God, wouldn't you? It would be a lot easier. I wish I was sure about God." She was quiet a minute. "You know what the only thing wrong with Joan is?"

I had a list as long as my arm, so I said the first thing on it. "She smokes."

"Worse. She's religious."

"Oh, no," I groaned. "What kind?"

"It's got a strange name, like Southern Eucalyptus of All the Saints. But it really has nothing to do with the saints," she said quickly, protectively. "It's not even a church, exactly, it's something else. They don't ever sit down in one place, they move around a lot and give things to people. That's why her car's so big, so she can just reach in the back and give someone something. That's how we met her. She tried to give me a bookmark."

"You could use a bookmark, Helen. What kind of a bookmark?"

"It was plastic with tassels. It said something about the universe on it, and there was a picture of the universe. Jordan said what she always says about things like that, 'You may keep it but the gift isn't free,' so I gave it back and we went on walking down the street."

That was her end of it, though soon enough I would hear a different story about that first encounter. As for the picture of the universe, to confine it to a bookmark seemed to defy the laws of the universe itself, and I asked my friend, "What kind of picture was it?" She went on to describe a giant, dripping heart lifted high on a sort of dinner plate by minions of angels. I was horrified.

Now as I crossed the river on my way to Helen's house, I wasn't thinking of the universe or, for that matter, of hearts that throbbed and sweated blood and stood for something we all agreed to call love. I was thinking only of spring, feeling my veins open to it, to these first days of it when it was both a child and not a child, like me; still slim as a reed but growing. I stopped on the footbridge and felt winter sliding off my back, summer's dizzying glare coming on, that familiar noise of heat—like a swarm of bees. But it was only the river shooting bright arrows of light skyward as I threw the rest of my breakfast roll down into a boiling eddy.

It was nothing like its languid winter self this morning, my river Harriet. It was high and swift and a soapy brown-black color where it overran its banks. It was up into the sycamore trees by the school, and I saw with dismay how quickly it had taken away the path Helen and I had followed every day until she got sick.

A small wind was blowing as I walked uphill towards the yellow house, and perhaps the goose bumps it raised on my bare arms offered me a chance to understand something: that who I was exceeded my skin; that nothing could contain me. Or was it the recent sight of the river? The sight of an old goalpost standing cockeyed in a flooded field behind the boys' school? Things toppled in the spring. Jordan said things came to their knees in a useful way. Spring kept us from feeling landlocked, she said. It was like spending a few weeks by the ocean, and nothing stirred things up quite like an ocean did. You needed to walk a clean, washed beach from time to time, just to see the waves land and scatter and disappear and come back again with a new load of dead eels or sea glass.

"Have you ever?" I asked her.

"Ever?"

"Walked on a beach?"

"No, but Joan has."

"Let's."

"Did you know, Augusta, there's a fish called a skate?"

I knew cod. I knew sharks had four hundred teeth. Skate I didn't know.

"We'll take you to the lake sometime. Helen and Harry and I can show you where we cut our teeth."

"Cut your teeth?"

"It's Joan's expression. It means grew up."

I looked forward to that day, though we had to wait for Helen to be well enough to travel and that might be weeks away. Or tomorrow. For she moved so swiftly in and out of her illness, one afternoon she seemed racked with fever and a burning in her joints, and the next day she greeted me like someone playing a long, luxurious game of hooky. Today I wanted her well. I was full of a happy, impatient feeling, and I let my knuckles tap out the chorus of "Lili Marlene" against her door. Julian used to play that song over and over again on our old record player while my mother and I sat with our hands over our ears, our faces twisted into grimaces, exaggerating our discomfort in every way possible in order to persuade him to stop. Yet I liked that song. After the record wore out I discovered I missed it. I'd only sided with Harriet to side with someone, otherwise I knew I'd be left out.

I knocked until both hands ached. I turned around to ask the street, Where is she? Where is my friend? when I noticed a car pulled up, not against the curb but onto it, as if it had been parked in a hurry. It had a license plate like my father's, the license plate of a doctor, and all of a sudden I felt so dizzy I had to lean against the house.

I wasn't a fainter. I'd only fainted once in first grade when a papier-mâché frying pan fell from the ceiling onto the stage right in front of me in the middle of a play called "The House Comes Alive." I was Mrs. Pencil and Helen was Mr. Piano, and though she was new at our school and I hardly knew her name, I was told she trundled out from backstage trying to look like a piano and knelt down and fanned me awake. I wanted to remember it. She remembered it. "Oh yes. You got that part because you had a tiny head," she replied when I reminded her of our early history together.

It did me no good now to think of her. My tiny head felt like a small white flag flapping at the top of a tall flagpole, and I was filled with the queer sensation that all my hair had come off and was hovering over my scalp. My knees too were floating somewhere, not attached to me, and as I started to slide down the side of the house I felt the sun, the steady sun, wobble and come loose. In the middle of a spring morning I felt daylight leaving the neighborhood, draining from it like a person losing interest. Or like rainwater draining out the back of the old rowboat pulled high up on the riverbank below the sanatorium. That boat had been there ever since I could remember, with oat grass and pampas grass, thistle and poison ivy all growing up around it and through it, wrapping its oars and oarlocks and rotting its seats and what Julian called gunwales. I'd named it *The Earthbound,* and to think of it now as I sat down hard on the ground gave me purpose and pleasure. It came out of nowhere and seemed to say to me, *I promise you, I promise you,* and whatever that meant it brought daylight back to that corner of our town. It put my hair on my head again and the dizziness passed.

"What in the world does that cold hard ground have to offer?"

I looked up as the door banged open, and there was Joan. She was wearing the same black stretch pants I'd seen last Saturday, and she had on a pair of hairy slippers with long plastic claws. Her white shirt was covered with green ponies, and every time she moved, the ponies all reared up in the same way as if they'd just seen a snake.

"I thought you were a little bird tapping, a little peckerwood," she said. "I came out to shoo you off the side of the house. They'll ruin a house. Why, up north I've seen them do to a house what carpenter ants do in the South. Though with carpenter ants your floors'll go first, then your walls. There ought to be some way to get the birds to eat the bugs that eat the house, instead of pecking at the house. I wonder why nature hasn't figured that one out yet." The ponies reared up as she swept her arm sharply in front of her—like someone hurling seeds down into the earth to grow. "Come on in! Aren't you going to come on in?"

I just sat there. "Where's Helen? Why's the doctor here?"

"Honey, there's no doctor here." She called inside, "Hey! Are we hiding a doctor? There's no doctor."

"There's a doctor's car across the street."

"People have to park, sweetheart."

"Not right here."

"I park here. There's my car." She pointed to a dark green station wagon with wood paneling, pulled up in front of Helen's house. "If the doctor's out there I don't see him. He drives a gray Valiant with the passenger side all smashed to bits. It gives me the goose bumps every time I see it. It doesn't seem right for a doctor somehow. Now maybe there is a doctor somewhere, but he's not our doctor. Maybe there's old people across the street in need of a doctor, I wouldn't know. The people in the pink house, I know they once accidentally swallowed poison. It could be something like that. Or a woman all of a sudden having a child, that'll bring the doctor. People in that kind of situation don't always make it to the hospital. I ought to know that. I wasn't born in the hospital."

"So what? Neither was I."

"Oh, for goodness sake! Where were you born? I was born on a boat."

"I was born at home. By a midwife."

"Well that sounds restful. My mother was a midwife, but of course she couldn't deliver me herself, so she got some help from the man who drove the boat. He was just a regular old sailor. It was a ferryboat, and we were crossing this big, wide Georgia river, the name of it's the Lame River. We were going, my momma and I, to meet my daddy on the other side of it. From there he was planning to rush

Momma to the hospital to have me. My daddy was full of plans. I was his first failed plan, that's what he always said. I always said, What's time to an itty-bitty child? There's no clocks in heaven. Did you ever stop to think of that?"

I never had, but the truth was I was burning to clear up a mystery of my own, one that went all the way back to my first soggy breath. "Her name wasn't Mrs. Della Foote, was it?"

"Whose name, honey? I don't believe I know a Della Foote. I do know a Della but she's not a Foote, she's a Piscina. And not a Mrs."

"The midwife. That lady. Your mother."

"Oh, Momma," Joan laughed. "No, she was a Parker, her maiden name, and never a Della that I know of."

"Good," I said. "Then she wasn't my midwife."

Joan might have said anything then. She might have said, "For a young person, you certainly have an overfed rude streak." Or she might have wondered, "Why so mean, Augusta? Why not gentle and easy, like a pastured cow?" Instead she told me, "Every time I step out of this house and step back into it, you know what I do? I say something. I say a little, I guess you'd call it a prayer. It goes like this: Peace be unto this house. I say it three times to myself and once out loud in case anybody's listening. Now if you leave that mouth of yours outside, you're welcome to come inside whenever you're ready. There's a friend of yours here who's been waiting all morning to lay eyes on you." Helen! I thought, and shot up and followed her into the house.

It wasn't Helen. I knew when a house had Helen in it, and she was a long way from this one. The kitchen was dark, almost black. Someone had hung blankets over the curtains, so the only light in the room ran in two gray lines down the sides of the windows.

"Don't even ask," said Joan. "There's already been a fight about it. We're on a mission of darkness, that's all we know." I could hear what sounded like a person rubbing their bare legs together, then a dry, smothered cough.

"What's that?" I asked.

"What's what?"

I waited for the rubbing sound to come again. "That."

"Oh, the poor thing's got a rash. They never fed them properly in that place, and he's been itching and scratching ever since he got home. If he's not itching and scratching he's putting stuff in his mouth. Pins and stuff. Sharp objects. I've never known anyone to like metal the way he likes metal. Yesterday, bless his heart, he tried to swallow one of my keys."

"He could choke!"

"I know it."

"I'd hate to die of choking," I said, suddenly remembering Helen's story about Harry and the rat. "It's a very mean way to die."

"I had a great-aunt died of choking once. She died in a little café called the Genevieve Hot Stop, named after the town it was in, Genevieve. This was the only café in all of south Georgia where you could bring in your own fish or chitlins or whatever, and they'd let you into the kitchen to cook it yourself."

"What's so great about that? What are chitlins anyway?"

"What's so great about that is you'd cook it just the way you liked it, and if you complained you complained to yourself. Even my great-aunt who died, she died on a piece of tough old pork, but there was no one to blame but herself for cooking it too long. She always did eat too rapidly. That had happened to her before in the Genevieve, but every other time she was with someone and they knew just how to whap her on the back so the meat flew out and landed clear across the café. I heard she always returned to eating her meal. She lowered her arms from the sky and picked up her fork and knife and went at it again. This, by the way, was my great-aunt Augusta."

"Not Augusta Cotton."

"No, not Augusta Cotton. We called her Auntie G, though for some reason her lady friends all called her Grover." I made a face in the dark. "Now Grover, that doesn't suit you, but not one minute before you came I finished telling Harry I'm searching for something to call you that isn't Augusta. It's such a pretty name, but my goodness what a mouthful! In fact we have more than one Augusta in our family. The one who died, then my daddy's momma, she was Augusta also. She was famous for not speaking her mind, that one. She saved every bit of it till the end, when she sat straight up in bed and said, 'I don't want to marry anyone.' What in the world did we call her? We called her Gus. I only saw her twice in my life, and both times I believe that's what we called her."

Before I could say that my name was Augusta or Gussy and I liked my name, Joan said, "It's just plain foolish, Harry. Only a fool waits in darkness. There's someone here who's come a long way to visit with you. You can cry and whine and carry on all you want, but count five and this light's going on."

She started patting the wall to find the light switch, and suddenly the kitchen was flooded with shape and color. Harry sat at the table. Even sitting down he was a tall boy, tall and thin. He wasn't much older than Helen and I, but he had the whitest hair I'd ever seen on a young person. It was cut short in a crew cut, so when the light hit it as it did now it looked like his head was glowing. He had a big head, like Helen did, a Walsh head. "You'll see," my friend had warned me, "his head looks like a light bulb. He used to have dark hair, it was black like Wallace's, but after the accident it all turned white. Something happened to his face too. He looks different. He looks—" She was quiet a minute, staring at a spot on her T-shirt. "I don't know, sort of like a murderer."

I said I didn't know many murderers, but she assured me I did. "Those pictures in the post office. They're all murderers."

"Your brother looks like that?"

"He looks like he sleeps in his clothes."

I searched Harry's face for whatever made him a murderer, but all I could find was the tail of a scar that started near his left temple and disappeared into his crew cut like a snake in the grass. It was an ordinary face. I was expecting it to be full of imperfection. I thought he'd be walleyed, or one eye would at least wander or droop, or the imperfect shape of his skull would show through his thin skin and his veins would be knotted and bulging. But he was just an ordinary-looking boy who looked like Jordan and Helen and someone else, and I liked that, seeing the people I knew in someone I'd just met.

"We're learning how to dress this week," said Joan. "We're learning how to match colors. His favorite color is— What's your favorite color, Harry? It's the color of your shorts, isn't it?" I couldn't see the shorts. She said, "They're plaid."

He was wearing a brown T-shirt and what looked like a string of small blue meatballs around his neck. Every time he leaned over to scratch his legs, the meatballs whacked the table.

"They're dung beads," Joan explained. "Made of dung and painted blue. This boy just loves jewelry." Before I could ask what dung was, Harry started rubbing his legs together, then rubbing them against the table leg so the whole table rocked. "Quit that. Sweetheart, cease. You're going to wear right through the wood."

"It looks like they itch more with the light on," I said.

"They itch more when we're nervous," said Joan. She moved behind him and took his hands and laid them palms down on the table. She put her own hands on top of them. "There's someone here I want you to meet. Are you ready to meet someone?" He shook his head. "Well, never mind then. We can wait. We can say our favorite poem, 'The Silent Poem.' Would you like that?"

Harry opened his mouth wide, then pressed his lips together and moved them in and out as if he were chewing some kind of sticky food.

"Doesn't he talk?"

"Oh, he's a prize talker, you'll see. Right now he's saying 'The Silent Poem.' That's his poem. It's the only poetry he learned in that place, can you imagine? Five years. All those magical children. When I think of the joy that could have come out of it and didn't, it makes my stomach flip over."

"What's he doing now? He looks like he's drowning."

"No, sweetheart, not drowning." She was talking to Harry. She wrapped her arms around his shoulders. "No more drowning. This is our way of getting ready for conversation. We have to breathe fire. The yogis knew about it. Are you breathing fire, Harry? That's right. Now close your mouth. Open it again. Wide. Wider. Exhale. I said exhale."

"Maybe he doesn't know exhale. Say blow out. Blow out, Harry."

Harry exhaled, and Joan took him through his exercises a few more times, then we were ready for conversation. I sat down across from him at the table. I noticed his ears were bigger and rounder than Helen's—hers were small and almost triangular—and they were scotch-taped to his head.

"They stick out," Joan explained. "They flap out and embarrass him. I used to have ears like his. Bigger than his, in fact. The size of pork chops. Every night I taped them to my head and take a look now." She pushed her hair back and showed me a very regular-sized ear. "My head was on the small side and it grew into them, that's what happened."

"But his isn't on the small side. If you ask me, I'd say his is already on the big side. Anyway," I turned to Harry, "ears are useful. If you didn't have them I know you'd wish you did. What's your favorite kind of music?" He said nothing. "Think of your favorite music, then think of what everything would sound like without it. Think of what everything would sound like if there wasn't any sound, if you couldn't hear anything. What sound would that be?"

"Is there a real answer?" asked Joan. "I love questions like this."

"Or let's say you had to choose between having ears and having a tongue. What would you choose? I'd choose having ears."

"I'd never give up my tongue," said Joan, "never in the world."

I glared at her. "I asked him."

"You hear that, Harry? She asked you. What have you got to say? Someone's trying to teach you how to compare." He turned his head away as if he were smelling his shoulder. "Who is this person? Do you know who this person is?" He shook his head. "Here's a hint. She's the girl we were just talking about, you and I. Who was it? Do you recall? Who's Helen's good friend?"

"Frankenstein!"

"No, precious. No, it wasn't Frankenstein. This was today. This was a little while ago. Harry could talk Frankenstein to death, couldn't you, handsome? And the queen of England, of all people. He loves the queen of England. Who's the queen, Harry? Does the queen have a name? What's her name?"

"Frankenstein!"

"Is the queen's name Elizabeth? It's Elizabeth, isn't it?"

He looked at the table. He took his dung beads off and put them on the table, and suddenly I thought of Helen's pearls. They were real pearls. She kept them in a baking soda box beside her bed. She liked to put them on if she was well enough to walk me to the door after one of our visits.

"Where is she?" I asked. "What happened to her?"

"Why, she's in England. You know that. She's in Buckingham Palace." I shook my head and kept shaking it until she said, "If it's Helen you mean, she's off with Jordan. Now, can you keep a secret? If you can keep a secret I'll tell you where they went."

"Who's it a secret from?"

"You."

"Oh. I can keep a secret."

"Well, they went across the river to see your daddy. He's a nice man, your daddy. Just yesterday he called up to say he was more or less available, and last night we had another scare, so this morning Jordan took her on over. Your two trains passed in the dawn."

"What kind of a scare?"

"She turned yellow, sugar. That's all we know about it."

"Yellow!"

"Not a yellow yellow. A beige." Then she added, "Your friend's going to be just fine. I'll tell you what. She'll be coming home soon and needing a lot of rest and nobody in her hair. Harry and I are planning on going to the cinema. There's a matinee. Why don't you come to a matinee with us? First we're going to climb up high and look down on the town from a place I know, one of my favorite places, and after the picture, if there's time, we're going for a boat ride."

"A boat ride?" I said. "Maybe you haven't seen the river." In my own thoughts I was rowing Helen through the sycamores. She stood in the front of the boat, pushing the trees away from us. "They're a beautiful color," I told her. "Beige," she smiled, and held up her palms to show me. "They come off on your hands!"

"Harry," said Joan. He was picking at the scotch tape that held his ears back. "You're tempting fate." She turned to me. "I'll tell you something about the pictures, Gus. They've saved our life this week. They're a good place for me to go because I've been trying to quit smoking, and a cinema, that's somewhere I can't smoke. They're a good place for Harry because he has to sit in the good company of language for an hour or two, even if it's not English. We take off in the evenings, he and I. I usually bring some sandwiches under my coat, then we wait for the lights to go out and have a picnic. I never go to the pictures, hardly ever. But this week we've seen the first half of *Children of Paradise* three times, and this afternoon will be the fourth. The pictures I like are the kind you have to read, and they come around so rarely. Maybe you know the way they work. The actors say a lot of long sentences in a foreign language, but on the screen you get a few words like 'Yes! and take her too!' So unless you understand the language you never know what you're missing. I truly like that. Though I've been tempted off and on to learn something like French well enough, and go and sit in the cinema and speak out the real words, everything they leave out. That way no one would be able to get the wrong idea of that picture and think it was about taking someone somewhere when what it was really about was a girl who dreamed of running away on a horse, and to buy that horse she stole money from her family and buried the money under a bush in a shallow hole, if you follow me."

It would have been easier to follow a bat in the rafters, but I nodded. I heard something rattle around in my head, and I knew what it wasn't: peace and quiet. I didn't feel like going home. I knew if I showed up at Julian's office on Tennessee Street I'd be very unpopular and perhaps cause trouble for my friend, who was troubled enough already, and yellow, and frightened. I couldn't stay here. I felt fairly certain Jordan would send me away if she found me lurking, and Helen would be all the wrong color, sleeping in her mother's arms. "I'll go with you," I heard myself say, and not five minutes later we were chugging uphill in the front seat of Joan's green station wagon with a bag of egg salad sandwiches on the backseat and a thermos of cool water. Harry sat between us, hugging a paper bag to his chest. He'd made himself Guardian of the Slippers.

"What do I need slippers for? I don't need slippers," I said.

But Joan had insisted. "You can be stubborn or you can be comfortable, Gus. It's nice to take your shoes off in a cinema. Unless you're pregnant and your feet swell, then you'll never get them back on again. Here. Borrow Helen's."

She searched the closet and threw a pair of Helen's winter slippers at me, and I clutched them to me, stroking the ragged wool with a sudden grief and confusion no one was meant to see. I thought I'd try and lift the weight of that grief alone for as long as I could, and that's what happened, though long wasn't more than a short car ride and the first hundred steps of the long climb up to the Corinth Sanatorium (I was quiet and counting), which turned out to be Joan's place of refuge before it ever was mine. I'd dodged around a gopher hole and was about to warn Harry to do the same, when I felt someone or something take a tuck in my throat. I said, "Joan, I can't swallow or breathe. Do you think it's the elevation?"

"The altitude? No, sugar, I don't see how it could be the altitude. We're no higher here than standing on a tall ladder."

"What should I do? Maybe I should go back to the car and lie down. How long can a person go without air anyway?"

"You've got air. As long as you're talking, you've got air. Keep talking, it'll pass. I haven't had air for close to twenty years on account of the cigarettes, and that's what I do, talk. Harry! Watch that gopher hole. You know who lives in a gopher hole? Gus'll tell us who lives in a gopher hole, and then she'll tell us a few other things so she can keep her lungs pumping that vital O-two."

I had one hand on my throat, trying to work loose whatever was in there, and I could feel my voice vibrate when I spoke. It was the first time I'd ever felt that, and it cheered me up in a small way. I told Joan what I could about gophers and gopher holes, including that a gopher meant one thing up north and another thing down south, a distinction I was proud of knowing. I told her I guessed a gopher lived in a gopher hole, and she said, "What if the gopher's died or gone away?" I said, "I guess another gopher." We left it at that, though the answer she was fishing for was a snake.

The twelve o'clock whistle blew, and all three of us turned to gaze at the factory. "What do they make in there?" I asked. "A long time ago Papa told me seat belts."

"They still do make seat belts."

"He said they make the belt part and they also make the metal clasp you click into. He thinks that someday we're all going to have to wear seat belts, it'll be a law, and this town will be rich again."

"Again? Were we ever rich? Rich I don't recall."

"If you're only thirty-three," I said, "it was probably before you were born."

"You angel! I like that, thirty-three!"

"Everyone was rich if they didn't have tuberculosis. If they had tuberculosis they were poor because they left all their money in the sanatorium, that's how the rich people got rich. He says, Papa says, that to make a living off sick people is one thing and troublesome enough, but to make a killing is another. He would be happier, I think, as an architect."

"He'd be happier, I think, as a saint."

"He'd be a good architect. He already knows all the different kinds of roofs there are. We used to walk down Flat Street and each roof we passed he'd say the name of it until I learned them by heart: gable, hip, gambrel and shed. It's called that because it sheds water," I added, "not the other kind of shed."

"My goodness, don't they all shed water?"

I thought a minute. "That one sheds water the quickest. He knows about weight-bearing walls, and this thing called the angle of repose. Things you can't see, he knows about them and he can explain them to make you see them. We used to come up to the sanatorium and he'd point at buildings that weren't here anymore, and it was as if they were. People too. One time I saw my aunt Kate who died. She was lying outside on a mattress and she got up and put her arms around me and passed right through, I swear it, Joan. I felt this heat in my chest and something salty in my mouth. What was that?"

"It's different in each case, honey. Did she die a peaceful death?"

I'd never thought about peace and death in the same bed together. I said, "No, a violent one."

"Well, was she a religious person? Did she believe in God?" I hesitated. "Did she wear a cross or keep a Bible or sing hymns or say grace at the table?"

"She never went to church, I know that. She sang some songs but they weren't religious, they were French."

"There's many French people who're religious."

"She wasn't." I shook my head, and the words *Elle avait de touts petits têtons* began to roll around between my ears, stirring a memory of Aunt Kate clinging to my arm and singing, smelling of talcum powder, flannel and urine as we made our slow way from bed to bathroom. "I learnt that song in the war," she shouted, and I shouted back, "What war?" and she laughed and wet the cool board floor, and I was barefoot.

"I'm not either," I said to Joan.

"Either what, sweetheart?"

"Religious."

"Well, good for you. That's God's business and nobody else's."

"What if I don't believe in God?"

"Well that's God's business too. Now I'll tell you what I know about that salty taste. Some people say it's the tears they shed waiting, if the death is violent and the person involved is not religious. If the death is peaceful, a natural death, you'll generally get something sweeter, and in my experience more aromatic. Like cider and nutmeg. I love spooks, don't you, Gus? I grew up on spooks. We lived between a cattail swamp and a graveyard, and sometimes instead of going off to school I'd hide myself in the graveyard and pray for a funeral."

"A funeral!"

"Our town, at that time, had a number of funerals. All kinds of people seemed to be dying in sympathy with the people who were dying. This was during the war."

"What war?"

She laughed, just as Kate had, and I wondered, Was it a joke then, war? I decided, No, how could it be? You only laughed if you survived it.

"What I call 'our war,' sugar. The Second War. Every generation has a war, is the way I think of it, and that war lets them know who they are and what life's worth to them, and with any luck they go out and live it."

"What if they die first?"

"Lord knows, it touches the dead as well."

We were quiet a minute, standing there inside our own thoughts, looking down at the town we lived in, though my eyes felt heavier and heavier and soon came to fasten on my own feet. I couldn't breathe again. I couldn't speak, but I must have looked wild because she said, "I'll tell you something. I'm no clairvoyant, but I can see what's clutching your throat and it's got a great big head of blue hair, it's got wide teeth and long white arms and it's called grief. Lady Grief. He's got it too."

She pointed to Harry, who had walked a few yards off and was waving his arms wildly and silently in the direction of the factory.

I managed to say, "Who's he waving at?"

"Who he's waving at is Wallace. Who he's waving at is not your problem. You've got someone else in your path, and you can be happy, child, because she's alive to contain you and all your happiness. Throw that weight off. Unbind yourself. You're not the Rock of Gibraltar, and you don't need to walk around dry-eyed all the time. In my family we took turns being unshakable, until one day I put my hand on the door and said, Friends, I want out. Do you know how it feels to feel? It feels good. It won't hurt anyone, I know this, it'll only help. Ask Harry. He's one big ball of feeling with arms and legs and a crew cut. You can see right through him. I believe that's why death stroked his head and moved on and took Wallace instead. That boy gave her nothing to grab onto. Why, most plants and animals and even small bugs have more, what do you call it? Anyway, more reason to get on over to eternity than that boy does. I love him, Gus. Did you know that? I love him in a clean way I've never known or loved anyone in all my life. Clean. Like weather. Like things that just are, without explanation or complaint." She made a little face, almost a grimace. "I don't believe I even love Jordan that way, do I?" I was about to tell her I hadn't a clue, when she answered her own question. "No, I don't. And why I don't is pride. Pride is that little old song telling the singer, 'I don't need you!' Well it's a damn fool, that song."

We started walking again. I walked ahead and managed

to let go of Lady Grief, and she came tumbling down my cheeks in thick tears. I sucked the last of these into my mouth to taste that salty taste, and it was exactly how I remembered Kate, her ghost at least.

Up at the top I hesitated, then took a long look around, not letting my eyes stop anywhere until I'd taken in every inch of rubble and felt my own long absence pass through me like the leanest ghost of all. It was long and lean and *sheer,* if I understood that word. There was nothing visible, nothing I could touch about the three and a half years since I'd last set foot up here. Things had happened. Helen had entered me; so had Jordan. But in that glance they were not of this place. No one was.

I took a few steps towards what I knew would soon be a solid bank of wild roses, then turned and found a bare bush of blueberries and put my hand on the cool stems: I was asking to be anchored. There had been too much talk of death that day, and I knew this bush inside out. I'd plunged into it a hundred times, full of good intentions, carrying Julian's hat for a bucket, and under the coolness it offered, I knew it was throbbing with sleepy life. "Please help me," I whispered. "Please remember me and help me and help my friend Helen and her mother." Out of one part courtesy and two parts superstition I added, "Help her brother, and help Joan the friend. If nothing else, could you get him to talk to me?"

I'd just finished my prayers when those two struggled over the the hill, Joan's shoulders heaving and Harry walking close as a shadow behind her, pushing his own shoulders up and down to match hers.

"Lord, I'm winded! Make fun all you want, but my advice to you, young man, is never let a neighbor child taunt you into smoking corn silk cigarettes in the tobacco field between your two homes. Portia Blunt. Now that's a name I won't forget if I live to be a hundred. It's carved in my lungs."

It made no sense to me why anyone would smoke corn silk in a field of tobacco, and I said as much.

"Oh, we were nowhere near old enough to smoke tobacco! Anyway, this was rough tobacco, a few rows of homegrown planted by Portia's daddy. He ran the Champs Cinema, Champs with an 's.' It's a French word meaning 'fields so green.'" She thumped her chest and took a long, deep breath. "My first real, honest-to-goodness cigarette was years later, a Lucky Strike, a brand you may not have heard of. I liked the artwork on the package and Portia did too. It used to be a green package, but during the war it turned white with the slogan 'Lucky Strike green has gone to war!' We liked that. We always bought Lucky Strikes and we always smoked them way back in the graveyard, as close as we could get to the body of Portia's first love, Danny Something-or-other. She was clairvoyant, Harry, Portia was. Just like you. She could raise up Danny in front of us so even I could see him, and I'd never laid eyes on that young boy. He was gone before I ever knew Portia. They were sweethearts at age six. The trouble was, he stayed six. He never got a minute older. We'd sit there smoking our Lucky Strikes with this child of a boy beaming white light down on us from the live oak tree where he used to appear, and poor old Portia would plead with him, 'Grow up, Danny, please! Grow up with me!' It was awful to hear. It broke her heart twice, is what it did. From what I know about Portia now, she's been married five or six times and left her gift to wither and die."

"What gift?" I asked. I asked sincerely, for the only gift I'd understood from that story was Danny's.

"Clairvoyance. Didn't I say that? She was clairvoyant."

"Isn't that something you can get arrested for?"

"Arrested for?"

"Isn't it like a Peeping Tom?"

"Oh, my goodness, no! I might know what you're talking about, but this isn't that. It means someone who's tuned in. Someone who's got a foot in each world. Like Harry. Only his trouble is he hasn't learned how to bring all that beauty and stuff he finds out there, back in here. It gets stuck in the middle." She looked at him. "Who am I fooling? I like to think it's beauty. I'm taught to think it's beauty. It's not all beauty, is it?"

He shook his head. "It's crap."

"What have I told you about the word 'crap,' Harry?"

"It's crap."

I was waiting to ask, A foot in each world? How many worlds are there? when he narrowed his eyes and shot me a look that for its coolness could have been packed in ice. "Two!" he said, and there was no mistake, he was talking to me. I knew then to watch my thoughts around him.

He was a funny boy, with not much there to grab onto, Joan was right. The only words he'd let loose in my presence were strange words, islands of thought, like "Frankenstein" and "Guardian of the Slippers," and now "crap" and his telepathic "two," which charged the early afternoon with meaning and made me nervous, wary. I even decided I disliked him. This didn't last long. It was a day in my life when I warmed to anyone who knew my right name and called me by it, whether they'd picked it up from the ether or stood and been introduced. Harry hadn't picked it up from the ether, he'd heard it from me. The first time he called me anything he called me Augusta Cotton, the whole mouthful, and that was what stuck.

We wound around the sanatorium for close to an hour. Each of us picked a different route. I don't know what the others did, but I was mostly still, sitting in the old operating room and counting my blessings. I started with: I don't have lupus, I was never in an accident, I'm not from the South. From there I went on to: Julian's still alive, so is Mother, we have enough food to eat, we have a garden, we have a hip roof that sheds water, we have more than one bathroom, we live on Flat Street instead of Accidental where all the buses turn around, I was never in a war, I like my name, it's unusual but not hard to pronounce, I have a friend, I've never seen a rat in our yard, I don't smoke cigarettes, I only once had an infected finger, I had TB, I survived it.

On the way down I asked Joan if she thought there was a family in the world that escaped accident or illness, and she answered a quick, flat "No." I told her that until this year I hadn't known anyone who was sick or hurt in any way, and she said, "You weren't thinking, sweetheart. Your own daddy's a doctor."

That quieted me for a minute, then I said, "I mean no one I knew well."

"You've never had a pain in your whole entire life?" I nodded. "And lost no loved ones?" I shook my head. "There's so few families can boast of perfect health. Yours could surely be one."

We went on in silence for a minute or two. Harry was ahead of us, searching the short, brown winter grass for turtles.

"I did have TB," I said.

"We won't hold that against you."

"My aunt Kate was in bed for a long time. She died of multiple sclerosis, but I don't remember it."

"Then that doesn't count."

"Harriet, my mother, she suffers from this thing with a French name, it begins with 'm.'"

"Not migraine headaches?"

"No, Julian gets those."

"Malaise?"

"It's malaise."

"Well, malaise. I hardly call that an illness."

"Mother has a glass eye," I said softly.

"I beg your pardon?"

"And I just got glasses."

"Everyone's got glasses." She stopped in her tracks and put her hands out, waiting, I thought, for that one cloud above us to rinse her palms with rain. "And if they don't have glasses, they can't hear well, or breathe right, or their nose is too big or too small, or they don't like their complexion. Or they suffer little pangs in their feet, mysterious pains, bad backs, sore arms, allergies, distress of the mouth. A tooth aches. Their belly aches. Their tonsils act up. They have gas. We are all human, Gus. We live inside human bodies that break down. They're not made to be foolproof. How uninteresting life would be if that were the case. We'd all live forever and torment each other every step of the way."

I was about to say I didn't think it would be uninteresting, I thought it would be interesting, but Joan put a finger to her lips to hush me and went on.

"Why you see disease this year is because you are becoming old enough to take in the whole picture of life. Don't forget that. It used to be rosy, I know it. It used to be a child's garden. Well, it's not quite like that. You see, on the flip side of every wellness is an illness. They share the same coin. We see what we need to see at the time. We go to where the lessons are. Sometimes it's not what we want to see, it feels all wrong. But it's a privilege just the same. It's what the big doctor ordered."

"What big doctor?"

"Up there." She squinted at the sky, and I saw two big drops of rain, the size of nails, fall out of it. "He ordered it for Helen, he ordered it for Harry, he ordered it for Jordan. He even ordered it for Wallace. And he ordered it for you and me. What recent life has dealt the Walsh family is as much our business as it is theirs. You know that old saying, Gus, 'The wages of love is love itself, through sorrow and joy, sickness and health'? Well, why don't we spend the rest of this day taking a long look at what's good and joyful and *easy* in our lives."

"Like what?" I asked sullenly. I didn't like being lectured to.

"Like the powerful size of the river today. Look out there. Harry! Come and see! There's a darling little row-boat pulled up in the high grass, not far from the water."

"I know," I said, "it's *The Earthbound*."

"It certainly is."

"I mean, that's its name."

"Where?" said Harry. I pointed and he said, "I'm fourteen, Augusta Cotton."

"That's good, Harry. When's your birthday?"

"All day."

"All day what day?"

"When I was born."

"Mr. Stubbornhead," said Joan, "tell her when you were born."

"On the eighty-fifth of July."

"Oh. I'm the eighty-fourth," I said.

"And I'm the queen of England," said Joan. "Let's take a detour. Who wants to take a little detour?" She started cutting down towards the river, and I wanted to tell her, That boat's not yours. That boat's my boat. But something heavy and small enough to be generosity pinned my tongue to the floor of my mouth, and the minute it did, someone spoke up for me.

"I don't," said Harry.

Joan hadn't gone five yards. "You don't what?"

"I don't," he repeated. "I do not."

"Sweetheart, it's just a little boat by the river, that's all. It's just an old wreck past fixing."

"You never cared about it."

"What didn't I care about?"

"The exit light," he said and flopped down on his stomach on the ground. He put his face to the ground and rubbed it back and forth in the short grass, then he lay still.

"Who said anything about the exit light? Did I say anything about the exit light? Get up before you find pneumonia in that grass, Harry."

"What's the exit light?" I asked. "Breathe, Harry. You're not breathing. Joan, he's not breathing."

"As long as he's talking, he's got air."

"He's not talking. You're the one talking."

The little first aid I knew from Julian failed me in that moment, a thing I was later ashamed of. I stood there gawking at Harry like the one unmerciful angel heaven ever produced. I remember thinking, Well, he's a long, flat envelope of a boy, forgetting he could see right into me and out the other side if he cared to with that clairvoyance of his, even with his eyes in the dirt. "Doomed to live" were the next words that came to me, and I aimed them right at his head, where I knew they'd do the most good, right where the scar was. I must have been in a trance because something solid and sweaty brushed my arm and I didn't even jump. I said, calm as could be, "Joan, you scared me halfway to death," and made a note to myself: Augusta, there's no such place.

"He's playing possum. This is something he does, Gus. All it means is he's unhappy." She kneeled down and rolled him onto his back. His eyes were wide open though the sky was empty of interesting things. Not even a bird or a bee drifted over us. "Look at me, precious. Now, tell me something. Why am I perspiring like an apple in a barrel when Old Man Winter hasn't been gone more than a week?"

He shook his head against the ground the way I'd seen Helen shake hers against the pillow. I thought the answer was easy and I said, "Simple: spring."

"Do you know why, Harry Walsh?"

"Catching flies?"

"Catching you."

"You're a turtle."

"I'm not either."

They compromised. Joan gave up on her adventure, but for that day only; we would come back. We each took a stone and dropped it on our left foot. This was Harry's way of sealing a pact.

On the way down to the car I said to Joan, "That war?" It seemed enough to me, at least I thought it asked what I meant to ask, but she said, "Spend one day with Harry and this is what happens. Use verbs, Gus. Make full sentences. God gave us verbs to use them. That's what makes us different from the animals."

"Verbs do?"

"You heard me." Before I could ask about nouns, adjectives, adverbs, and those little pests, prepositions, she said,

"Jordan tells me that boy was the best friend language ever had, and I believe it. What's most precious is often the first to go. A painter will lose their sight, a musician their hearing. Or Portia. She lost Danny. It happens all the time. Don't misunderstand me. You can't spend your whole life preparing for the loss, or you wouldn't have a love in the world. The fact is, trouble haunts a stingy person and lets a generous one go free."

"That's what I was asking."

"Not free, exactly. 'Far' might be a better word."

"I was asking if you ever lost someone you loved. I mean to that war."

"I never did. I lost an uncle and I lost two cousins, but a real love no. The real loves all stayed home like I did, collecting bits of tinfoil and making gardens, and sending off care packages to soldiers we never met or knew—though I always threw a note in and signed it 'love.' It didn't mean anything. Shoot, we weren't more than girls when the war broke out, though I'd have to say we were mostly grown-up women by the time it was over. Until Pearl Harbor we'd never heard of the Pacific Ocean except once when Amelia Earhart stumbled into it and it ended up taking a big long drink of her plane. We thought the whole world was Georgia."

"That was back in nineteen thirty-seven," I said. I felt old and important saying it. "We're reading about Amelia Earhart in a book called *Warriors Aloft*. We have someone at school we think might *be* Amelia Earhart. She's the oldest teacher in the school. Her name is Miss St. John."

"Gertie!"

"You know her?"

"I know her dog better. He used to be my dog. He may be

the oldest dog in the school. His name is Charles Darwin. I'll tell you who loved that dog is Helen."

"My Helen?"

"Everyone else in the world called him Darwin, but that wasn't good enough for Helen. You have to imagine this great big dog, Gus, not one bit a Charles, but that's what she went ahead and called him. She said if she was Helen then he was Charles. Bless her heart, she's Wallace all over when she says stuff like that. She never talked about that dog to you?"

I shook my head, then remembered, "Once. She thought she heard the dog but it was a radiator banging. Most of the time we don't talk about dogs."

"Most of the time I don't either. Who does? But that was the way I met Helen. I met and loved someone who belonged to her, and she met and loved someone who belonged to me—my dog. Darwin, big oaf that he is, won her heart in a trice."

"I thought you met on the street. I thought you gave her a—" I hesitated. "A religious bookmark."

"Whose version of which story is that? The truth is so seldom one thing, but honey, if I told you we met in a Russian beauty parlor, would you have to believe it? No, you would not. Now, banish all thought of religious bookmarks from your head. We met at Della Piscina's house on Guy Street. Your friend and her mother were two live sparks in a room full of deadly company. The first thing she said to me I'll never forget: 'If you're going to smoke, smoke outside,' and I did and she came with me. That's where she fell in love with Darwin."

We were almost at the car and I said, "I don't see why a person would lie."

"You mean Helen?" I didn't answer. "Helen doesn't lie. She makes things up in the morning to get her through the afternoon, and by the time afternoon rolls around she forgets she made it all up."

"But it's a bookmark. Nobody makes up a bookmark. Why make up a bookmark?"

"Because I never was easy for Helen, and in the beginning she needed to make one thing easier, so she took me out of her world and put me in a make-believe place. Don't you ever make believe?"

I thought a minute. "I worry about the future a lot. Is that the same thing? I do something with the five o'clock whistle."

I explained how I gave the whistle powers I never gave to any person, such as, If it blows before I count ten, I will do well on the earthquake quiz; or, If I reach the end of this block at a normal walking pace before it quits blowing, I'll never break a bone in my body. I let it promise me many things, and well into my future, and it must have been natural to bargain and wonder and wish, because just before five o'clock a desire to know would come up in me. I could feel it bother my jaw, like an ache. This was often the exact moment when the whistle began to blow, so there was never time to take it back, to unwonder or unwish, though if I had tried something too grand I was always sorry. School business was usually safe, the business of this or that test, or even as far ahead as how seventh grade would go. But people were tricky. Helen especially was tricky. Happy and live a long time were tricky. Anything with the word "forever" in it was slow poison, and it began to be that when this kind of wish came up in me, I would open my mouth and sing something louder than the sound of the wish in my head, and I would do this until the whistle stopped blowing.

I didn't tell Joan that Helen had become entangled in the promises made to me by the whistle. I simply said that I was trying to learn how to draw the future closer to me, and at the same time keep it small. She suggested I aim for the size of a lime.

"Don't you want to know the future, Joan?"

She laughed. "I couldn't if I tried." We walked a few steps more. "I know that's not what you're asking." I asked again, and she said, "Yes. Oh Lord, yes."

"You've tried then?"

"Ever since the gypsies used to come and beg water from my momma—a couple by the name of De'Ath, a man and his wife. She'd grab my hand and tell me how many husbands I'd tear through, and Mr. De'Ath, he'd stand outside the door making clucking noises at the road to calm his invisible horses."

"What made them invisible?"

"Same as what makes anyone. They were just a dream he was dreaming."

"The husbands were invisible too, right?"

"Who made you such a Nosy Parker?"

Later I discovered we weren't the only two people on earth drawn to the future that day. The three things that impressed Helen most about her visit to Dr. Cotton were that he smelled of a certain kind of nut she was allergic to, that in the middle of everything he asked Jordan if she'd like to water the plants (there were twenty-eight plants and two small trees in that office), and that he hadn't asked any of the standard how-are-you-feeling questions. Instead, he'd wondered about her plans for the future. Had she any idea what she wanted to be when she grew up? Helen, caught off guard, answered the first thing that came to mind, which happened to be, "A veterinarian."

I sat on her bed at the end of that afternoon. I noticed with relief that she looked pale but not yellow. I pulled the sheet up to her chin and tucked the blankets around her, and I would have left then but she said, "If I got glasses and didn't tell you, how would you feel?"

She pushed the covers down to her waist, and I stared at her T-shirt. It was the old one with the cosmonauts, but the faces were on the front this time. "They're just for reading, Helen. Anyway, you got lupus and didn't tell me."

"If I didn't tell you, how do you know?"

I couldn't argue with that, but I said, "There's other things. Harry and Wallace. The accident. Charles Darwin. You never talk about those things."

"I tried to talk about Charles," she said, and lowered her eyes so we were both looking at her T-shirt. "Harry can talk. Let him talk about the accident. He's the only one who knows about it anyway—if you don't count Wallace." We were quiet a minute, then she said, "Gussy? Do you see what I see on one of these cosmonauts?" She pointed at one of the heads inside its space helmet, and sure enough, this one had something the others did not.

"Hair?"

Helen smiled and nodded. "Hair."

"It's a she!" I cried, full of a sudden, happy enthusiasm I didn't quite understand until Helen said, "So now we don't have to be veterinarians."

Her sudden dream of becoming an astronaut surprised everyone but Julian. He was on his knees, weeding a bed of pennyroyal when I came home. He looked up at me with that faint smile that meant I was interrupting him, calling him back from the only place he ever really rested, a place I imagined to be full of glorious weeds, nurtured outcasts from all the world's gardens—this time, said the smile, I'll allow it; next time, it warned, you take your chances.

"I'm glad to hear it. That's good news, Gussy. You're on my pennyroyal." It was a strange, sparse ground cover that smelled strongly of turpentine and peppermint when you trampled it. I was hit with its astringent odor and moved my feet.

"Doesn't it seem kind of odd to you, Papa?"

"Odd? It seems the most natural thing in the world. It seems healthy. Outer space could use a few girls like you." He laughed, and I knew he hadn't come back yet, not entirely, from his own private orbit. "If nothing else, it will get you off Flat Street."

"Helen doesn't live on Flat Street," I reminded him.

"No, but you do. Aren't you going to join her?"

"Well, no. Not exactly. I'm interested in becoming a marine biologist." I was pleased with the way that sounded, but Julian seemed unimpressed.

"Do that some other time. Science alone can be grueling. And insulting," he said softly, "to a person of intelligence and imagination." It was one of the first personal things my father ever said to me.

Harriet's response was "Astronaut? Your friend's off her rocker if you ask me. She can't even get up off her bed and she's planning to walk on the moon. What a *meshuggas*! What fool would let her set her heart on such a thing?"

My mother rarely resorted to Yiddish in my presence, though it seemed to fly out of her often enough when she argued with my father. I was too busy being surprised by that to notice she'd asked a question. Julian answered it. "This fool, Harriet."

"And for what, may I ask?"

"For the simple reason that nobody has ever said the word 'hope' to that girl. She comes from a family where parents are untrustworthy and children are cut down in their youth—"

"Pss!" she hissed and pointed. Julian turned and saw me trying to make myself small in a corner.

"Gussy," he said wearily, "it's unprofessional, that's all. I can't speak about her in front of you, you know that. The trouble is—" he tugged his earlobe—"I think you should hear it. Go to the kitchen and eavesdrop. It will make me feel better."

I went, still shaken by the phrase "cut down in their youth"—I imagined a giant blade slicing Harry at the ankles; all that was left of him were his big feet. Then I saw the terrifying blade take Helen, and after Helen it took me. We were lying next to each other in a huge field of other broken children, and for some reason she was telling me the best way to make a bread and butter sandwich. She liked a little salt on the butter, and the crusts cut off, and the sandwich cut diagonally. If you spent an afternoon with Helen, you knew this about her.

"She's a challenging patient," said Julian. I knew he meant stubborn. "She's thoroughly educated about her illness. In fact, she seems less afraid of lupus and the possibility of dying than she is of a long, unpredictable future, a future which may involve accounting for her past; I can't quite make it out. Her psychosomatic response is extremely well developed. For example, she arrived in my office this morning, jaundiced from head to toe, yet her color was close to normal by the time she left, and her blood work was negative." Harriet opened her mouth to speak, but he put his hand up. "It's not unusual or even significant in and of itself. What's important is that the child chose yellow. Cowardice. Bitterness. Some say jealousy. She has a brother at home, a retarded boy, as far as I understand, and whether she feels she has to compete with him for her mother's attention, I don't know."

"Retarded, no." I stuck my head out of the kitchen. "He's clairvoyant."

Harriet shushed me and asked, "What's the father, a traveling salesman? We never hear about him. Where's he?"

I gave Julian one full second to answer. When he didn't, I said, "Dead."

My mother looked at me sternly.

"Well, he is."

"I don't care if he is. It's not what you say, it's how you say it, Augusta."

I hung my head for a second or two, then asked Julian if he thought a person could be jealous of someone who wasn't around.

"Don't ask the doctor," said Harriet. "He doesn't know. Anyone can be jealous of anyone at any time, believe me."

"Then I think the person in her family Helen is jealous of is Wallace."

"Who?" asked Harriet. "The brother?"

"No, her father. Her brother's name is Harry, almost like your name."

"Wallace," said Julian, deep in thought. "Wallace. Of course. She'd like to keep him buried, but at the same time she feels guilty for it. Her illness is her unwillingness to move forward. On bad days, in fact, her lupus enables her not to move at all."

"You're thinking aloud," snapped Harriet. She took up her crossword. "Give me a Eurasian plant, beginning with 'f' and ending with 'k.' Nine letters, Augusta."

"I don't even know where that is!"

"Fenugreek," said Julian, and that day was over.

# *Chapter Six*

Whenever a bee or a wasp found its way in through an open window, Mother would drop everything and follow it around the rooms of our house. "Look, family!" she would cry. "Teddy's back! Augusta, your uncle Theodore!" She'd laugh and offer a spatula to the poor trapped insect as a landing platform, and with great care carry it outdoors to freedom.

Uncle Teddy was Aunt Kate's husband. During the war he'd been a tail gunner aboard a bomber called *The Great Artiste,* and in the sky over Nagasaki, Japan, he'd lost all control of his bowels and bladder—a fact which impressed me so deeply as a child, the shame of incontinence was all I could conjure up whenever I heard the words "nuclear age."

One day when Teddy was still alive, I said to Harriet, "He's different, isn't he?"

"Different from when?"

"Different from the beginning of the war."

"He used to be thin," she smiled, "thin and handsome.

We all used to be thin. And dance! He could dance circles around your father."

"Isn't there something else?" I asked.

"What else would there be?"

"He doesn't use the toilet, Mama!"

She lowered her face to mine and whispered—almost fiercely, "Every day I'm alive, I thank God he's alive, Augusta. Of what great importance is the toilet in such a world as this?"

I was not expected to understand such a world, this world I lived in, a world which put grown men in diapers though once they'd hummed like a top on a dance floor. I knew Teddy only as my girlish uncle who wept easily and couldn't drive a car, and was allergic to everything, including toothpaste and stones. He was a Christian Scientist, whatever that meant, and he had a war wound in a place that didn't show with his clothes on, a place that according to Harriet made a bedroom widow of my aunt Kate. His body had an almost planetary roundness that excited and repelled me, and in mean, dispirited moments I imagined *The Great Artiste* in trouble and her crew members parachuting to the earth, all except Theodore, who rose up like a hot-air balloon and disappeared into heaven.

"He was in hell, Gussy. For the rest of his life, the man was in hell. He was one of those the war should have killed," said Julian, retreating behind the evening paper. "I'm sorry to say it."

"He liked animals," I said. "He was good with animals."

"He was allergic to everything that moved. His own heartbeat, his own blood frightened him. Look," he lowered the paper, "if we're lucky we'll never know what it was like to be Ted. If we're lucky."

The bombing itself was never talked about—I was told

Uncle Teddy didn't remember a thing; I asked him once and for an answer got the ticking of the clock—and in that vacuum of information, I created for myself and for the world a benevolent bomb. I imagined it vividly as one of Julian's leggy gladioli, sucking in light and warm, endless spring rain until one morning on my way to school I'd catch my breath before the first flower exploding from a green stem, the sudden, hot fragrance of the blossom bringing me to my knees on the path that led to the gate that connected our yard to Flat Street and the world.

If you're a child and are not told otherwise, a whole crying city may be reduced to the beauty of a flower. A flash of white light, a blaze of heat, these may be the color and fragrance of the petals of the flower, and until someone tells you or you find out for yourself, a thing of infinite destructive power can be defined in your heart as the act of creation itself.

What didn't I learn that spring? The hard rain began on April Fool's Day and didn't stop until the wreckage of Murdoch was complete, which meant the last goose of that tiny Czechoslovakian community—our upstream neighbor—passed beneath the footbridge that crossed our river. It wasn't swimming, it was balanced on an old refrigerator swept down by the flood. It was a white goose, roughly the color of the refrigerator, and if Helen hadn't spotted it I never would have. I was gazing upward into a tear in the clouds, wondering at the unfamiliar sight. "Blue!" I cried out. "Enough for a Dutchman's breeches!"

"It can't fly," said Helen. She had to shout over the noise of the water.

"What can't fly?"

She pointed at the refrigerator before it vanished under

our feet. Connie Browne was with us, bobbing her blond head up and down as the goose reappeared on the downstream side of the bridge.

"How do you know it can't fly?" I shouted.

"If you were that goose and you could fly, wouldn't you have flown?"

"They clip their wings," said Connie gravely. "We had geese. I didn't like them one bit. They're almost all dark meat and very fatty."

The last we saw of the goose it was flapping its useless wings, trying to stay upright on the rolling refrigerator. It looked like a circus bear riding a ball, and I felt sorry for it the way I always did for the bears. Back when the pearly everlasting still grew in our yard, I sat under it and wished them their freedom.

"It can swim, right?" I asked Helen. "Why doesn't it swim?"

She shrugged, and looked down into the racing water. "The lake was this color."

"What lake?" asked Constance.

"Where we used to live."

"Aren't you glad you don't live in Murdoch?" said Constance.

"No one lives in Murdoch anymore," I reminded her. "There isn't a Murdoch."

It was as if that town had been tipped up and shaken out over the river, spilling, among other things, chairs more numerous than fish. "All they ever did there was sit," Constance decided. She and Helen and I watched from the bridge every day after school, and by the time the sun came out, moments after the refrigerator and its lonely passenger touched our lives, we'd counted forty-two chairs, each one looking more and more human as it made its stiff way downstream. One afternoon, four porches swept by, and close behind them four wicker rockers and what Helen swore were the tangled remains of an old fire escape. My prize was a whole section of floor covered with linoleum. Connie Browne attracted the smaller, more buoyant and personal things, such as lampshades, and one old stand-up radio that looked like it might have fallen right out of her mother's English girlhood and landed in our river. It got trapped in an eddy, and after the three of us waded out through the sycamores and dragged it to dry ground, I looked up and saw an inauspicious flock of dark birds wheel across the surface of the water.

"Let's drag it back," I said.

"Relax," said Constance. She and Helen already had the back off the radio and were fiddling with the wires.

"How can I relax? The river never floods like this. It's ruined a whole town! I don't think we're meant to be taking things out of it, Constance. I know I'm not touching that damn radio."

"I saw what you saw. It was nothing but a bunch of black umbrellas."

"Gussy, take a look at what's inside here!" cried Helen. She'd changed overnight into someone with a purpose and a passion: an unquenchable thirst for flight. Flight, she explained, might have to include unlofty things in the beginning, like tinkering with soggy old radios or taking lawn mowers apart, anything to get at the root of order from which mechanical knowledge sprung. To our great surprise, Constance had wandered down the seemingly random path of electricity years ago, and could be counted on to know how things worked. Though, when it came to the more elaborate business of internal combustion, she offered her older sister Patience—the one who could sit on her braids. "She's the real grease monkey. We had a boat with a ninety-horsepower Evinrude engine that she fixed when she was seven."

"What was the problem?" asked Helen.

"Cavitation."

"Oh," she nodded, "our boat has the same engine."

"What boat?" I said. "You don't have a boat, Helen."

"Does it cavitate?" asked Connie.

"It doesn't anything," said Helen. "It sits at the bottom of the lake."

Connie whistled the way a boy whistles, through a gap in her teeth. I laughed uneasily.

The sound of that spring for me was uneasy laughter, behind which the river ran. It was as if I'd forgotten how to set my mouth or contract my throat to express exuberance, and instead uttered a cry as double-edged and haunting as the air raid siren that shook us from our seats at school. There was a problem with the siren that spring, something mechanical that Patience Browne might have fixed in a minute had anyone heard the story of the Evinrude and invited her to. Because of this problem the siren wailed frequently and unexpectedly and with a vengeance, disrupting classes two or three times a week until they got the bugs out of it—which meant someone came and went with a monkey wrench and changed nothing but the pitch of the siren, so now it sounded like a dog howling inside a barrel, mournful as ever.

Helen loved it. She loved the possibility it promised. While the rest of us ducked and covered according to the strict rules for air raid drills at Pacific No. 9, she slipped outside and stood in a corner of the dirt lot, head back, waiting for planes.

"You should at least wear a hat," I told her crossly.

"I don't have a hat. What would a hat do?"

"It would protect your head."

"From what?"

"From a bomb, I guess. I don't know."

It was a foolish thing to say. Better than most I knew how war was run, and a hat didn't make much difference anymore, no difference at all. A person's life didn't make much difference; their death didn't either. Things were done in a bigger way, which made all our dropping to hands and knees and crawling under lockers hopelessly old-fashioned—or painful if you were Deirdre George and had warts on your knees. That girl suddenly stood up one day in the middle of an air raid drill and cried, "What's the point of this? We're all sitting ducks!" It occurred to me: She's dead right. Nothing will save us from what we know exists already. The power to kill and utterly destroy from above is great. No matter how many coats we fling over our heads as we sit in enforced silence in our lockers, we will surely perish. That flower, that gladiola was a child's fairy tale.

Sometimes I felt lonely with this knowledge and sat in the back of the bus and hugged myself. Or the sight of our neighbor's cherry tree, its blossoms lost to the constant rain, put me in a mood I had no explanation for. Whenever the siren blew at school, I wanted to break free and follow Helen outside just to stand beside her, to feel the great happiness of having her back again, here in the dirt lot. I thought it would make a future I couldn't imagine, bearable, to have had that moment with her. I thought if Uncle Teddy had had a moment like that with Aunt Kate, he wouldn't have had to sneeze and shake all his life. He would have been able to drive downtown in his own car, and feed a heartworm pill to his dog Dolly without crying. Poor

Teddy. Every time a stump or barrel passed under the footbridge, I thought of him. And that old refrigerator bearing the goose, that was Teddy. He surfaced often that spring. I never knew where to expect him. I liked him better as a ghost—or a bee—than I ever had as a man, though his last visit was more man than ghost, and I made peace with that all right.

It happened on a Wednesday. I loved that word, "Wednesday." It was one of those fine, lively words that could take you so far into itself you lost its meaning. The harder you looked, the less you saw. Wednesday. Wednesday. I'd open my *Funk and Wagnall's* for the hundredth time and there, between "wedlock" and "wee," I'd wonder again at the simple facts of it: "The fourth day of the week, occurring after Tuesday and before Thursday." Helen understood what I meant by Wednesday. The word "was" had the same effect on her, and we agreed maybe it was something peculiar to the W's.

This was a warm Wednesday at the end of April. That morning I'd carried my coat to the attic with a crisp new dollar bill pinned to the lining. "I gift you," said Harriet as she did every spring, and shooed me up the attic stairs with the first cold November day already and happily in my heart—a day when a simple greeting of friends sent you reeling under the spell of mothballs, a day with a dollar to look forward to. The rain had finally broken up, but the river was still making history. From the school yard, Helen and I watched the swift current peel away the bark of the sycamores.

Suddenly she said, "At the lake there were plenty of those trees. Harry and I used to take our chairs out and sit in the forest and pretend we were living in an old house where the wallpaper was so old it was peeling off the walls.

We called it the old home game. We had another game where we'd sit in the car—"

"Harry loves to sit," I said. "He should have been born in Murdoch."

"He'd sit and I'd hold the steering wheel, and you know we weren't going anywhere but where we pretended to go because we were too little, but still sometimes he'd tap my arm and tell me, 'Slow down, Helen. The road might be slippery here.' Or, 'There's a bridge coming up, Helen. Bridges freeze.' He hated to drive, but he loved telling other people how to drive. Except Wallace." She frowned. "No one told Wallace. Whatever you told Wallace, he'd do the opposite, unless you told him to speed up. I always asked him to speed up, and Harry and Jordan asked him to slow down. For all of us he'd speed up. He wasn't a bad person, Gussy. He just wasn't careful all the time and sometimes he was reckless."

"You miss him," I said, looking out at the river and the trees. "You must miss him."

"I miss someone," she nodded, "but it's the same someone I always missed when Wallace was alive, and that's a father."

Just then the siren blew for the second time that day. "We'll have to go in!" I shouted over the noise. "I wish they'd figure out the damn problem with the mechanism and fix it!"

"Joan says it's triggered by dampness," said Helen, and we turned our backs on the hungry river.

As we crossed the school yard I noticed for the first time that my shoulder was a good six inches below hers. How she'd grown, my friend! How she'd shot up! Soon she'd be as tall as Jordan. We fell in step behind a pack of girls as reluctant as we were to come in out of the day, and she whispered, "You know what they're doing? They're gossiping." I raised my eyebrows. "About the *f* word."

"What *f* word?"

"It ends with 'k.'"

"Oh, I know." Of course I thought of "fenugreek." "It's a Eurasian plant."

She was kind enough not to laugh out loud, and she could have. "The other *f* word," she said.

"What's that all over Deirdre's arms?"

"Eczema."

"It looks like heartbreak of psoriasis to me."

Helen stopped and cocked her head. "She doesn't live at the morgue!" she whispered vehemently.

"Who doesn't live at the morgue?"

"Agnes. Deirdre just said, 'How's life at the morgue?' She doesn't live at the morgue, she lives at the mortuary. There's a big difference."

"Helen." I grabbed her sleeve. "Let's not go in. Let's stay out here and watch for planes." We were close to the steps of the school, and I couldn't imagine saying good-bye to her at the W's and crawling all the way to the other end of the alphabet to bury myself in my locker, which was next to Connie Browne's. Sheer proximity had finally made me friends with that girl, but it seemed a waste to die in her arms simply because C followed B.

Helen had a better idea. We'd head for the footbridge, where one of us could watch for planes, the other for useful junk borne down by the river. I agreed, and we ducked out of sight behind the corner of the school. "What if we're caught?" I whispered. She shushed me. I put my forehead against the warm bricks and said a prayer I'd learned, Peace be to this house, meaning: To Whom It May Concern, Bless our truancy. And keep Miss St. John away from the windows on the river side. Very Truly Yours. Amen.

We took the long way around to the river. I kept looking back over my shoulder until the school disappeared, and even then I had the sense it was following us.

"In that case, it is," said my friend. She'd clearly left it behind in the school yard. As we walked, she searched the edge of the sycamores where the water had receded. "We're looking for an antenna, Gussy. Or something to make one out of."

"For what? For that stupid radio?"

"Connie's a ham. She's got a ham operator's license. With an antenna she says we can get Europe and Russia and Florida. Maybe even Eurasia. Where is that?"

"Who would want to talk to Russia?"

"I would."

"What would you say?"

"I'd ask them about the cosmonauts. I'd ask them about Valentina Tereshkova, the lady cosmonaut. I'd ask them what they ate for lunch, and if their house was warm, and what they were reading, and if they'd ever seen a television. I'd ask them what they thought about Americans. I'd ask them if they'd heard of Amelia Earhart."

"I'd ask them about the Cuban Missile Crisis," I said.

"No you wouldn't. Anyway, they wouldn't know about it."

"We know about it, and we're only children." I was watching the wet ground travel beneath my feet; then for no reason I looked up. I looked ahead of us, through the trees. "Isn't that Jordan?"

"That tiny person?"

"She's a long way off."

"She looks like a clothespin," said Helen, and stopped

walking. She didn't say anything for a minute, then she said, "All summer at the lake she looked like that, like a clothespin. She was always a long way off, down at the water teaching Harry to swim."

"How long does it take to teach a person to swim?"

"He was a lazy swimmer. Every summer he learned, but every winter he forgot. I was a good swimmer. It made Harry embarrassed, so when he was swimming I stayed in the house reading, or I sat on the screened-in porch listening to the owls. At the lake the owls were noisy all day long. It's probably the only place in the world where that's so, that's what Wallace said. When she was a clothespin, Gussy, I'd do this." She brought her hand up to her eye. "I'd hold her between my finger and my thumb and I'd say, 'She had me. I came out of her.' Then I'd cross over to Harry and say, 'He came out of her too.'"

"The woods were dark around the house, that's why."

"That's why what?"

"That's why the owls were there in the daytime." We started walking again and I said, "What do you think she's doing?"

"She's just walking. She likes the river when it floods. She's doing what we're doing."

"I bet she's not looking for some stupid antenna," I laughed, then caught my breath at the sight of a human skeleton hung in a tree. Another look and I thought, No, it can't be. Bones don't rust. "There's your antenna, Helen. But it'll take somebody taller than you or me to shake it out of there."

We settled on Jordan.

She had long legs and a good head start—as far as we were from the footbridge, she was the same distance beyond it and walking away from us, not towards. We were all three headed for Murdoch. At the same time, Murdoch was headed for us and had been for as long as I could remember—at least three weeks. We could still look out across the water and watch pieces of its post office glide by, or the upturned ceiling of the Czech Brotherhood Hall, where Harriet had once taken me to play bingo. There were fans on that ceiling, I remembered, and my mother wore an embarrassing hat—it looked like a jawbone. It was a hot, smoky place, full of noise and laughter and a strange form of English I didn't understand. Neither of us felt at home there. She kept patting the back of her neck with one of Julian's handkerchiefs, and I knew I'd been brought along to protect her (possibly the handkerchief, smelling deeply of my father, served the same purpose), but from what or whom puzzled me all evening. The men—one man in particular who sat between us and polished his blood-red shoes, then mine, with a cold biscuit—looked like Uncle Teddy; they were all younger, happier Teds. The women looked a good deal like Harriet. Whether we won or lost or broke even that night, I had no idea. I assumed we lost, because Julian greeted us home without one bit of warmth whatsoever. "I was worried sick," he said, and pointed at the clock and shooed me off to bed all in one motion.

If anyone ever asked—and no one ever did—whether I'd traveled beyond the slim borders of my home to a foreign country, I would have answered, "Yes. Murdoch." And at the end of that day, that Wednesday, I would have meant it in more ways than one.

We decided to trot after Jordan, but first Helen gripped my arm. "Look!" She pointed to the middle of the river.

"Look yourself. I don't see a thing."

"Yes! It's a barber chair!"

That made the forty-third chair to have touched our lives.

"There's someone in it!" I cried, but it was only a trick of sunlight and a towel.

"Yesterday Joan found a box with a perfectly good wig in it," she laughed, "and Jordan said the river gives you what you need."

"What does Harry need?"

"Oh, turtles. But he won't go anywhere near the water."

We started to run, and suddenly something came to me. It unbound itself and flew up into my mouth and out through my teeth before I could stop it. "Helen? What's the exit light? It's something in the river, isn't it? It's something you have to be careful about, that could hurt someone."

She didn't hedge, she just said, "It means God. When Harry says he saw the exit light, he means the accident."

We ran along in silence after that. The ground was tricky, covered with wet and mostly meaningless junk. Helen kicked things, I left them alone, that was the difference. She discovered a few old, waterlogged books this way. Soft as mushrooms, they fell apart right there on the toe of her shoe.

At the footbridge we stopped to catch our breath. Mine was nowhere to be found, but I managed to ask, "What about your planes?"

"They'll wait. Let's go."

"She won't mind that we're not in school?"

"Jordan? She's vague about things like that."

We could see her ahead of us from time to time, but there were whole minutes when she vanished in the forest. The trees grew closely here—stands of willow, box elder, poplar, some young oak and hickory; we'd left the sycamores behind. This was no longer the path to anywhere, and soon Helen and I were traveling like shadows in a shadowy darkness, through tunnels of branches and vines, not running, but stumbling over the roots of the trees exposed by the flood. It was midafternoon, the foliage was slight, and still we could see neither light nor sky above us. We both felt it, but I was the one to say it: "Let's turn back."

Helen squeezed my hand, Yes, then remembered, "Oh, but Gussy! Jordan!"

"She's thirty-seven. She can walk home by herself." To this day I'm ashamed to have said it.

We walked on, fighting our way through the tangled sumac, traveling farther and farther away from the river. I was beginning to think no human being had ever set foot in these woods, that Jordan had certainly found an easier way upstream, when a clearing discovered us. I say discovered us because we were standing perfectly still when all of a sudden the place behind Helen's ear began to shine, then her whole head was covered with a sort of platinum light. Something the size of a jail window opened above us. It wasn't much, but it let the air and sky in, and we both smiled widely and breathed relief—though clearings that come to you leave you, and this one was traveling fast. There was enough time to notice a big beech tree on the edge of the clearing. It seemed to face us—if a tree can face. What it said to us, besides Come lie in my fertile shade and climb my wandering branches when summer comes, was

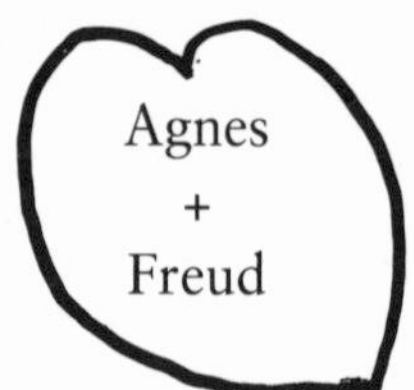


The heart was lopsided and true to life. Helen went to it immediately.

"It's recent," she said.

"Do you know Freud?"

"She talks about him. I know what a Freudian slip is. She told me."

"I like Agnes," I said. I was thinking of her patience, and how she probably came out here and clawed away at that tree with her own nails.

"I like her too. She explained tapeworms to me."

"I once asked her about prehensile thumbs."

"When I was sick she made me a shoe-box camera."

"That seems like a long time ago."

"Harry keeps his turtles in it now."

We stood with our heads bowed to the ground, made suddenly shy by that heart, now that we were done with its occupants. I said "Helen" and she said "Gussy" at the same time. "Go ahead," I told her.

"No, you go."

"It was nothing," I said. "I was just going to say nothing."

"Me too."

"We can find this place again if you want to."

"Please!" It meant yes. "All I have now is a key and it wouldn't cut butter."

I never wondered, not even for a minute, whether we'd return to that spot again, or whether there was a spot to return to. As far as the first goes, we never did, though we left our names somewhere else (in wet cement) without cutting into a live thing. As far as the second: no map I know of ever called true moments between people *geography*. Our clearing rolled away behind us. Maybe a hand passed over the sun; maybe we dreamt the whole thing anyway. The next part we didn't dream. Helen wished she had. I was satisfied to go through it. I had just ducked under an evergreen's low branch—we were coming into the territory of the spruces—and as I turned to ask my friend whether we should call out to Jordan, a high, piercing scream hit us from the direction of the river.

"The siren," I said, then covered my face with my hands and shook my head.

"Of course it's not," Helen whispered. She put both arms around me and we stood still, waiting to know what to do or where to go, but it didn't come again.

We set out to our left, thrashing through the underbrush, shoving at full-grown trees as if we believed they'd move. Helen kept calling out, and her voice was surely drowned by the river, but I kept thinking, there's only her and me and something so needy around the next bend it can't even say its own name.

We stopped on the riverbank. She looked upstream, I looked down. I know now that I did it to get ready—there was no other reason to look away from where the future lay. Helen had had a whole second or two of that sight before my eyes came around, and all she said was "I'd have died if it was Jordan."

Jordan was walking towards us along the edge of the water. She looked like she was drunk or in love. She was carrying a pair of muddy shoes—they were men's shoes—in one hand, and with the other she was clinging to the thin young trees that lined the bank. The river was almost placid here. It bent away from the main current and circled back on itself, creating an eddy deep and slow as a lagoon. Helen said her name, but she was still too far away to hear it. I shouted, "Jordan!" then wished I hadn't. I knew what it was like to be shaken from a solid sleep, and she had that same vague look on her face that sleepers have.

"Look behind her," said Helen.

"What is it, another chair?"

"Don't you see that?"

I saw nothing.

My friend took off along the bank and threw herself into her mother's arms. Jordan passed one arm around her and rocked her. Her right hand still clutched the shoes. She pressed her forehead against Helen's, then raised her head and kissed Helen's hair. It was the first time in a long time I'd seen anyone kiss anyone. They walked slowly back to me and I said, "Harry," meaning the shoes.

"No." Jordan shook her head. Her lips were almost white. Her face was divided by a long piece of hair. "A man," she said. "A human being."

"There's a body up there," said Helen.

"Thank you," I said. "I understand it."

He had not just arrived. The back of his head was eaten away, and I guessed that was enough to cause anyone to scream, even Jordan. In spite of it, she'd rolled him over to see his face, to identify him. I didn't know it at the time, but it was an instinct as strong in her as survival.

I said I'd walk back there alone to see what a dead man looked like.

"Don't let her!" cried Helen. She held the shoes now and was rubbing them all over with the palms of her hands. Under the mud they were a reddish color and looked like someone had taken good care of them.

"How can I not let her?" said Jordan.

"Go with her!" She motioned us away. There were tears running down her cheeks. "She shouldn't be alone!"

"Neither should you," I said. "I'll go myself. Halfway."

I picked a point on the bank, a certain tree that leaned over, and steered for it. I could see all I needed to see from there. The wind, small as it was, came at my back and carried the part of him I dreaded most back upstream to

Murdoch, where he'd come from. He was a large man, as large as my uncle Teddy. He looked like Teddy, and I wondered why some haunt us and some don't. That side of the family surely did. He'd swallowed half the river, and it still ran from his mouth and nostrils and a place I hadn't counted on, his open eyes. I knew so little about human death, but I'd heard that corpses gasped and even urinated, even eliminated, and I wondered if emotion wasn't possible. I walked back and said, "Hey, he's crying."

Jordan stood up next to me and held my hand. "No, sweetie. It's the river trying to get out."

We took an easier route home—easier and harder. We followed the river and were reminded every step of the way of its power to take and keep—"And give," said Jordan. I assumed she meant the shoes. How I tied it up with *gift* I don't remember, but I told her that body looked like an uncle of mine, my father's sister's husband, Uncle Teddy who was dead now.

"I'm sorry," she said.

"Oh, it wasn't your fault."

She looked puzzled. "Blaming anyone was the farthest thing from my mind."

"My mother loved him, Jordan. She may have been *in* love with him."

"Love never killed a soul, Gussy. People die of everything but love."

All the way back, Helen walked ahead of us, her arms stiffly by her sides, spreading and clenching her hands as if she were leaving an invisible, sporadic trail of bread crumbs, a trail we followed. She hadn't said a word or reached out to me in any way since I went to take a look at the body. At the bridge she was still crying, and when Jordan asked if she couldn't say good-bye, nicely, to her friend who'd seen a lot that afternoon too, more, much more than she bargained for, Helen looked at the ground and said, "Nicely, Jordan? I don't get that."

"See you tomorrow," I said. "We'll get that antenna tomorrow, Helen, I promise you."

She nodded without looking up.

I asked Jordan what time it was and she said, "Five o'clock. Will anyone be frantic? I'll call the school the minute we get home."

"And the police," I reminded her.

"Not the police!" Helen said quickly.

"Why not the police?" asked Jordan. "He's got a family, just like you do, just like Gussy does. They're worried sick by now. You can understand that. If we hadn't met in the woods, and I got home and Joan and Harry said you were gone from school all afternoon with no trace of you anywhere, I'd be worried sick, wouldn't you?"

"You were the reason we were gone all afternoon."

"I heard a different story, Helen."

"I already explained to her about the antenna," I said.

"The antenna was only part of it, a small part of it," she said hoarsely. "You led us to him, Jordan."

"Helen." Jordan put her arms around her. "Helen."

My friend started to cry again. She looked like a little girl, a long, tall little girl, chewing on her lip and leaning into her mother. "You don't believe that," Jordan said softly. She pushed the hair off Helen's forehead. All the damp weather had made it wavy. I liked it that way. "You're tired," said Jordan. "We're all tired. You're exhausted, Helen."

"She didn't have any lunch," I said. Then I remembered, "She had my lunch."

"Whose lunch did you have?"

"Hers. Harry made it. It was a lettuce and tomato and paper towel sandwich."

"On buttered bread," said Jordan. "That's what I had. I think he puts the paper towel in there to dry the lettuce, don't you? But he forgets to take it out. He's our new cook. He was our old cook, but this one's teaching him how to cook again." She nodded so her chin hit the top of Helen's head. "She's the best cook we have."

"Better than Joan," said Helen, sniffling and mopping her face with her hand.

"Much better than Joan. Ten times better than Joan."

"Better than you?" I asked. It was the closest I ever came to trying to be polite to Jordan. I knew she could barely put together a tuna fish sandwich.

"A hundred times better than me. A hundred thousand times better than me. I'm the worst cook in the world. Hasn't Helen told you?"

"I told her," said Helen. "She forgot. Jordan?"

"Mm?"

"What's caviar exactly?"

"Caviar exactly." She laughed and gave Helen a squeeze. "Did I ever tell you I love your questions?"

"No."

"Well, I do. Caviar exactly is something you eat. It's expensive. The best caviar comes from Russia. It's black. It looks like—"

"We know all that," I said. "We've seen it. A girl, Deirdre, brought it to school, a sandwich of it. She ate half the sandwich, then she dared another girl, Connie—"

"Constance," Helen explained. "Constance Browne. You know her, Jordan."

"Do I?"

"She dared this girl Constance to eat the other half," I continued, "and she did, and Deirdre said, 'You know what you just ate?' Connie said, 'Yes.' Deirdre said, 'What?' Connie said, 'I don't have to tell you.' Deirdre said, 'You don't know then, because if you knew you'd be sick all over the floor.' " Suddenly I realized I'd never spoken like this in front of Jordan before, and the worst part was coming up. I said, "Helen, you finish it."

"Deirdre told us it was the chopped-up private parts of lady fish," said Helen, and Jordan tipped her head back, laughing deeply and noiselessly, and I was aware of the river again, the high hissing sound of it under the bridge. Yet out there in the sycamores it lapped the ground like a tame dog. Every passing second took it farther from us, I could feel that, and though it came as a relief, like the end of any long day, it was sad too.

I said, "Something's changing."

We all looked around, and Jordan said, "It's the light."

"I think it's the river," said Helen. "I think it's giving up."

"Good," said Jordan. "We can all go home now."

"We can't," said Helen.

"Why can't we?"

"I promised Gussy the good river."

"The good river can wait."

"It's waited," said Helen.

"It can wait some more. Other people are waiting."

"Please, Jordan. We haven't done it in a long time and she's never seen it. We could be halfway through it by now. The short good river?"

She looked skeptical and I said, "They're never home before six, Jordan, ever." This seemed to surprise her, and

I explained, "My mother works at the Woolworth's store and the drugstore and the fire department."

Helen was impatient. "Come on, Jordan. The short good river. Just say yes."

"What does she do in all those places?"

"She puts out fires," Helen answered for me.

"She's a bookkeeper," I said.

"She's a very important person," said Jordan. I started to shake my head, but she said, "Yes."

"Now me, yes," said Helen. The back of her head rested against her mother's shoulder. She had her eyes closed and her face tilted up like a sunbather.

"Unlean, Helen. You have to be standing on your own two feet to say it," said Jordan. She gave her a push, and Helen stood on her own two feet with her own two arms out to the sides and slightly up, as if she were lifting a very light world. She stood between us and we faced the river and the bridge, and she began, "What's so good about a river?"

"Tell us," said Jordan.

Helen nudged me with her foot. "You say 'Tell us,' Gussy."

"Tell us, Gussy."

"No! Just say 'Tell us.'"

"What difference does it make? Tell us."

That seemed to satisfy her, and she went on. "What's so good about a river is it's full of life. Fish and grass and big birds come to it. Crops grow and animals come right down to it and drink. People live near it and do their laundry in it, out on big rocks."

"Not here they don't," I said.

"It doesn't matter," she said sharply. "It's part of the song."

"It's a song?"

"Yes! No! Not the kind of song that's meant to be sung."

"Go on and finish," said Jordan.

"How did I know she was going to have so many questions?"

I'd thrown her off enough so she had to adjust her feet and shake out her arms. She put her arms back up in the sky and said, "What's so good about the river?"

"Tell us," said Jordan and I together.

"It divides countries and carries passengers" (I thought of the goose, I thought of the empty barber chair, I thought of the dead man) "and you can stand still and never see the same water twice. Without this river, we wouldn't have this bridge. We'd all live in the same place, on the same side of town."

"There wouldn't be sides," I said.

Helen lowered her arms and turned to me. "That was the last line. You ruined it."

"Oh, it wasn't the last line, Helen. It was time for the last line anyway," said Jordan. "Joan has to go to work."

"She drives a taxi," I said to Helen, but of course she knew.

"Come here," said Jordan, "right here, Gussy." She held me close for a second or two, a brief, distracted hug that fell far short of the only other time we'd done that.

She went on ahead and left Helen to say good-bye—which meant my friend found a hangnail to pick at and said nothing. I thought, She can do what she's doing and speak at the same time. I'll stay and wait for a kind word. It never came. When it was time to go and she only nodded, I pointed back at the hill to my house and said, "Look, I have to go up there alone, there's two of you." I felt stark naked saying it.

But she couldn't come any closer. She was hurt and stubborn herself. She leaned down and swooped something off the ground—those terrible red shoes—lifting them up by their tongues. I felt my heart beating in my stomach and I said, "Who needs them?"

"They'll fit Harry."

"Don't be an idiot. Leave all the bad luck on this side of the river."

"Then you'll have it."

"I won't. It falls right off me. Helen, I *knew* him." I pointed to the shoes, to the sudden ghost who filled them—not Teddy this time, but a man who sat between me and Harriet at the Czech Brotherhood Hall; Ted's look-alike. I saw him with a cold biscuit in one hand, Harriet's knee in the other.

She didn't leave them, but she didn't take them either. From the middle of the bridge she dropped them into the river. They were the only part of him that got away.

I was wrong about the bad luck. It walked right home with me. From the front yard I could taste the grease and smell the warm smell of flour, the fresh-dirt smell of potatoes. Harriet was frying latkes in the kitchen. She glanced up as I came in. Her face was streaked with heat and onion tears, and her hair flew about her head. She was arched slightly backwards, holding her head away from the spitting grease. One hand rested on the long handle of the frying pan, the other held a spatula.

I made my voice as neutral as I knew how. "You're home early, Mother. Mmm, latkes. My favorite." For a second I let myself believe I was the luckiest person on earth. Here was my mother, cooking a meal I loved. She didn't care where I'd been or what I'd seen. There was nothing to forgive. It was all forgiven.

I turned to leave the kitchen, to hang my sweater up. Harriet said something in a thick voice I barely recognized as hers. She cleared her throat, but the only word she could manage before her voice cracked again was "*Where?*"

I heard a hissing in the pan, the potatoes losing their moisture too fast to the grease. "You're burning something," I said, my back still to her. "You're about to burn something, Moth——"

"Never, ever, put me through that again, Augusta." The spatula clattered to the stove. "Two and a half hours I stand here waiting by that front door. Waiting. I am beside myself. Your father's delivering. He doesn't even know you're gone. The school hasn't seen you since who knows when, and they notify me at work and I'm supposed to do what? Tell them not to worry? Tell them no, not Augusta Cotton, not possible? Tell them, look around. She's got to be there somewhere because she isn't here? What do I tell them? I tell them I'm going home to Flat Street and if she's not home by three hours from now I call the police."

"Jordan's calling the police," I said. I was staring at my hands, which were chapped and dirty and didn't seem like any part of my body.

"She's human," said Harriet. "She's a mother. I know who was with you, Augusta. For a part of this day she lost a daughter too."

I nodded, more in confusion than agreement. A sweet, almost chocolaty smell rose from the stove. Neither of us moved and the smell turned quickly bitter as the latkes scorched, then blackened. Harriet put a lid on the frying pan and shut off the flame.

"What are we going to do?" I asked, though I didn't understand the question any more than she did. Food had been ruined before in that house, it couldn't have been that. She looked at me as if she'd never seen me before, and maybe she wished she hadn't; I don't think so. "Go away from me," she said, and clutched me to her, and the sobs that rose the whole length of her shaking body broke hot and sharply against my cheek.

I went to my room and sat on my bed. There were two beds in my room, and I sat on the one I never slept in. I pretended I was in prison and the high window above my head was a prison window. It faced our yard, Julian's careful flower beds, and in my mind I dug them up and covered them with tar. I put a ball and chain on my ankle. I gave myself a striped prisoner's hat and prison pajamas, and I needed a shave as all prisoners did. I lay on my back wondering what had gone wrong, and when exactly, and how someone like my mother could love or even like someone like me. It seemed a mistake. It seemed a waste that a girl like Agnes Mill couldn't be her daughter. Agnes was humble. Agnes had glasses and wore them. Agnes ate a big, predictable lunch every day. She ate neatly, on top of her lunch sack, so the food never even touched the table. I was about as neat as a bowling alley. Agnes didn't love the sanatorium. She didn't have the wrong friends. It occurred to me she didn't really have a friend in the world. People liked her—some did and some didn't—but no one reached right out to her and touched what they could only see with their eyes closed.

I looked up at the ceiling. There was an electrical outlet there, and the sight of it always baffled me. As a child I'd believed in some vague way that my dreams were powered by it. When I was older I'd seen ordinary wasps crawl through it, drunk on winter sleep, and hurtle to the floor.

Harriet had taped it shut for one whole year of my life (she was always climbing around on ladders, rooting out drafts in that house), but the tape had frightened me and caused insomnia. It looked too much like a bandage.

I wondered if Agnes Mill ever suffered from insomnia. If I lived at the morgue, I thought, you'd never catch me napping. Mortuary. She lives at the mortuary, Gussy. I turned my head aside and tried not to imagine what he looked like, our man by the river, stretched out in the living room of Agnes's house.

Then I remembered I was in prison. I'd heard how in prison your own thoughts could turn against you and do you actual harm. *Actual harm,* I said to myself, and the minute I said it I felt the first tingly ache of the flu hit me, that balloon in my head that meant fever and no turning back. I never moved from my bed. Harriet fed me aspirin for supper and rubbed my shoulders with witch hazel, and by the time Julian came home at midnight, I was warming up to some of the worst nightmares I ever care to walk through.

Some people say you make peace with things in your sleep, in your dreams. I say, try and make peace with a wide open wormy place on the back of a dead man's head, and that peace looks like a pomegranate split in two. He'd been down on the ground so long, what was left of his hair had taken root, and it fanned out around his head, short and soft and sickly green as a bed of moss. I looked around and there were clumps of moss scattered all through those woods—wherever an animal had chewed off and dragged a piece of his scalp and left it.

He never came alive the way some characters need to do in a dream, though his shoes got up and circled him from time to time, crying and calling out like a couple of orphans. He didn't bat an eye or move a limb. I was thankful for that. In the end that was the peace we made between us: the dead stay dead and the living wake up, and the lost souls walk in circles.

I was in and out of a feverish sleep for a couple of days, and I didn't even know it. I woke early Saturday morning, guessing it was Thursday around five o'clock and in a few hours I'd be getting up and going to school. The daylight was forming pockets in the sky outside my window and I thought, *I must have swum to China and back. My pajamas feel loose.* I could have been a wet rag someone's big hands took and wrung dry. I'd dropped three pounds of sweat right into the mattress.

There was a tall glass of lime juice by my bed, a few bottles of pills, a box of baking soda and a thermometer. Under the bed I discovered a bowl of water and a heap of dry washcloths. One damp washcloth lay beside me on the pillow. *Somebody has cared for me,* I said in wonder, and sat up. I was half afraid I'd fall back down into the burning well of my own bad dreams if I didn't push myself upright.

I didn't wait to feel better. I slipped my knees over the side of the bed and felt around for my feet, the way I usually blindly searched for my slippers, then I rose up and took a few steps towards the chair where all my clothes still lay (Harriet had husked me like an ear of corn). I didn't bother with a shirt or school tunic. I pulled on socks, shoes and a sweater over my pajamas. I had to rest on the chair for a minute, chewing on the painted wood to keep my balance. It seemed incredible that young children everywhere had the strength to rise up each morning and dress.

I made my way to the door of my room and down the hall

and out of the house. The heaviness of the dew lay across the steps of the house, darkening the bricks. It was fading from the grass, the pennyroyal, Julian's peppermint and chamomile, but it shone like a quiet white fire in the waxy head of a new tulip. I could have drunk from the bowl of its petals right then and there.

Nothing I know rings as clear as those first hours after an illness, especially if you go outside your bed and house where your prison's been and walk in an isolated place full of nature. That morning in Julian's garden, I felt each blade of grass, each stone under my shoe as if it lay at the heart of the world as I knew it. The Johnny-jump-ups, the wild orchids hiding in the shadow of a peony bush, the slow marigolds, the strawberry plants, a tall, exceedingly frail-looking plant we'd puzzled over and finally named conundrum; each one and all together seemed to incline their shy, budded faces towards me (even the orchids), until I was certain the absence of a single stamen, pistil, stem or leaf would throw the whole world off by a second or two. The hill to the river would never be quite what it was, nor the alignment of bricks in the factory wall. Whatever could accommodate would, and what couldn't would shatter.

I walked to the gate and leaned on it and watched the light gather and fall across Flat Street in creamy, languorous stripes. There was nothing and no one on the street, and I stepped out onto the sidewalk and moved slowly away from home. I felt like a tired king walking my kingdom, surprised to find it not only intact after a war or famine but flourishing with birdsong (cardinals!) and the taste of earth that a heavy dew brings; the taste of worms at work, as Julian called it. And the smell of kitchen gardens as well as flowers. Nothing rivals the smell of spinach and chard in the early morning.

I walked away from Second Street, a direction I didn't usually travel, and halfway down the block I came to a place I loved where an ancient oak tree grew in someone's yard, and the root of the oak had traveled underground and sprung up like an old knee out of the asphalt. Cars had driven over it, making it lie down like the asphalt, though its livingness kept urging it to spring up over and over again. It grew at night, I imagined, when the street was empty and exhausted from the struggle of the life of the day. We all grew at night. We went to school in the day. People who had a lot of growing to do slept longer and harder than people who were small and short. If you took their sleep away, I'd read this in a magazine, you could kill them, though usually you just made them very unhappy.

Somewhere at the end of the block the first car of the day coughed to life. It drove slowly past me, and I watched its front and back tires flatten the knee of the oak. I knew the car. It had a terrible paint job, and it belonged to a man who painted cars. It was pale blue in some places and gray in others, and there were streaks of fiery orange all over the hood, and the doors were the color of eggplants. I remembered an argument my parents had about the man who owned it. Harriet said this was not a neighborhood which called for the kind of big, square-jawed dogs he liked to carry around in the back of his car, so anyone who approached it might be torn in half, and Julian defended a person's right to keep animals, as long as they were under control. This morning the two dogs sat in the front seat, next to a woman who was driving, and a boy sat in the back with his pale arm dangling out the window.

I followed the progress of the car, wondering at the light morning traffic and searching the mouth of Flat Street for a distant glimpse of a bus on Second. I always loved the sight of that first morning bus with its dirty puff of exhaust, and the way the air turned glassy in its wake. At that time of the day I liked to share my world with something big and dumb on wheels. I still hadn't a clue it was Saturday. To me it was Thursday, after seven o'clock, and that boy was dragging his pale arm to school. I went home and dressed in a cotton jumper and a clean shirt. When the room began to spin I lay down on my bed to rest.

Children are strong as horses. They catch everything in sight, but throw it off again with the force of a new shoot scrambling palely upwards. I was so seldom sick I didn't know how to be, which is why I could walk outside in the late spring morning after an illness that might have killed a small animal—and some adults (they'd have died of fright with those nightmares)—and come home and put my feet up for a second or two, then wake up feeling recovered and refreshed. Harriet said as much. I came to as she was tugging my shoes off. There were clumps of black dirt all over the sheet, but that didn't seem to bother her. Where I'd been and where I thought I was going was her main concern, and when we cleared that up she insisted I be an invalid until suppertime.

"We'll ask the doctor," I argued.

"What doctor?"

"Papa."

"We won't ask the doctor. He's dead to the world. Since Wednesday, Augusta, he's brought in guess how many babies?"

I shook my head.

"Six!"

"Six!"

"Why they all want out at the same time is beyond me. That Mrs. Plante had twins."

"She had twins last year."

"She must have liked it, she had them again."

She was in a funny, girlish mood, and I asked her, "Do you believe in astrology?"

"I mix them up. Which one's the hocus-pocus?"

"Astrology."

"That, I believe in."

She bent down to pick up the wad of my pajamas, and I said, "It's Saturday, Mother? You're sure?"

"Five minutes ago it was. It still is."

"But you're dressed."

"So?"

"You don't usually get dressed on Saturday."

"Maybe you can teach an old dog a new trick," she smiled.

That smile was so unlike her, I smiled too.

She had her hand up, the one that wasn't clutching the pajamas; I think it was on its way to secure a bobby pin at the back of her head, when suddenly her face darkened and she said, "Augusta. I know all about the corpse. You can put it from your mind now, you poor children. It's over."

"Corpse?" I whispered. Body, yes. Dead man, yes. But corpse? I hadn't thought of him that way. "Oh, the corpse."

"The corpse," she nodded, and her hand came to rest on her cheek.

"You know he looked just like Ted," I said, then covered my mouth. I hadn't meant to say it.

"Like who?"

"Like a kid at school."

"He looked like one of your friends? How could he? He was a big grown man when he left Murdoch."

"He looked like Helen's father," I lied, and promised myself that was the end of it, I'd never use Wallace again that way.

The paper had carried the news on the front page, in what was called the human interest column. This was a place where you could find the name of any dog or boy who fell through the ice, those rare winters when the river froze, or a list of the best students, or brides-to-be, or organ donors. That week, six newborns had shared the column with a dead man. Helen's name, and mine, also appeared in the column, though Harriet had already heard the news by the time she read about it. She had it from Jordan, whose name appeared in the paper as Mr. Jordan Walsh. She paid a visit to my mother on the night I went down with the flu.

I tried to imagine it, but all I saw was Jordan, her face and hair streaked with mud, looking wild and fearless, towering over my mother in the doorway while Harriet groped for the phone book and rolled it into a makeshift weapon. (In our town it was as thin as a magazine, and for some reason we kept it by the front door.) "An intruder!" I could almost hear her cry. She was terrified of burglars. Whenever Julian worked late and we two were alone in the house, she'd clutch her heart at every unfamiliar noise. Or she'd walk back and forth in front of the windows and instruct me to do the same in a different part of the house. This was to make the ones outside in the shadows think there were plenty of us inside, and we were all restless, alert and—what was Julian's word? Intrepid. Returning home one night, he watched this behavior from the darkness of our yard and laughed until he gave himself away. "Did we look like a crowd?" I asked him.

"A crowd of two, yes."

"No, a crowd, Papa. Lots of people."

"You looked like you and your mother trying to look like lots of people. You need to change your height or weight, or your clothes would be enough. Put on a different hat every time you pass in front of a window. Burglars notice things like that, Gussy. They're receptive to detail."

"A hat inside, Papa?"

"Yes, well."

We never had much of an arsenal: the rolling pin, the cast-iron skillet, a few evil-looking kitchen knives. When my mother and I rehearsed for burglary, we agreed she'd sound the alarm with "Augusta! Grab the ax!" The closest ax I knew of was only the head of an ax, and dull and rusty. It lived down at the old bus barn, where I'd once found pleasure in any object designed to move through the air—bat or windshield or ax. The word "ax" would be my signal to call the operator, and our neighbor and Julian's office; or, if the lines were cut, I was to climb out a window at the back of the house (we had no back door) and run for help.

How elaborate our plans were, and how active our imaginations! My mother and I came together over burglars the way I imagined other mothers and daughters shared the pleasure of gossip or shopping for makeup and clothes. "If they break and enter," she'd remind me, "our lives come first, remember?" Our lives come first. I liked those words. There hadn't been a burglary in our neighborhood since the day after the day I was born, when a rocking chair was taken from the front porch of a house at the end of the block.

Sometimes I wondered if whoever had burned down our pearly everlasting bush had intended to burgle us but lost their nerve. I never wondered at Jordan Walsh's nerve, though much later she confessed to me she stood outside our gate for ten or fifteen minutes, her hand on the gate and her heart pounding in her ears, waiting for the courage to cross our yard. She kept thinking about her children. Why weren't they at home like other children? It was a mild evening, as mild as the day had been warm, and she thought of Helen and Harry asleep on their backs with their windows open, in their beds. It was wishful thinking.

Joan was on-duty. She had picked them up in the taxi, and Harry's joy had at least outweighed Helen's gloom. Poor Helen. She was impossible to console. "It's just an hour, Helen. Ride with Jazie for an hour, I have an errand to do," said Jordan.

"I want to go to bed, I don't want to go to work with Joan."

"Sugar." Joan had tried her best. "Honey, believe me. Joan doesn't much want to go to work with Joan either, but we'll do it because we have to do it. Otherwise we'll be wearing flour sacks and eating dog food, and I know you wouldn't like that."

Helen sulking: "I wouldn't mind it."

"Well you can't stay in this spooky old house alone tonight. You heard your momma. Now pile in here. Harry, let Helen sit by the door. That's her spot. You can sit right here by my leg, and we'll teach you how to drive."

"You can't. It's the company car," Helen had pointed out, and scuffled with her brother when he told her to zip her lip. My family, thought Jordan as she stood at our gate, isn't like any other family I know. It was a comforting thought in the dark spring night, and it gave her the courage she was waiting for.

She used the doorbell—no one but the census taker ever used our doorbell—and she could hear it screech like a wild bird somewhere deep in the house. She wasn't sure there was anyone at home. The blinds were up, and she could see right through the sitting room into the kitchen, where a light was on, a standing lamp. That seemed unusual to Jordan, a lamp in a kitchen. She rang again and waited. When nobody came she turned her back to the door and stood on the brick steps and happened to see the moon rise over the house across the street.

Harriet watched the moon from my bedroom window. She couldn't remember the last time she'd watched the moon come up. It was something, wasn't it? No wonder those people wrote songs about it. The doorbell rang again, and she eased the thermometer out from under my tongue and went to answer it. She squinted at the mercury in the poor light of the sitting room, then glanced out the window at the figure in our yard. She saw Jordan's square back, her height and her long, drab raincoat and tried to decide, man or woman? Even so, it was the wrong year for the census, and a sudden cold sweat tickled her forehead. She whispered to no one, "Grab the ax!" and crept to the door and cracked it open. Her only weapon was in her hand: she held the thermometer up to the moon.

She didn't know what to call Jordan, so she called her nothing. She didn't know who Jordan was until she introduced herself as Helen's mother. "I'll get the lights," said Harriet, recovering from her fright. She motioned Jordan inside, where the darkness of her own sitting room suddenly embarrassed her.

"It's quite a moon," said Jordan. "It flattens everything."

What did she mean by that? Harriet wondered, and looked out at the garden to see if it was still there.

She snapped on the overheads. It wasn't right to bring a stranger into such gloom. Jordan sat in the doctor's chair, Harriet sat in her old seat by the record player. "That's where my husband usually sits," she said, feeling for the right thing to say to such a person at such a moment. She found herself hoping Helen's mother wouldn't start another conversation that went nowhere, like the one about the moon.

Finally Jordan said, "I love Elgar. Do you?"

Elgar. Harriet racked her brain. Elgar. A politician? No. Who loved a politician? An actor maybe. A comedian. She said, "Oh, we don't keep a television. My husband can't stand them."

"No," said Jordan, "we don't either."

They had, in the end, listened to a scratchy Liberace record turned down low. It must have soothed Harriet. She wasn't used to company, and she'd never met anyone like Jordan before, anyone who so compelled and terrified her at the same time. She saw in Jordan her own younger self; all that potential, that willful independence. She could well understand why a woman would walk by a river on a warm spring day and discover a body. It made sense to her. I never told her what I knew: that she, Harriet, had met that body long before Jordan had, at the Czech Brotherhood Hall, when a person still lived inside it.

Now it was close to noon on Saturday. Julian was still asleep—delivering babies always brought out his mortal side. Harriet fixed me some chicken soup and a plate of saltines, and I ate sitting up in bed with my school clothes on under the covers. I felt the deep pleasure of food after an illness, the warmth and flavor of the dry saltine in my mouth and the sweet, unfamiliar motion of my lips and my tongue as it slid across my back teeth, searching.

"What was it like?" I asked her.

"What was what like?"

"You know. Meeting Jordan."

She smoothed the cover on the other bed and sat down on it. She smoothed her apron and picked a thread from its hem.

"Was she wearing her yellow sweater?"

"I told you. That drab raincoat. With what underneath it, who's to say?"

"If she didn't unbutton it," I said as brightly as I knew how, "it wouldn't be the first time."

"The coat could have sailed with Columbus," Harriet said sadly. "The buttons looked like old tuna cans."

We were quiet a minute. Finally she said, "It's none of my business, but she could really do something with herself, fix herself up. She could make herself look nice. She's a handsome woman, Augusta, and she's young. She's the same age I was when I married your father."

"She's already been married. What good would that do?"

"Who said good? I didn't say good. She seems lonely, that's all."

"Everybody's a little lonely."

"Tss—" She dismissed this with a wave of her hand.

"I bet Mrs. Plante's lonely," I said.

"Homely," said Harriet.

"Lonely," I insisted. "She just had twins twice."

"Children are a comfort. If they aren't, they ought to be."

"I thought you didn't like babies."

"I don't mean babies. Someone about your age is who I mean. Eat that soup before it's stone cold."

I took a long, luxurious drink of it. It was cool and it tasted of celery and salt, and there were golden, buttery globs of chicken fat floating in it.

"Is the fat bad for you? It's my favorite part."

"It's good for you."

"I thought too much fat was bad for you."

"Too much of anything is."

"Say more about Jordan," I said. "After she gave you the fright, she came in and sat down, then what?"

Harriet thought a minute. "You want the whole thing?"

I nodded.

"Okay. We had a conversation. It went like this. I said, 'I'll take your coat.' She said no, she'd keep it on. So I thought, she's cold-blooded. 'How about a nice cup of hot, sweet tea to take the chill off?' "

"Jordan doesn't like hot drinks. Didn't she tell you?"

"Whose story is this?"

"I can't believe she didn't tell you."

"I'm waiting."

I shrugged. "Okay, go on."

"She said no thank you to the tea—"

"There! She told you."

Harriet glared at me. "She said she didn't feel chilled, if anything she felt warm. Walking made her warm, and wasn't it a warm night out? I said, 'In that coat, yes. I can take it and hang it by the door.' I thought maybe there were valuables involved and she had to have it in sight. 'All our coats went up to the attic today, the whole Cotton family,' I said. She said, 'What a good idea, an attic,' like I'd invented it. I had to say, 'Not my idea of a good idea, thank you. Up and down those stairs!' She said, 'I never have lived with an attic. It's so easy to like something you don't know anything about.' 'There's a few things I don't know beans about,' I told her, 'and for me it works better to know them, then like them.' 'Like me,' she said, and I said, 'Yes. Like you.' "

Harriet leaned back on her elbows on the bed. In that position she looked like a much younger person. I remembered the green dress, the green flame I always thought her spirit to be. It seemed to well up in her as she spoke of Jordan.

"What did she come over here for?" I asked.

"She wanted to tell me what I had a right to know. Where you'd been all afternoon and the sight you'd seen."

"I was going to tell you."

"No you weren't. She said you wouldn't tell me. She said you wouldn't know how."

"Well, she could have called. Hasn't anybody ever heard of a telephone?"

"She's like I am, old-fashioned."

"She's not old-fashioned!" I dug at my soup. "Didn't she want to see *me* at all?"

"She saw you, Miss Jealous, what there was of you to see. A hot lump in the covers. Friends are not to have like things, to own. You don't own her, Augusta."

She pushed herself to her feet. I heard a distant toilet flush.

"You don't either."

"And you don't make sense," she said. "Who do you think brought you that lime juice? And the Arm & Hammer? Twice she came back."

"Jordan brought me baking soda?" I reached for the box by my bed. It rattled. I looked inside, and there were Helen's pearls, the ones she wore to walk me to the door after a visit. I knew it meant get well soon.

"What's in there, teeth?"

"Helen's teeth." I don't know why I lied.

"Teeth!" laughed Harriet. "I think I was never a girl like

you." She stood for a second or two with her hand on the covers. "What's this?"

"It's my knee."

"You're a good knee." She squeezed it. "Good-bye, knee. Your father needs his breakfast."

I lay there for a long time after she was gone, waiting for her to come back again.

# Chapter Seven

Our town was ruled by the alphabet. The only way to escape it was to cross the river to Helen's side, where the streets were messy and human; that is, they were named for the people who lived on them and in no particular order. Or they were named for what you'd find if you followed each to its end: Factory Street, Sanatorium Street, Coward Park Street, Murdoch Way. That spring, after the town of Murdoch disappeared into the river, no one thought to change the name of the way. It wasn't the first time a path had lost its destination. Helen's street, Coward Park, no longer led anywhere but to the top of the hill where her yellow house sat, and next to it a purple wall.

I asked her one day who Mr. Coward Park was.

"He had cows, but he's dead."

"Mr. Coward," said Joan. "No Park. Mr. Coward."

"He isn't dead," said Jordan. "His wife is dead."

Helen turned to me. "A family of know-it-alls."

Whenever I walked the streets on my side of the river, from Accidental all the way down to Zoroaster, if I had nothing in particular to think about and no company but my own, I'd let myself sink into the name of each street as I passed it. Sometimes a song would come to me, a song about Dorothy or Tennessee, a small song as long as the length of a block. Or a street would brag. Guy and I Streets were braggarts; so was Mozart. And if Entire Street chose to talk, there was no shaking it. I never liked the name of that street, Entire. It was the only one I found cold and useless. Helen suggested we call it Earhart Avenue instead, though the truth was it was closer to an alley than an avenue. It ran behind my house and was the hunting ground for skunks and raccoons—and one lucky night in the moonlight I spotted a porcupine.

One day as I walked east from Flat Street, it occurred to me that everyone I loved, everyone who mattered to me, happened in these four blocks of the alphabet. G was Gussy. H was Helen, Harriet and Harry. I was Gussy. J was Jordan, Julian and Joan. The only one off somewhere by himself was Wallace. Did I love Wallace? Yes! I stopped walking. I loved Wallace. This was news to me, and I sat on the curb for a minute or two with my head down, pretending to look for a marble, until the druggist's wife passed and the whole empty street was mine to wander and brood in.

How could a person love someone they didn't know? Not possible, said Harriet. It happens all the time, said Jordan. I suppose it's possible, said Julian, though it seems unlikely. I loved Danny, said Joan. I love Queen Elizabeth, the queen of England, said Harry. I only like people I know, said Helen. For example, I like you.

Apparently, there were things I had to make up my own mind about. This was the difference between being a child and being grown. I knew it wasn't the only difference, but I prayed on my actual knees that the rest of the difference, all the things that happened below the neck, would simply lose interest in me and pass me by. So far so good—though others like Deirdre, Ashley, Agnes and even poor Connie Browne weren't so lucky. Connie suddenly had what my mother called a bust, and she smelled faintly of onions all the time.

Out of the blue, my mother told me a story I thought must be made up. It was about a panicked doe that crossed a street and entered a busy department store. At the end of the story the doe came out of the store with a child's dress streaming from its neck. That part I remembered.

"That was Robichaud's," I said. "We went there to buy shoes for school."

"Of course it was Robichaud's. I'll never forget that doe."

Forget her? I thought. Oh, impossible! I loved that animal. I felt just like her.

Robichaud's had the only escalator in town. It moved sluggishly and made such a flapping noise most customers avoided it altogether. I lived to ride it. I'd heard about a boy in the city whose shoelace got caught in an escalator and at the top he was dragged under to his death. I was careful to tie my laces, and I always kept my feet moving in place as the staircase rose.

Old Mr. Robichaud liked children; he had a certain radar for them. You could come into his store hidden under your mother's coat and within seconds he'd be out of his office, dragging a bucket of candy. He'd kneel down with his face so close to your own you could feel his damp breath in your mouth. I imagined it falling into my lungs and giving me tuberculosis all over again.

"How's Mama?" he'd ask me.

"She's the same."

"How's daughter?"

"Stinky."

At this point my mother always pulled me away—"Shoes to buy, Mr. Robichaud! Say thank you for the butterscotch, Augusta." He'd reach out his skinny arm, his face as sad as an old dog's, and whatever I was wearing he'd touch it. He'd hold me to him and say for the whole store to hear, "Such a pretty girl! I'd marry you in a minute!"

One night after supper I said to Julian, "Papa?"

"What is it, my earnest girl?"

"Mr. Robichaud wants to marry me."

"And what did you say?"

"I didn't say yes."

"You're how old, Gustopher?"

I counted on my fingers and held up five.

"Noxious little man," said Harriet.

"Oh?" said Julian.

She held her nose and pointed to her hip and mouthed the word "gas."

"Oh!" said my father.

"Upright he's tight as a drum—but get him on his knees!"

"It's a good thing he's a businessman, not a bricklayer," said Julian.

"We would all soon be dead."

About once a year I thought about getting married. It was a thought that touched the top of my head like a finger skimming my hair. I usually thought about who I would marry, and tried to draw a picture of that person in my mind. Once I drew Julian. I'd seen a picture of him as a little boy, and I drew that. Another time I drew the man who came to cane our chairs. He was an old man with a long, fuzzy white beard, which made it seem like I was marrying

God. But most of the time, no picture came to me. Where a face should have been, I was left with a grayish blur. Or I was left with only the thought, Who marries? Why? How can two people love each other enough to share a bathroom? This puzzled me for a long time.

My parents shared a bathroom, but Harriet was always running into my bathroom to do this or that. She'd lock the door and turn the tap on full force. We were meant to think she wasn't in there.

Julian played the radio in the bathroom in the morning while he shaved. I was afraid he'd get electrocuted. I sometimes sat on the toilet and did my homework.

Once my parents had a party for the neighborhood. It was the only party I ever remembered. I was very young and sure of myself, and people asked me all the foolish questions a child can never answer.

"How is school?"

I didn't go to school at the time. "School is fine, thank you."

"What's your favorite subject?"

"Urinalysis." I must have heard the word from Julian.

"What will you be when you grown up?"

"Who will you marry?"

"Are you a good girl?"

"Do you love your parents very much?"

When they were done, I climbed up into an armchair and went to sleep. Harriet woke me and carried me to my bed. "Mama?" I said. I felt an urgency without words. "Mama? I won't ever marry, will I?"

"Of course you will! Sleep now. Forget this nonsense."

"No!" I cried. I clung to her hand. I put it to my mouth. I kissed it.

* * *

One of our favorite places to drive to was the dump. It was a pretty little dump on the edge of a swamp, and in May the swamp was full of the sound of tree toads. A certain temperature made them sing, and they sang in the evening and all through the night, quitting when the air warmed up in the morning.

One time I was there early enough to hear them quit. Joan stopped the car on top of the hill that overlooked the swamp and the dump. Jordan said, "This is it?" It was her first time there.

"*It?*" Joan laughed. "I give you the world, Jordie, I give you Eden. Now go out and enjoy it."

"I'll stay in and enjoy it, thank you." She put her head on Joan's shoulder and closed her eyes.

It was beginning to get light. Helen and Harry and I walked down to the edge of the water, almost deafened by the crying of the toads. Across the swamp, hundreds of white paper bags clung to the trees, up in the highest branches. I knew what Harry was thinking, and I said right into his ear, "They're not birds."

There was a mist on the water. An old kitchen stove stuck up out of the middle of the swamp, its oven door wide open and the mist seeming to come from inside it. I thought, Someone is burning a pie.

It was the kind of swamp that looks solid but isn't. We walked around to the dump. The sky was almost yellow, and the trees were white with bags. The swamp was choked with magenta lily pads. Two ducks made a whistling sound right over our heads. "Foxes!" cried Harry.

I looked at him. "Foxes?"

Helen picked up an old bicycle pedal and threw it into the

swamp. The tree toads stopped singing. "They were ducks, nitwit."

"Don't call him nitwit, Helen."

"Sometimes he's a nitwit."

"I don't care. Don't call him that."

We climbed over the fence, and I said, "Why fence a dump?" The dump keeper's dog came over to greet us. It was a short dog with a face like dried fruit and a corkscrew tail. Harry had named it Muscles. It was chained to the dump keeper's shack, and the shack was surrounded by pale plastic flowers. They formed a border between the dump keeper and his dump. We could see him inside the shack, moving around making coffee in his striped pajamas.

He was a funny, ugly little man with blue lips and a wen on his forehead. He liked us. He didn't bother us and we didn't bother him. We could take anything we wanted from the dump, he didn't care. Once he set aside some golf clubs for Harry. For me and Helen he saved *National Geographics*. As we passed the shack I shouted, "Good morning, Mr. Karabulut! Kiwi birds weigh four pounds and their eggs weigh one. They can lay up to five eggs a year. Isn't that something!"

He came out and stood in the yard. "Good children! You like coffee? I make coffee. Come, come." He waved us in.

"Do we like coffee?" I whispered.

Helen said, "I love coffee."

"We're not old enough," said Harry. "He's in his pajamas."

"He sleeps in his pajamas, nitwit. He just woke up."

"We don't actually know him," I said.

"We practically know him," said Helen.

Mr. Karabulut went back inside and came out with a

table and a chair. He brought out a pot of coffee and four glass jars.

"You see?" said Helen.

"No, I don't see."

"He's from Turkey. They drink from glasses."

He filled the glasses, then walked back into the dump to look for more chairs.

Besides his dog, he had two cows. They wandered around wherever they pleased, with bells around their necks. "Do you milk them?" I asked. I would have liked some milk in that bitter, strong coffee.

"Milk is for children," said Mr. Karabulut.

I asked him what the fence was for if it wasn't for the cows.

He looked surprised. "A man must have a country."

He took Harry inside. Helen and I sat with our backs to the shack, looking through the fence at the swamp. It looked like a plate of purple hash. Grass and logs and purple lily pads and brown water, that's all it was.

After a minute I said, "What do you think they're doing in there?"

"They pray after each meal."

"Who does?"

"Turks."

"Harry's no Turk."

"They're praying. I can hear them praying."

I could hear them too.

Mr. Karabulut was saying, "Where's you dad?"

"Wallace," said Harry.

"You like him, you dad?"

"I don't know."

Finally they came out of the shack. We said good-bye,

and as soon as we climbed back over the fence, Helen said, "He's so tiny, Harry. He only came up to your armpit."

Harry looked at the ground. "I'm embarrassed."

"Did he do anything to you?" I asked.

"I'm just embarrassed."

There was a cow standing in the middle of the swamp. It shook its big, long neck and a bell rang.

I asked my father, "Who is Gypsy Rose Lee?"

He thought a moment. "Gypsy Rose Lee is an artist."

"Let's say I went to a costume party dressed as her. Why would that win me a prize?"

He began to laugh. He laughed until suppertime. After supper I said, "You still didn't answer my question, Papa."

"What question is this?" Harriet wanted to know.

"About Gypsy Rose Lee," I said. "She's a painter."

"A painter!"

Julian said quickly, "She's not a painter, Gussy."

"You said she was an artist."

"She's not a painter."

"An artist!" cried Harriet. "What's the matter with you? What are you filling her head with?"

"It's a wonderful, intelligent head," said Julian. "When it wants to know something, it asks."

"And you give answers like that? An artist? Some artist! A woman who undresses for a crowd."

"It's her profession, Harriet."

"A professional artist! Huh!" My mother jumped to her feet. "You don't know one single thing about children, do you? Not one iota!" She fled from the room.

After a minute I said, "But you're the doctor. You know all about children. You delivered a hundred babies."

"I didn't deliver you."

"I'm glad you didn't," I lied. "I like a midwife." He said nothing, and I finally had to know, "That's what she does, really? She takes her clothes off in front of people?"

"She assists in childbirth, Gussy. That's her job."

"I meant the gypsy," I said, looking down at my shoe.

"Ah, the gypsy," said Julian.

The next day, Helen and I were standing in the school yard aiming stones at the sun. She'd been sick again. Her lupus had flared up. It was a mild flare-up, but she was back on her pills and they made her feel lazy and irritable. We kept on throwing our stones until one of the younger girls came hopping over to us, crying and pointing at her shoe. "Stop throwing those things! You made a dent in my shoe!"

"We hit your shoe?" asked Helen, incredulous.

The girl nodded. "I live next door to you. You have lupus. When will you die of it?"

"She's not going to die of it," I said.

"I might die of it. People die of it. How old are you?" Helen asked the girl.

"Six."

"That's funny. I was six when I got it."

"*How* did you get it?"

"I was playing in the school yard, this school yard, and a stone fell out of the sky and dropped on my foot. It dented my shoe."

"Like this?"

"Like that."

"Oh, no!" cried the girl, and she limped away to join her friends.

Helen picked up another stone, and I said, "My father told me all about Gypsy Rose Lee. He explained striptease. You didn't really do that, did you?"

"I already told you, I won a prize." I must have looked

doubtful because she said, "It wasn't my idea, it was Wallace's."

"Wallace's!"

"How would I know who Gypsy Rose Lee was? I was only as old as she is." She pointed across the school yard at our friend with the dented shoe.

"What did you have on?"

"Oh, lots of things. A bathing suit, an old slip, some stockings, some high-heeled shoes, some black underwear."

"What did you take off?"

"Everything except the bathing suit."

"Did Jordan mind you throwing her clothes everywhere?"

"Oh, they weren't her clothes! She didn't know about it. I don't know where the clothes came from. Wallace got the clothes."

I looked at my friend. "She's your mother, Helen. Where was your mother?"

"She wasn't with me every minute, Gussy. She thought I was going as Zorro, but if I'd gone as Zorro I never would have won a prize. Wallace was right. There were already three Zorros."

Harry remembered that costume party. It was one of the first things he was able to remember about life before the accident. He went as Frankenstein and sat under a table with his eyes closed while his sister danced on top of the table in front of all their friends.

He was in charge of the radio. He was meant to use common sense and choose a station that played the right kind of music to undress to. When the second shoe came off, he was to count to twenty-five slowly, then switch off the music. Those were Wallace's firm instructions. And Jordan was not to know.

What is the right kind of music to undress to? Harry was nine years old and towered over every other child at the party, but this was something he'd never thought about in his life. The lake was in a hollow. The house where the party was lay in the deepest part of the hollow. The only radio station Harry could find was a religious station out of New Chaldea, with a man yelling about sin and hell and damn this and damn that. He was swearing, thought Harry. All right. If Helen could take her clothes off to anything, she could take them off to that.

He closed his eyes right after the underwear fell to the floor. It fell right in front of his eyes, like a crow landing, then another one. With his eyes shut he imagined himself leaning out to feed them corn.

Finally Helen had to shout down to him to turn off the radio. "Hey! I'm freezing up here!" Poor Helen, shivering in her bathing suit. She thought he was sleeping.

"I wasn't sleeping," he told her. "Don't tell Wallace."

"What were you doing under there? You had your eyes closed."

"I was embarrassed."

"Embarrassed!"

"I hated to see you fall."

"I didn't fall. I won a prize. They loved me!"

"I can't explain it, Helen. I don't necessarily like being older than you."

That night, at home in his own bed with the sound of the lake like a big wet tongue licking the shore, and his sister in the next bed sleeping, Harry closed his eyes and felt safe. But something woke him up. It woke Helen too. She said, "I can't sleep. Can you? What is that? Listen."

"It's a whippoorwill."

"How do you know so much about birds?"

"That one's easy. It tells you its name."

"Harry?"

"What?"

"Nothing. I just wanted to keep you awake."

A little while later she padded over to his bed and sat down on it. When he said, "You're sitting on my legs, Helen," she moved an inch.

"Harry?"

"What?"

"Do you think Wallace is happy? I don't."

"He drives too fast, I think."

"That's because he isn't happy. Happy people drive slow."

"Who told you that?"

"I just know."

"Go to sleep, Helen."

"Harry?"

"What?"

"Can I stay right here?"

"You'll be cold."

"Can I climb in?"

He moved all the way over in the bed, and she got under the covers with him. "You smell of cheese," she said.

He put his hand over his mouth. "It's my breath."

"I'm sorry for what happened in the car."

"I knew it would happen."

"Why does he yell at you?"

"Jordan says he's yelling at himself."

"It doesn't matter one bit about the eyes closed, Harry, or that crazy radio station. I still won a prize." She rolled over onto her side. "Harry?"

"I'm sleeping, Helen."

"If Wallace asks you to go out in the boat tomorrow, will you go?"

"Yes."

"How come?"

"Because Wallace doesn't ask."

"When he was so sick he asked. He asked for everything, remember? Even to pee in the pot. Did you ever think he'd die of being so sick?"

"No. Did you?"

"I was too young. Harry?"

"No more, Helen."

"When we wake up I'm going to ask Wallace if I can go out in the boat with him. I'll say you have to stay home and learn to swim."

"He'll just get mad at you."

"When he gets mad at me, I get mad back. Whatever he tells me to do, I do the opposite."

"You're just like him."

"Jordan says that. But I'm not just like him. He'd never be lying in this bed with you."

Harry felt his sister go to sleep. He heard the whippoorwill again. It was much closer this time, and he whispered, "Good bird, good bird, the life of my night, I like you."

In the morning she was back in her own bed, and Wallace was already down at the water waiting for him.

Another place we liked to drive to was the old airfield on the edge of town. On a Sunday, Joan would pick me up in the taxi with the off-duty light glowing on the roof. After she sold the station wagon and bought the taxi, we went everywhere in it. Sometimes she had Jordan, Helen, Harry and Connie Browne with her; or else I was the first stop, and I'd sit in the backseat and pretend I was a paying passenger, which meant I didn't talk to the driver except to say, "Coward Park Street, please. The yellow house on top of the hill, and step on it."

I'd never ridden in a taxi until I rode with Joan. There were many things I didn't know and couldn't have guessed about taxis, such as their seats are often old and cracked and patched with silver tape that makes the whole inside of the cab smell like the bottom of your shoes. The meter ticks just like a bomb, and the cents roll around on the face of the bomb until you have a dollar. When will this bomb explode? I wondered, the first time Joan gave me what she called a metered ride.

She explained tipping to me, and how to figure out percents of things without a piece of paper and a pencil. Ten percent was easier than fifteen. Ladies tipped ten, men tipped fifteen, that's what Julian said.

"That's a bunch of hot air. He ever drive a taxi, honey?"

She looked at me in the rearview. I shook my head.

"I wouldn't know a gallstone from a pebble on the beach. Same exact difference."

When she drove she kept one hand on the wheel and the other ran along the back of the front seat. She liked to chew gum, and she liked to have the radio on softly. She wore blue jeans and her hair was always pulled back and tucked up into a baseball cap.

One day, though it was against my rules, I started a conversation. I said, "Joan?"

"Well, aren't you a chatterbox."

We were flying over the bridge, through light traffic. All the windows were open, and the air smelled of rotting vegetables. That was the river.

I said, "Do you ever do this? Do you ever go somewhere

by yourself and think about all the things you've said that day that you didn't mean to say, and all the ways you've hurt people by thinking a bad thought about them? Then in your mind you fix the whole day by imagining the way it should have been, and having the conversations over again? I do that. I just began to do it and I don't like it, but I can't stop doing it."

She drove on. I hung over the front seat. Finally she said, "Every day you do this?"

"Yes."

"So what you're fixing doesn't stay fixed."

"It stays fixed. But every time I open my mouth or see someone I don't like, there's more to fix."

"You do it at night?"

"In bed at night."

"Tonight, will you try not to fix this, this talk we're having? Will you try to say to yourself instead, 'Joan loves me with all her might. Helen and Harry and Jordan Walsh love me with all their might. My own daddy and momma love me with all their might. They always have and they always will, no matter what I do or say. My friends and teachers at school love me, and if they don't that's their problem. I, Augusta Cotton, am trying as hard as I know how to love them, and let's face it, they're not all that lovable.' Will you say that, Gus? Will you try and say, 'I love me. I think I'm the greatest'? That's what I say. Every morning I say, 'Joan, I love you, you are my best friend, you are the greatest, and I'll kill you if you smoke a cigarette.'"

We were at Helen's house. She stopped the taxi, and we sat there looking at the windshield like we were at a drive-in movie. She said, "It's not just your body growing, Gus, it's your soul. The whole notion of thinking evil, or doing evil, is not a child's notion. You're like Helen. Sometimes I want to shake her and say, 'Be kind to yourself, for pete's sake! Trust yourself! Get yourself up and out of that bed! It's only Wallace keeping you there, and you didn't kill him, he killed himself.' "

"How, Joan?"

"He drowned. Didn't you know that?"

"In the lake?"

"Yes."

There were all kinds of wildflowers growing in the woods around the airfield. It was a four-acre field surrounded by pine trees, and straight down the middle ran an old, broken-up runway. The grass had taken over the runway, just as the pines had stepped forward from the shade they created and taken over the grass. Nature moved slowly at the airfield, but it moved. It wasn't like the river. It was a quiet, hopeful place.

It had served the sanatorium in the days when illness was the commerce of our little town. Now it served the woodchucks. The dandelions commanded the grass. In a month, buttercups and clover would flower here. If I lived a long life, the field would disappear under the snaking roots of the pines by the time I died. Someone eating a picnic in the forest might find a chunk of asphalt and wonder how it found its way there.

Years ago a plane had missed the runway, flipped over and skidded towards the woods. We called it the ghost plane because all that was left of it was the engine. It was hardly an engine anymore. The first time we saw it Jordan said, "What is that, a meteor?" It was just a brown lump at the far end of the field, but Helen loved it. She climbed all over it. Constance had a camera that hung from her neck, and Helen said, "Take my picture, Connie." She laid her arm across the top of the engine and dropped her head sideways on her arm. I have that picture.

One day in the forest the three of us uncovered a propeller. It was such a huge thing, a propeller. I had no idea. Constance tripped and fell on something too sharp to belong to those woods. We dug it out. It weighed so much it took all of us to lift it, and it left a great hole, a dangerous hole. We brought Jordan out there and she said, "I like the propeller, you three, but I don't like the hole." She helped us fill it with pine branches and the little dirt we could scrape bare-handed from the ground. Our hands smelled of vanilla. They were black with sap, and on the way home we were not allowed to touch anything inside the taxi. We had to press them together as if we were praying.

I thought poor people had taken the seats from the plane and used the wings and body to make roofs for their houses.

"We're poor people," said Helen. "We never did anything like that."

"I meant in Murdoch."

"Mrs. Alexander's house didn't have any seats. And her roof was made of tar."

"She lives in Murdoch?"

"Lived," said Constance, drawing out the "d" at the end. "Remember? Murdoch's kaput."

We usually brought lunch and sat around in the grass, eating and drinking, then went off to look for lady slippers in the woods. Harry sat in the taxi and ate his sandwich and listened to the radio. He got rashes from the long grass, and he was frightened by the possibility of ticks.

Sometimes he called out, "You have one life to live, why not live it as a blonde?" or he asked, "What is a nudist colony?" It was hard to believe he heard these things on the radio.

"You wouldn't like it," said Joan. "It's where people go bare naked."

I said I wasn't allowed to say certain words at home, and that was one of them.

"Nudist?" asked Jordan in surprise.

I nodded.

Joan said, "Every family has words like that. In my family it was f-a-r-t, a word I still cannot say out loud without feeling my great-aunt Augusta's cane on the back of my knees. Break wind, we had to say, or say nothing."

"We have to say excuse me," said Constance, smiling at the ground.

Helen laughed. "Jordan says, 'Who dropped a rose?'"

"I stole that from Eleanor Roosevelt."

"Jordie, you didn't!"

"I did. She was famous for 'Who dropped a rose?'"

"She's my mother's favorite person," I said.

Jordan looked at me and shook her head. "No. You are."

Joan taught Harry how to drive on what was left of the runway. They crept from one end of it to the other, turned around and crept back. She sat beside him, and we could hear her urging him to use more gas, but to me it seemed a fitting speed for an old runway. The soft *puck puck*ing of tires over the brittle asphalt, this was right, this was as it should be. I was glad to see a cautious boy learning how to drive out there on the broken back of an old, once useful thing.

Queen Anne's lace ran neat and white as a painted line down the middle of it. I knew late summer would bring a beacon of yellow goldenrod. I loved that runway. In my love and in my life I have often confused things with people, loving a bush and a friend equally until, as I grew up, I was told this was wrong. I was told a thing is not something you can learn from. A thing takes and takes, it has a mute face, it will never say the words "I love you." It will never have an original thought, or any thought, and never a feeling. I didn't believe it.

Once I asked Harriet, "Where do the animals fit in?"

She said in this case to think of them as people.

Why? I have never heard a dog say I love you, but plenty of trees talk, boulders do, and the river chatters incessantly. I understand the ocean sings with a deep, unforgettable voice.

I have learned more from certain songs, doors, hills, plants, cracks in the ceiling and runways than I have from most people. I like nature's patience. And I like the freedom of objects not in nature: they don't have death hanging over their heads. I like their muteness. I call it silence. I like their *it*ness. The word "it" is a beautiful word. To not bother with human gender seemed extremely wise to me at age eleven. Like a cool cave on a sunny coast, the sea pounding below, the sky vibrant with heat, light, birds, air. A refuge from thought and life: it. Dark, soothing.

One day I lay down on the runway. It was late in the afternoon, and its blackness held the day's heat, releasing it through the bare backs of my legs and arms until I was as warm as noontime.

I was surprised when Harry came and lay next to me. "Hello," I said, "how are you?"

"Is this a tick?"

I looked. "It's a scab."

I had my shoes off; I was using them as a pillow. He stretched out on his side, and his knee touched the bottom of my foot. I moved my foot, but there came the knee again, inching across the runway. It was a bare knee, the color of bone, and bone thin. It found the arch of my foot and brushed against it like a rabbit passing a rock.

"Your knee is touching my foot."

He looked down; I did too. There was his knee, there was my foot. They could have belonged to anyone, any boy and girl, but they were ours. My foot, plump and white as a fish; his knee, square as an ashtray.

Of all the joints in the body the knee was my least favorite. The kneecap was a heap of flaws. A knuckle was better than a knee. The only thing worse was a foot. Oh, feet! Oh, doughy lumps! I looked at mine every night as I brushed my teeth, hoping for some improvement in overall shape and size. I prayed to God for bones that showed, little foot bones and squarish toes and toenails that looked soft and human. Nothing changed.

"So maybe God likes those feet on you," said Harriet.

"Two eggplants, Mother! It's like walking on whales!"

"Who has to see them? That's what shoes are for. Be happy they live such a long way from your head. There's closer things you could like less."

I told Julian my prayers, and he said, "That's not praying, that's begging. I've never known God to be much interested in personal affairs."

I was astonished. "Then what is he interested in?"

"I don't know. Balance."

"You're kidding. Balance?"

"Look at the body, look at anything in nature. It's all built around the principle of balance. That's why you have two feet, two legs, two arms and hands and a sensible little head on top. Balance. Give and take. Active, passive. Extension, contraction. It's an old, old idea, Gussy. In Chinese, the yin and the yang. The male and the female."

And these aren't personal affairs? I thought. I could do

with a little less balance. One foot, one dough lump, one eyesore. Wasn't that enough?

We are never prepared for love from a familiar quarter. When Harry reached out, took my foot in his hand, brought his lips to it and kissed it right there on the runway, I thought he'd been struck by lightning, though not one single cloud occurred in the sky, a sky of such deliberate blue it might have been painted on. I said, "You're crazy. Look how crazy you are. You're crazy." He looked at my foot, then far away at the green woods that said nothing. He got up the way he always did, like a sticky umbrella unfolding. I watched him cross the grass slowly, pensively, his head down as if it weighed a hundred pounds.

I looked out the window and saw a boy I hated kicking a stone down Flat Street. "What a spaz," I said.

"What a what?" asked Julian.

"A spaz. A spastic."

"He looks like a perfectly healthy child to me."

"He's mean, papa. He rides the bus. He lit a girl's hair on fire. He puts hot matches on your skin, on your knee. I hate him."

"You hate what he does," said my father.

"Who wants their hair on fire? Not me."

The boy passed in front of our gate, kicked his stone into our yard where Julian couldn't fail to hit it with the mower, then threw another rock at our neighbor's cherry tree.

"Do you hate him now, Papa?"

He didn't answer. He stepped outside and called, "Son!"

Son? I thought. That would make me his sister. He was a tall boy. His legs were long and skinny. He had a face as big and pale as an ugly moon, with a crater where his mouth was. His mouth was always open, and a sneery laugh came out of it. He laughed at our house, at Julian standing in his scrub suit in front of the house, at me inside the house, and ran away.

My father chased him. I couldn't believe my eyes! He ran to the fence, vaulted it and was gone.

Harriet came into the room. She had a small, L-shaped piece of metal in her hand. It fit right in her palm. "What does this do?"

It was an allen wrench. Patience Browne had a set of them.

"An Allen who? Why would I find it in my bed?"

"Papa's running around the block, chasing a boy," I told her.

She narrowed her eyes. "And I can jump to the moon."

He came home a few minutes later. He came through the gate and walked slowly up to the house.

"Well?" I said. He looked less like an athlete and more like my father.

"You're soaked through!" cried Harriet. "Where have you been?"

"It's sweat, Mother. I told you he was chasing a boy."

"Don't say 'sweat,' Augusta, say 'perspiration.' And enough with the boy. It's time you chased a boy. Where are all the nice young men, the boys? My life at your age was full of them."

"Don't chase that one," Julian said hoarsely. "What's his name, Gussy?"

"Donald."

"Donald's a biter."

He showed us his hand. It was covered back and front with tiny red tooth marks, some of which had punctured the skin. Harriet's knees went wobbly. She had to sit down in a chair. My father pointed to his hand as if it were an exhibit in a museum. "Do you notice anything unusual about Donald?"

I thought it was all unusual.

"Look closely. He has a mouth full of baby teeth!"

Who could explain that? The next day Jordan tried. We were lazing around after lunch up at the airfield, watching Harry learn to drive in reverse. She said to Helen, "He drives like an old man, your brother."

Helen looked at Connie, who laughed nervously. "Connie thinks he's attractive."

"He is attractive," said Jordan. "You're right to think he's attractive, Connie, I think so too."

This was too much for Constance. She wrung her hands and stared at a piece of windblown wax paper on the ground. It was exactly the color of her hair.

Jordan said, "What on earth is that in your back pocket, Helen? It's not cigarettes, is it?"

Helen pulled it out. It was Prudence Browne's transistor radio. "Are you coming, Gussy?"

I shook my head, and she and Constance started down the field towards the ghost plane.

"Why don't you go?" asked Jordan.

"No one asked me to." I let a long minute go by, then I said, "Anyway, I don't like the music they play. When she gets around Connie she acts just like a teenager."

"I hated being a teenager."

"You did?"

"Oh, yes! No one likes being a teenager. It's like living with a thief in your house."

I said I couldn't imagine that, we'd never been robbed. "Yesterday my father chased a bully." I told her all about mean Donald and his baby teeth.

"No wonder he's so mean, he's guarding the moat," said Jordan.

"What moat?"

She drew a circle around her heart. "That moat."

"Oh." What does that have to do with teeth? I wondered.

"You have a moat, I have a moat, everybody has one. Donald has one."

"Does Helen have one?"

"She certainly does."

"Joan has one?"

"Joan has a thin one. She and Harry have thin, shallow moats. They wear themselves all on the outside. Harry wasn't always that way. He used to hide behind his sister."

"Then she was his moat."

"That's right. Until he went away."

"Why did he go away, Jordan?"

She looked out over the bumpy, green ground to where the taxi moved in reverse with a certain new assuredness. I wanted to put my arms around her, but something stopped me. It must have been her moat.

"Because I couldn't help him," she said flatly.

"Then why did he come back?"

"Because he's our boy. He's our brother and our boy and we wanted him back again."

"Helen didn't."

"Don't be fooled by Helen."

"She says it was money, and when she got sick you couldn't afford to keep him where he was. It was a hospital, wasn't it?"

"It wasn't called a hospital, it was called a facility. It was called a rehabilitation facility, and yes, it was a hospital."

"Joan said he was in a place where they didn't feed him or

teach him much poetry. She said that's why he itched so much when he first came home."

"Not enough poetry?"

"Not enough food. He was so hungry he ate metal. He ate her keys!"

"Oh, he did not." She laughed. "Anyway, he's always loved metal. Ask him about the man who ate the car, that's Harry's hero."

Strange hero, I thought. Helen's was Amelia Earhart or Valentina Tereshkova, it changed from week to week. I asked Jordan if she had a hero.

"Yes."

"Who?"

"Dag Hammarskjöld."

"What kind of a name is that? I've never heard of that person." I was visibly disappointed.

"Who's your hero?" she asked.

The truth was I had no idea. There were things about heroes that made me uncomfortable. Did they have to be dead? Did they have to be brave? Did they have to be old? I shook my head sadly. "A hero is one thing I never had."

One day a man came up to me on the street. He was a friend of my father's, and his wife was one of Julian's patients.

"How are you?" he asked.

"I'm fine. How is your wife?" I suddenly remembered Harriet had gone to her funeral, and I blurted out, "Is she still dead?"

I told Julian the story. I had to clear my conscience. "Are you mad, Papa?"

"I'm not mad."

"Are you sad?"

"Sad about Dan and Caroline. Not sad about anything you said or did. It was an innocent mistake."

"I should have remembered she was dead."

"There's no reason in the world you should remember the death of someone you hardly knew."

"You were her doctor, Papa."

"Someone had to be."

"What's that like when a person dies and you're their doctor?"

"You don't like it. You never like it when a human being can't get well. You feel mad at them, then mad at yourself for feeling mad at them. Is this about your friend Helen?"

He startled me. I shook my head, though it took all my will to shake it.

"Because Helen is not going to die. She's going to get better then worse, better then worse, over and over again for a long time. Her life won't be very different from anybody else's life, at least not as different as it's already been. She'll have lupus. She'll always have lupus. But even sickness and pain can be a friend. Even death can. I can't explain it, Gussy."

He was in a reflective, melancholy mood, and there was no point reminding him he was my father and he could explain everything. Maybe I have grown up, I thought. Maybe we are talking about grown-up things that have no answer or explanation. What did that mean, Death can be a friend? What did that mean?

When I was little I loved the butcher shop. It was a tiny, narrow shop on Knife Street, right around the corner from the public library. The same Mr. Sweet who owned it owned the dry cleaners next door and a linen service called Sweets Sheets.

Mrs. Sweet, his wife, worked in the butcher shop. Her husband was a dour, anemic man, thin as a chop, but she had large bones, big teeth and fair hair. She was as tall as my father and her voice was deep and runny. She was Norwegian, and sometimes she spoke Norwegian to me as she wrapped our chicken thighs or breasts.

*"God dag, frøken!"*

"Good dog!"

*"Er ikke Deres far doktor?"*

"Good dog!"

Later she taught me how to say "This tobacco is too mild," and "Why did you bring your umbrella?"

I was possibly the only child in the world who ever lingered in a butcher shop, but it was an unusual butcher shop. The front window was clean and bare, without hooks or bodies. Plenty of sun came in and lit up a couple of wooden bowls of white eggs and a cardboard sign that said CHOICE CUTS WE HAVE THEM. There were comfortable chairs to sit in while you waited, and magazines to read. Mrs. Sweet clomped around in galoshes and a white coat, eating marshmallows! If it wasn't busy she'd make little butcher paper animals for me and tie them to my fingers with string.

One day she confessed to me she'd always wanted to be a doctor. In Norway she'd studied to be a doctor, but Mr. Sweet had come all the way from America to marry her, and look what happened. Now she was a butcher.

She was a good butcher. My father once called her a stevedore, and I asked, "What's that?"

"It's a man," said Harriet.

He ignored her. "It's someone who can throw a whole side of lamb on her shoulder, carry it out of the walk-in cooler and slap it down on the butcher block without even breathing hard. It's a compliment, Gussy."

I wasn't so sure.

I watched her work. Or I sat in a chair and watched the dust ride the sunlight down to the floor. Or I read *Life* magazine.

Eventually Mrs. Sweet would say, "Your mom, she knows you're here?"

"She sent me here."

"How much long ago though? One hour?"

"She knows I'll come home. I'll beat her home."

"If anyone ask me I say you are too much by yourself."

Sometimes in the summer the air smelled of blood and marrow, and a few fat flies buzzed at the window. But most of the time the shop smelled of sawdust. Mrs. Sweet smelled of scented soap in the morning. By the afternoon she smelled of rubber and sawdust and sweat.

The only time I ever saw something in the butcher shop that turned my stomach was the day a man came in with a pretty bird hanging from his belt. The head was a brilliant blue-green, and I recognized it right away. "A peacock!" I cried, jumping to my feet.

The man laughed. "It's a regular pheasant."

"Oh," I said, sitting down again. "Its head looked like a peacock's head."

"You're some kid." He sat down next to me. "What do you know about peacocks?"

I told him what I knew. It wasn't much. I'd never been to a zoo, and this was years before Mr. Karabulut at the dump made a present to Helen and me of those *National Geographics*. The bird hung between us. Its eyes were shut, and its feathers looked soft and inviting. "Touch it," said the man. "You want to touch it, touch it. Here." He undid his belt and slipped the bird loose and placed it across my lap. I stroked it, but all the brilliant, hopeful colors seemed to come off in my hand.

"It's fading," I said. I started to give it back to him, but he pushed it into my lap.

"Keep touching it. It'll come back."

I stroked it some more, but it was no use.

Mrs. Sweet came out of the cooler and went back in again. She didn't look up, and she didn't see the man.

"Are you a friend of hers?" I asked.

He laughed again. "Let's say I'm her brother-in-law." He put his hands on my hands. He held my wrists and pushed them across the bird's body. "Nice, huh?"

I said I didn't think it was nice, and I wanted to go home.

"Oh, not yet," he said. "The bird needs you. Don't you want to help the bird? Look, its eyes are opening!"

They weren't opening. It was dead as dead, that bird. I told the man so.

He wouldn't believe it. "This is where the bird lives. This is where the bird goes in and goes to sleep." He opened his zipper and his penis flew out. It was dark purple, and it seemed as long as a leg.

He brought my hand over to it, and I dug in my nails and squeezed as hard as I could. I ran out of the shop and looked back through the clean, empty window. Mrs. Sweet came running out of the cooler. The man was folded over. The pheasant had dropped to the floor.

Our music teacher, Miss Harriet Blue Teal, left school that spring and never came back. One day she was there, the next she wasn't. No *may I*? No *because* . . .

Helen said she was off to get married. Ashley Hobb insisted she was off to have a b-a-b-y. I, who never really cared for Harriet Blue Teal, not since the day the submarine came up the river, dreamt she moved to Indiana and joined the Army. When I woke up I was drenched with sweat and my pajama top was turned around backwards, choking me.

I thought about her again only once, briefly, one Sunday evening driving home from the airfield. This was always my favorite time of the week, a time when I felt most open to suggestion or surprise. I think we all did, because we often discussed important things on those return journeys, such as the reason and cure for dandruff, or the purpose of the UN. The sky with its dome shape—unlike the flat noon sky—seemed so impressionable to me. Its clouds, thin and gauzy, hung without earthly shadow. The taxi cast a long and humorous shadow, like a galloping horse pulling us home behind it.

We could see great flocks of birds at that time of day, long-necked herons, rising from the river. We could see crows diving for bottle caps on the road.

"What do birds think about?" asked Harry.

"The exact same things you do," said his sister.

"There's not much *to* think about," said Constance.

"There's a lot to think about," said Jordan.

"There's bottle caps," said Joan, "and bottle caps."

"We had a bird once," I said. "After a week it flew away."

"If a bird flies away in Georgia, you find it at the airport. They go directly to the airport."

"And get on the plane," said Harry.

I thought about Oiseau sitting in a pine tree up at the airfield, watching over me. He was the only pet I'd ever had, an ordinary budgie, but it had been a solid week of good news in my life.

"We had a bird that flew away," said Constance, "but really the cat ate it. Did you have a cat, Gussy?"

"My mother did."

"I bet the cat ate it. They don't like to tell you that, they think you'll feel bad."

We reached what Jordan called "the town proper." This was the line where nature stopped, the birds flew backwards, even the clouds lost their fugitive look and drifted like hats in the sky. Helen sat forward and poked the driver. "Joan?"

"What is it, sugar? What is it, Stella D'oro?"

"Why do you call me Stella D'oro?"

"Because it's your name. It's what I've always called you. Because you're a sweet cookie."

"What does it mean?"

"It means 'I love you like I love the stars.'"

"In Greek," laughed Jordan.

"Joan?"

"I'm right here, darling."

"Let's sing the alphabet of the streets, okay?"

Helen was a good singer, and I loved to hear her sing. It reminded me of that time not too long ago when she played the cello with a beauty and talent praised by many adults, and soothing to children.

Every week it was the same. They'd run from A to Z, paralleling the progress of the taxi. Harry would join them, his voice deep, scratchy and unpredictable. Constance, who was a high soprano, often joined them, which left only Jordan and me, dumb as stones. I don't know why she didn't open her mouth, unless it was to keep me company.

"I never hear you sing, Gus. Don't you ever sing?" Joan finally asked.

"Her voice isn't that great," said Helen.

"I sing when I'm by myself," I said.

"What a shame! All that light and you're hiding it under a barrel."

"It's not much light. Even the music teacher says so."

"Well, it's a great big barrel. Now pull it off!"

I said I'd pull it off if Jordan did. I was counting on her to say no, we'd gone that far together. When she said yes, I wanted to climb right out of the taxi, right out through the window. But Helen started up, and it seemed so easy, like walking, you just put one sound after another and came out with a song. We took turns.

"Accidental."

"B Street."

"Cherry Street."

"Dorothy!"

"Entire."

"Entire? That's Earhart Avenue."

"Flat Street."

"That's my street."

"Guy."

"High."

"I!"

"Too loud, Harry."

"Juniper."

"Knife. Knife?"

"Because of the butcher's."

"Locust."

"Named after a bug?"

"I call it Lemon."

"I call it Lois Lane—ha!"

"Mozart."

"Nancy."

"Orchard!"

"Pine. Boring."

"Redjay."

"Why isn't there a 'q'? I hate that."

"Saint Elmo."

"Constance calls it Sweet Potato."

"Tennessee."

"That's where I go to the doctor."

"Ukiah."

"Vine."

"West Vine."

"Why isn't it East Vine? It's east of Vine."

"It has to be 'w.'"

"Xavier."

"Yarrow!"

"Zoroaster."

"Finally."

Joan caught my eye in the rearview mirror. "Well, you're no Leontyne Price, but sweetheart, there's nothing the matter with your voice. I could shoot people who tell a child they can't." I felt a subtle moment of revenge, then laid Miss Harriet Blue Teal to rest.

A motorcycle cut in front of us as we joined a slow line of cars crossing the bridge. Joan braked and swore softly at the driver. "Are we scaring you, Jordie?"

Jordan was gripping the dashboard. "This is exactly why I don't drive."

"That little motorcycle? He misjudged, that's all. It's easy to do."

"I know how easy it is to do. You forget, I lived with misjudgment on a daily basis."

"Wallace drove like a bat out of hell," said Helen. I was sitting by the open window, and she was stroking my hair.

Maybe she just liked the feel of the wind on her hand. Then why didn't she stroke Connie's hair? Could I tell her I liked it? "If you never had to drive with Wallace, Jordan, you'd probably drive now, right?"

"I used to drive. I used to drive you two everywhere."

"Everywhere where?" asked Harry.

"All around. Do you remember Frank Moss, Harry?"

"No."

"Do you remember Walter?"

"His brother."

"Right. So you remember Frank."

"No."

"I remember Frank," said Helen.

"He was your best friend, Harry."

"I know."

"He was your friend and Walter was Helen's, and sometimes I drove you to their house to see them."

"Frank had no ears," said Harry.

"He had ears. Of course he had ears. He just couldn't hear. The boys were deaf. That's what 'deaf' means."

"They taught me how to swim," said Helen.

Jordan half-turned around in her seat. "I taught you how to swim."

"You didn't, Jordan."

"Of course I did."

Helen shook her head.

"I did, Helen. You're sure I didn't?"

"I know you didn't."

She turned back to the front of the taxi and said something to Joan, and Joan said, "Daily? Never mind daily. It rewrites itself by the minute, Jordie." She reached across Harry and touched Jordan's chin. "Now look at me. Who cares who taught her? She wouldn't be such a water rat if she didn't come out of you."

"Harry came out of her and he's no water rat," Helen said softly. She cleared her throat. "I'd like to go back to the lake, Jordan. That's what I'd like."

# Chapter Eight

Helen got her wish, but not until school was out and one precious month of our summer vacation had slipped away. It was the hottest summer of the decade. The days melted down and pooled like butter in a tub. I spent my time reading, my bare feet propped up in front of the rickety window fan in my room and the rest of my body draped with damp towels. I got up for meals, and sometimes I met Helen and Harry at the movie theater on Saint Elmo Street.

It was one of two places in town that had air-conditioning; the other was the morgue. The movies, while never great, were seldom horrible, and the popcorn was stale but heavily buttered, and the drinks were sweet. It was an old Catholic church, and we sat in the pews on green velveteen cushions that scratched our bare legs and looked mossy in the dim theater light. The organ still occupied the balcony, and some troublemaker would regularly find his way upstairs and walk on the keyboard during a love scene. Sometimes, in boredom, I'd wander out to the lobby and watch old Mrs. Snow, who sold tickets, inch her wig around until it sat correctly on her head, or I'd stand in front of the long windows looking out at the couples waiting in the rain that fell dark and steaming from a hot, black summer sky, and I'd think, *This is the end of the world and I am Noah.*

He captured my imagination, Noah, at least the Noah of Julian's rare bedtime stories. He was an old, old veterinarian—six hundred and one at the time of the flood! He lived to be nine hundred and fifty! God knocked on his door one day and said, "I like you, Noah. Got any plans for that great big pile of gopher wood in the backyard?" Noah said, "Not especially. Gee, you look familiar." That's how they got going on the ark, according to my father. He always ended the story with a stampede. They'd been cooped up for a year, those animals. All the different species roared out with a great thunder of hooves and flapping of wings, and Julian named each one as they scattered themselves across the face of the earth. Somewhere in the middle of that long list of living things that poured from the ark, I'd fall asleep. ". . . ibis, iguana, jackal, jackrabbit, junco, kangaroo, kestrel, kinkajou, kite, koala bear," my father would say. It was the closest thing to a lullaby I ever knew. In my sleep I always heard him whisper, "Your life doesn't have to look like anybody else's, my little human, my little girl," then he'd kiss me and turn off the light.

That summer of being eleven, I knew two things: my life wasn't going to look like lonely Mrs. Snow's, with her yellow wig and that same flower print dress week after week, and her stash of comic books and *Soldier of Fortune* magazines under the steep stairs that led to the balcony; and it wasn't going to look like Prudence Browne's, or Ashley's older sister Gloria's. They came to the late show and stood outside and smoked until the theater doors opened at exactly twelve minutes before showtime, then they came inside and smoked in the lobby, blowing the blue smoke out through their nostrils or rolling it off their tongues. They came with a different boy each time, though one night Gloria came with the boy who came with Prudence the night before. The boys used their own hands as ashtrays. At the end of each cigarette they rubbed their palms on their blues jeans and started all over again.

For a long time I thought my life would look like Helen's. After she got lupus, I still believed we were as close as any two creatures with skin. When she was sick, and she was sick twice in June, it caused me actual pain. I'd stand at her bed and feel my own joints on fire, and once my hands swelled up like hers did. (Later I found out I was allergic to Fels Naptha soap.) One day, in the middle of *King Kong,* she left her seat and was gone a long time. This was unusual for her; she could sit through almost any movie—my own patience hung on a thread. I told Harry I was going to see what the matter was. He said he'd come with me, and he hopped up out of his seat. His head got in the way of the projector, and a boy behind us yelled, "Siddown, Frank!" I looked at Harry. "Siddown, Frankenstein!" I told the boy it was a mean thing to say. I took Harry's hand, and we walked to the back of the theater, past one of the old confessionals. Helen wasn't in the lobby or anywhere in sight.

"We can't find my sister," Harry said to Mrs. Snow.

"Try the powder room, hon. Not you. Your friend."

I went into the bathroom, and there were Helen's feet showing under the stall.

"Helen?"

She didn't answer.

"I know it's you, I can see your feet."

"Well, help me," she said. "There's blood everywhere."

"Blood!"

"Shh!"

"I'll call a doctor!"

"I don't need a doctor."

"I'll call Jordan."

"You won't find Jordan."

"I'll call Joan."

"*She* calls it 'the British have arrived.'"

I looked at my friend's feet, then down at my own hands, which were knotted together. "Helen. It's not—?"

She said nothing.

"Does it hurt?"

"No."

I didn't know what to say, so I said the only thing I remembered from a little pamphlet called *Welcome to Womanhood!* "You can play team sports, but you should stop if you feel dizzy."

"I don't want to play team sports, Gussy. I want to go back in and see *King Kong*."

It was an old church bathroom, and this church wasn't equipped for puberty; there was barely a sink and a toilet. So I took off the undershirt I always wore against the chill of the air-conditioning and passed it under the stall to my friend.

"Can you believe it, Helen? Some girls look forward to this."

"Who?"

"I read about a tribe in Africa."

She sent me out of the bathroom while she did something at the sink. When I came back she was back in her stall, and I said, "I wish I could have it for you."

"No you don't, not really. Anyway, you'll have it soon enough."

"You already have lupus."

"So? You had TB. You've got glasses. Your hair is straight. You're short. Your teeth are big."

"Helen!"

"It's all the same, Gussy. It's all something to live with. I'm surprised you don't know that yet, considering who told me. Your father."

That picture of Helen's feet in their dark socks and white sneakers showing under the stall in the bathroom of the movie theater on Saint Elmo Street, the first summer of her lupus, the hottest summer of our lives, appears often in my dreams as a photograph floating on water. Just her feet; the rest of her cut off by the stall like the hem of a heavy wooden dress. I don't know why that day needed to be a turning point for me. It couldn't have had much to do with her messy coming of age and my lagging behind, because physically she was always ahead of me and it didn't mean much to either of us. As we got up to leave the theater at the end of *King Kong,* I thought of her wearing my wadded undershirt, and it gave me an interesting, unsettling feeling, nothing more than that. But in the weeks that followed, whenever I was around Helen this feeling increased. I felt the known parts of her dissolve, exposing all I didn't know. I felt her history chasing me, and because I could avoid it no longer, I began to put together pieces of her life at the lake.

It looked nothing like a picture, this puzzle; it looked like blankness upon which small stories and objects were laid, islands in the same shared sea. I was no cartographer. I didn't even know what the word meant. I was eleven, almost twelve, and maps that led the way back held no interest for me. History, I believed, was incidental. I was a scientist, involved with visible, tangible things. I was a marine biologist—landlocked, yes, but I could and did walk to the river and chalk my name on the stone bridge built by my grandfather, and feel whole.

Augusta Cotton
3:30 afternoon June 24, 1964

No child is pure anything. If I clung to science with my teeth and will, the rest of me—at least three quarters—was imagination. I was an architect. I could raise a sanatorium from a pile of rubble. I was clairvoyant. I saw ghosts, I heard voices in the wind. My father tells this story. He came into my room one bitter cold night when I was very young, to find my window open and a lump of sugar on the sill. Closing the window he woke me.

"What is it, Papa?"

"Your window. It was wide open. What's this sugar doing here?"

"Leave it! I'm feeding the moon."

I fed the stars too. I fed them with my attention. Lying on my back in the yard, surrounded by my father's garden, the smell of chives and honeysuckle thick on the air, that mysterious mingling of sour and sweet, I watched over them. I talked to them as if they were mine. I called them by name, names I'd invented, simple names like Paul, Liza, Susan, John, Sarah. Simplicity, I hoped, would bring them nearer. The constellations were families. The Little Dipper was the Peterson family, and all the Petersons had names. For some reason, the North Star was Betty Peterson. Maybe I'd stumbled over a Betty Peterson in a book or a magazine.

Each one that fell, each star that shot off into the darkness, blazing a bright trail into nothing, registered as an irreparable loss inside me. I clearly remember one summer night on Flat Street. Harriet's brother, my uncle Jerome, and his wife, Bella, were there for a visit. They sat in lawn chairs on either side of me, their heads tilted back, gazing up at the sky. Suddenly it was as if the entire Milky Way had come unpinned. Star after star streaked across the heavens. At first I thought someone had come up behind us and was tossing lit matches. Uncle Jerome shot up out of his chair, yelling for my parents to come out and see the spectacle. Aunt Bella just kept repeating the word, "Oh," over and over again, while I turned on my side, away from the night, pretending more interest in a firefly.

It was like losing dozens of my dearest possessions in less than a minute. Other people felt lucky or chosen whenever a star dropped in front of them; I felt bereft. They were so irreplaceable, these igneous chunks of the universe. The thought of a shrinking galaxy left a cool, clammy feeling inside me, a lonely feeling. We were so small, so small.

Stella D'oro, Joan had called Helen. I love you like I love the stars. I understood that. One hot night at the end of June, when after an early movie I walked Helen and Harry to their footbridge and stayed there, long after our good-bye, too wakeful to go home, I met someone else who understood it. It was a quiet evening. The neighborhood hose fights had ended, and it was too humid to be anywhere but inside in front of a fan. The river curled beneath me like a loving, sighing animal, and I hung my head over the bridge railing to breathe its cool, dirty smell.

I hadn't seen Jordan in what seemed like a long time. The afternoons were too hot to pile into the taxi and drive to the airfield, and I never went to Coward Park Street anymore, but instead met my friends at the movies. I didn't recognize her as she approached me. In fact, the memory of the only other time we met on the bridge came to me before I knew who I was looking at. She'd done something with all her hair, put it up in a twist I imagined. A few short wisps clung to her face as if whipped up by a private wind. She looked taller than usual—a trick of the twilight—and pale as the moon. She made an imposing man, and at first I was frightened and started walking quickly towards my side of the river. Then some inner voice told me to stop, turn around and look down. I did, and saw that whoever it was was barefoot beneath an old, familiar raincoat.

"Look what I've done!" she called out. That was her greeting. "I've cut off my hair!"

She showed me the back, which was chopped unevenly an inch below her ears. All that long, beautiful hair! I was stunned speechless.

"You're the very first to see it. Do you like it? I like it. I couldn't stand that weight on my head one minute longer. You don't like it, do you?"

I said it was new and I wasn't used to it.

"It isn't the first time. At the lake it was always short because I swam. Did you know I swam, Augusta? I used to swim one mile out and one mile back, every single day, in any weather, from the day the ice broke up in the spring until it froze in the winter. If there wasn't ice, I swam all winter long. I can see you don't believe it."

I didn't know what I believed. It didn't matter what I believed. I heard what I was told, that in the past there were certain times of day that depleted Jordan of her sense of well-being, and at these times she would go to the lake and stand beside it, then remove her clothes and gratefully sink below the surface, feeling ease return to her body as she spread her arms and kicked her legs, giving the limbs purpose.

"No wonder Helen loved it," she said. "I loved it. To see my shadow skim along the bottom and rise up to me in rays of light. And that feeling of being wrapped in silk, touched all over by a sheer fabric."

Luminous, the body. Tactile, the world. She rose up out of the water each time with a candle burning in her chest.

Sometimes Wallace watched her from the porch. She sensed this with her back to the house. Earlier in their marriage he used to row out on the lake in the dinghy, row hard and far to exhaust himself and return home cleansed, his own candle burning in his lungs and in the muscles of his upper arms.

One summer he made a rowboat for Helen, a smaller version of his own. "Made out of bulrushes," said Jordan, "and together they would go out and play on the lake. That's where he gave her the name Saint Oar. She always did love the saints, and that made her one of them. Do you know," she said, combing her fingers through what was left of her hair, "I have never said this to anyone, Augusta, but when I hear someone say they feel like they're standing at the center of their life, that there is such a place and it comes only once and they're now in it, my heart sinks for them. It falls right to the bottom of me. Because I remember feeling that way for one summer. Wallace was faithful—that terrible word—and Harry was Harry, and Helen was Saint Oar out on the lake. We were all at the center of a life, I felt that so strongly. I felt it daily, like a thick, warm syrup all through me. It was a very, I guess I could only call it joyful, time. That word 'enjoy,' I do so know what that means, deep deep down in me. My heart sinks for them, Gussy, because the joy of it can't prepare you for the next thing;

that it is its own place, high and separate, its own—what? unbidden—time, that's the joy of it. It doesn't know of any future. Real joy can't. For me it was a great rest, but one I made the mistake of thinking would never, ever end."

We were looking down into the water, which was one shade darker than the dusk, into the river that kept moving away from us with a will and power equal to its arriving at our feet again. "The only way things last, Jordan, is that they end and they don't quit coming back again."

"Wallace does that. He keeps me awake at night."

"Is that why you walk? Helen says in the summer you walk all night."

"I walk the way I used to swim. I try not to think and I try not to remember things. I go where I go. I seldom meet anyone. Though one night I found myself at your front gate. It was the funniest thing. I wanted to wake you all up and bring you out to see the beauty of your own house in the moonlight. Can you imagine? I had to stop myself from throwing a pebble at the window. I had to say 'Jordan Walsh, you're a grown woman. There's a family inside, two parents and a child, and a child's business is sleep.'"

I could imagine. I could well imagine, but instead of saying, I wish you had, I said, "You were just lonely."

She looked at me long and hard, then back at the river. "Never say 'just' when you say 'lonely.'"

Every summer for six summers since the accident, he inhabited her thoughts and dreams as he never had alive, and his company, come too late, made her a nocturnal animal spurred on by the need and desire to leave him behind. Like an animal, she went barefoot. Like an animal, she walked the civilized ground of our town, her shoes in her pocket, silent in her wandering and in her standing before the darkened windows of homes and people dear to her and unapproachable. Like a hurt animal, chewing her way out of the teeth of a trap, she took blunt scissors to her head and sawed away what had first made her Jordan to me, her long, beautiful, powerful hair. On her knees on the bank of the river, she offered it to the water in long, dark handfuls, and watched in awe as her gift was taken.

She was more than a bit mad. I didn't know it that night, although her bare feet surprised me and I was frightened and deeply disappointed by her hair. She was still Jordan to me, a restless, mournful Jordan. She was still Helen's mother, and she held the key to whole parts of my friend I'd never before encountered.

"Even in the womb she took charge. She carried off her own birth," said Jordan. "I could never have done it without her. It was a twenty-two-hour labor—with a second child, unheard of!—and every time, *every* time I lagged, Helen reached up and pinched me. She pinched me!"

"There was a midwife, wasn't there?"

"Midwife? Wallace was the midwife. Catching a baby might have been a simple, soothing act to anyone else, but he was a man forever involved in cutting out his own heart. This almost shattered him. He took Helen in his hands, he took life in his hands, a life he had made with me. He despaired and rejoiced. I don't believe he ever forgave me."

"For what?"

"For bringing him someone he loved."

"You brought him Harry. Didn't he love Harry?"

"Harry was all the parts of Wallace that Wallace refused to love in himself. Helen was different. She was and is more like me, though she seemed more like her father because they got along. She was stubborn and brave—"

"She still is."

"She still is," Jordan agreed.

"Are they home alone when you're out walking?"

"No. Joan's with them."

"She sleeps there, Jordan?"

She looked at me, then high up over the trees at the sky, glowing green and silver in the endless, midsummer dusk. "She sleeps there, yes. I always find her asleep. I find my children asleep. They've kicked the covers off and their arms wave off intruders in their dreams. I'm the intruder, Augusta. At this time of year I'm always the intruder. Now you must go home."

"I only have to be home before dark."

"Well, you've missed that. It's dark."

"No, dark is when the stars come out."

"Don't I see one now?"

"That's a planet."

She pointed above us. "That's not a planet."

I had to admit it was a star, the star I called Victoria.

"Victoria? It's Arcturus."

"I don't know their real names," I said sheepishly. "I just call them what they feel like to me."

I told her what I had never told anyone, all my deepest, most sympathetic feelings about the stars. She listened intently and laughed only once, when I spoke perhaps too earnestly about Betty Peterson. She knew a great deal about the stars. She knew their proper names, but more important, she sensed their dimensions; she knew the value of the space they occupied.

"The galaxy is shrinking!" I complained, with an urgency I didn't understand myself.

"We are not so small. We are in no way small. Look up there," she said sternly.

I looked. But for Arcturus and Vega, it was all blankness.

"They're there," she said, "you know they're there. In a

while Scorpio will rise, Hercules will show, and dear old Berenice's Hair. The stars require great faith, Gussy. To believe in something so many light-years away, requires faith. The ones we see may have sputtered out already. That twinkle, the message of their existence, left their shore so long ago, when we look up and love them we may be loving only a ghost."

She took her head in her hands. Her neck looked so long and vulnerable, like a taut, white bow in the last light of that day. Finally she said, "I love him. What does it matter? I forgive him. This is more. I'm not a jealous woman, Augusta, unless I feel I'm dealing with an equal. I was never jealous of Audrey Alexander. I may have pitied her, but she was simple, limited. She was a known quantity. I understood her. Who understands a mistress better than a wife? He came home one weekend, and I don't know what saint of irony kept him on the road. His usual Friday headlights set two translucent swans on the lake for the children to delight in—I always wondered what part of their joy in his arrival was really Wallace, and what part swan. When they went out to greet him he collapsed across the seat of the car with a fever of one hundred and four. This was the first clue I had of what a long, dark distance he'd crossed to lead the life he was leading.

"It was winter. Our house, our tiny three-room tinderbox, became a hospital ward. His body was covered with a rash and his gums were a mass of lesions. His joints ached, his fever rose, but he didn't want the doctor—oh no. He wouldn't allow it. He would fight it off himself, whatever it was. I think he knew what it was, but could not look his life in the face. One day I said, 'You'd rather punish yourself than ask forgiveness, Wallace.' I called him a coward. He asked me if I had ever loved him. I said I had. Sick as he was, he got up out of his bed, got dressed and went to the doctor."

"How old were you?" I asked. I don't know what made me ask it.

"Old?" She laughed. "I was two hundred years old, that's what it felt like. I was thirty-one. The children were eight and five. Harry was in the third grade, and Helen didn't go to school, she stayed home with me. She took care of her father that winter. She was a better nurse to him than I could ever be. She was his little Saint Oar, his friend; they were best friends. She washed his hair, she shaved him, she learned to read at home and read to him. One day it dawned on me she was just a child doing a grown woman's work; she'd taken my place. The very next morning I sent her off to school. Call it jealousy—it might have been. We were equals after all. But she seemed relieved to go, and my reward for a sullen husband was at least a happy child. After her first day she came racing home up the dirt lane, lunch box flapping open, big brother in tow. 'Jordan!' she cried. I'll never forget it. 'They named a river after you! We sang it in school!'

"My two tributaries, my children. Every afternoon I sat with a sick man at my back and waited for the house to flood with life again. Harry cut his knee, Helen lost a tooth. They bled and grew. Everything in and around them breathed life. Yet what was it in me that couldn't or wouldn't, in the dead center of February, look out any one of my own thirteen windows and see for myself that all was neither cruel nor beautiful; that there were clouds of sackcloth worn intimately against a sky of silk; that the lake, my lake, was a living, breathing thing under its skin of ice? It was dark and bright and breathtaking, and longing for us.

"I stood up. Distorted by an ancient windowpane I

caught sight of two children crossing the lake; rippled, underwater children—the glass made them swimmers in their boots and coats. They'd found a faster way home from school and dragged me with them out across the ice. One day we skated, cut up the front of an old window fan and wrapped our feet in runners. Another time Helen instructed us in the delicate art of packing small lumps of ice inside snowballs. 'I can't believe you're with us, Jordan!' Were these my children? I left the sickroom, joined a tribe of wellness, saw them at real play for the first time in their lives out on the solid safety of the lake. This went on until the ice broke up in the spring and Wallace staggered from his bed and pronounced himself cured. Then an early darkness seemed to fall upon the house, though the days were longer coming out of winter, the sky was generous, the ground warm. A chill fell across our lives again. He went back to work at the factory, and of course he saw Audrey. We had very little money, yet suddenly there was something about flying lessons. I couldn't imagine him learning to fly, except to endanger. Caution meant nothing to Wallace. It was a lie for the sake of the children, to be somebody for the sake of the children, when what they needed was a father, not a hero. He never understood that."

It was true dark by now, a dark that brought a subtle coolness with it and the nasal cry of a nighthawk somewhere between our hair and the stars. Jordan said she would walk me home.

"Why? I'm not afraid." But I was thinking of her bare feet, her ragged head and that terrible raincoat she wore, the one that sailed with Columbus. I didn't want to be seen with her and questioned, as I surely would be by my mother, who sat with her face to the yard at the stroke of dark if I wasn't home yet. I couldn't explain the night. I felt protective of it. The streets on my side of the river were well lit, and the movie would be letting out so I could walk uphill with the couples.

"I know you're not afraid. You have no reason to be," said Jordan. "It's your mother who's afraid." She took my arm and led me over the bridge, and we walked arm in arm along Zoroaster Street. A gentle, wet breeze touched the back of my legs, and I bowed my head to invite it onto my neck. The river had a certain wet ripeness that came to us more and more as we walked farther from it. It smelled green. It smelled of summer. It smelled of earth and ammonia. We could hear it running beyond the sycamore trees, and between the trunks of the trees we could make out its dark form and the darker shape of its banks.

I said, "This reminds me of Paris, France."

"It's just like Paris."

"I've never been to Paris."

"No, I haven't either."

We turned right on Second Street, and I asked, "How do you know she's afraid?"

"She's a mother, isn't she?"

"You're a mother."

"That's how I know she's afraid. She held you in her arms, though you don't remember it. You were pink and new, you were helpless. She wanted to keep you from harm forever—but you were held to this world by a thread and she knew it. All mothers know it. I wanted only to be outlived by my children, that was the extent of my selfishness."

She stopped and took her shoes out of her pocket and put them on. "Before the accident I believed in goodness, in a certain goodwill at the heart of creation. I believed in the power of appeal. I used to say to the air in the room, 'Let the fates be kind! Look kindly on us!' Well, they tipped the boat with all their attention, and out fell Wallace. Out fell Wallace and Harry, out fell the lie of happiness and family. It was a white lie, a good lie, a small lie, Augusta. That's what I thought until it almost killed my son. Now I don't know what to think, so I try not to think at all."

We came to Saint Elmo Street, and I steered us across Second to avoid the small but garrulous crowd of people exiting the movie theater. Jordan kept looking over her shoulder at the crowd, as if she expected to be followed. All of a sudden she tugged my arm and cried, "Let's go to the movies! Can we? Everybody goes to the movies but me!"

I looked at her in surprise. She was pouting like a child. "It's over, Jordan. It's finished. You're walking me home, remember?"

"Walking you home? Yes, yes, walking you home. What a good idea," she said, and laughed like a person hearing a joke in a language they are only awkwardly familiar with, laughing to hide their confusion.

If I didn't understand her confusion, it was only because I didn't understand how completely he inhabited her at night, how his presence inside her waxed like the moon. He was unable to relinquish some earthly form, and if it could not be his own it would be hers. Every year for six years, every summer, he called her away from her life, he played her in like a fish, and she fought him as she could and she weakened and often thought she might die.

He had been killed in July. Each year on the date of his death he let go of her. She felt him knock three times inside her, three sharp blows that knocked the wind out of her—it felt like a block of ice had fallen from a high place and shattered on her chest. It felt like her heart had grown huge and cumbersome and had fallen right through her, and if she looked down she might see it jerking and throbbing between her feet. After that she would fall asleep for days, a sleep from which no one and nothing could rouse her, and only when she woke up at last would she understand, by the absence of dreams, which side of death she was on.

That's how she described it, but it puzzled me. As far as I knew, the dead didn't dream; that was an entertainment for the living. Though I'd heard someone say, When God dreams we get weather, and Harriet once said, God had a dream and called it Liberace. But that was God, and God wasn't dead, was he? just because I didn't know what to do with him. No, dead was dead and God was God, and if I was stumped by both that still didn't make them the same.

These troublesome thoughts disappeared as we came to the corner of Flat Street. I told Jordan I'd run the rest of the way to the gate myself. "In that case, I'll stand right here and watch you." I turned to go, and she said, "You're growing up, Gussy. I enjoy watching you grow."

I looked at her blankly. I think I touched my chest to see if I'd suddenly sprouted breasts, but she explained, "You're developing a conscience, that's what I mean. At times it may feel like a curse to know right from wrong, but in the end your joy will be greater and your grief will have meaning. You're an extraordinary person, don't forget that."

"Okay."

"Just okay?"

"Thank you, I guess. Good night, Jordan." I flew through the dark towards my own front yard with a mixture of dread and relief.

In bed that night I lay awake and listened to the dogs bark. There seemed to be a pack of them, at least half a dozen distinct voices in the alley behind our house. Had they treed a porcupine? If so, I knew they'd be sorry. Or a skunk? The two big dogs down the street had a skunk habit; they were always being disgraced by skunks. The neighbor's dog was in with raccoons the minute you turned your back on him. He was a shifty, disagreeable character who refused to be trained, though he stood only eight inches high and gave the misleading impression of being harmless. The raccoons loved our garbage for its plenitude of chicken bones, and maybe it was a raccoon they'd found tonight and chased to its hole.

It was the first night in weeks our house wasn't filled with the purr of fans. A cool breeze poured through one of my two windows, carrying with it the scent of mint and roses and new onions from the garden. The racket outside went on for a long time. Finally I heard my father get out of bed. He said something to my mother, and I heard their bedroom door open and close. His footsteps disappeared towards the front of the house, then I watched him come around outside until he stood at the back of the house, facing the alley. He was wearing pajamas and an old pair of shoes, and his hair stood up comically all around his head.

The moonlight was thick and bright, like a coat of new white paint over everything. As my eyes grew accustomed to it, I could make out different shades of color. The grass was dark green, and my father was a pale human color, dressed in faintly yellow pajamas. There was even a touch of blue to the blackness of the sky. The tall trees that bordered the alley were a wall of gray-green leaves and cream-colored branches. They grew in so close to the house (we had nothing you could call a backyard), in summer the catalpa's heavy leaves and cigar-shaped pods brushed the roof and deepened the sparser shade of the maples, which we were grateful for that summer in particular.

Tonight there was something treacherous about the foliage. I hated to see Julian disappear into it as the excitement of the dogs increased and their barking became a lugubrious baying. They had cornered something for sure. Why didn't he leave them to it? He reappeared briefly, snatched a hoe from where it leaned against the house and disappeared again.

There was an old shed back there. Years ago, on a rainy day I used to play house by myself in its musty darkness, pretending I was father, mother and child in my family of one. The roof leaked, the floor was dirt and there wasn't a single window. The door latched on the outside with a heavy, rusty latch, impossible to open from the inside unless you knew just how to work the handle. It wasn't our shed, but no one else seemed to claim it, so I was allowed to play there. This was before the pearly everlasting bush became my refuge. (It was just a forlorn little scrub at the time, about waist high.)

I learned to read in that shed, or rather I discovered that I had somehow absorbed an understanding of letters in relation to one another, which meant their order could never again be random to me. I might have been the only first-grader in the world to feel a certain loss when finally the shapes on a written page gave up their secret. It happened one day when I brought a broom and flashlight to the shed, determined to clear out the black widow spiders. The open door let in enough light to play by but not enough to get a good look at who lived in the corners. I beamed the flashlight across the floor. I'd made a cardboard table and chair, and a rope bed with no mattress, and Julian helped me build a shelf where I kept a jar of peppercorns and a pack of cards. I looked at all my handiwork in the light of the flashlight and felt proud and settled and happy for a moment, then I flicked the beam onto the wall and discovered, to my amazement, that it was covered with faded newspapers. They dated from 1932; the numbers were easy enough to read. Some of the headlines were set in type the size of my fist. There seemed to be a story that ran across the wall, because the pictures beneath the headlines were of the same two people, a man and a woman in what looked like different stages of an adventure. Sometimes they waved from a plane, sometimes they held a baby and finally they clung to each other like two people on the edge of the world, afraid of the dark.

I played my flashlight across the newsprint, looking at the photographs and observing the pattern of the columns. I loved the design of a newspaper, the crisp black against the white. I loved the dark smudge on your fingers and the taste of ink in your mouth. Before I could read I used to sit beside my father and memorize the lay of each page, fascinated by something I didn't have the words for then: the tidiness of organized thought. That day in the shed, I wasn't looking for more than that. I was admiring the landscape, lightly exploring it, not looking for a way in. But suddenly it was given to me in the form of the word "kidnap." I had never read that word before; I had never read any word before, yet here it was, clear as day. Kidnap. There was no mistaking it. It sounded just like it looked. Sound and look—and this was the moment I've always thought of as learning to read—were connected.

I went on from there to unravel other words, including the word "Augustus"—almost my own name. I worked slowly, with my face close to the wall, laboring over each letter until a word had meaning or didn't, and if it didn't I left it and went on to the next. At first I felt excited, like a decoder making sense of nonsense, and then I felt uneasy, then frightened as the unhappy story unfolded. Exhausted,

I left the shed and walked back to the house. Julian was in his garden, and I went and stood next to him and said, "Papa, I just learned to read. I wish I hadn't."

"Just like that you learned to read?"

"I must have known how all along."

"Well, what did you read?"

"About a stolen baby. It died. Someone killed it and put it in the woods, and someone found it. I don't like reading, Papa. You can sound out almost any word and put it with the word before it and the word after it and then you have things you don't want to hear. Is there a way to stop knowing how to read?"

He considered this, then said no, there wasn't. He asked me where I'd read such a story and I told him, and he got up off his knees and went to see for himself.

When he came back his face was the color of chalk. "I'm sorry you had to see that, Gussy. It was a terrible thing that happened."

"Could it happen again?"

"Yes."

"Could it happen here?"

"I doubt it."

"Could it happen to me?"

"No."

"How come?"

He managed to smile. "Because I'm no Charles Lindbergh."

I never set foot in that shed again, though some time later I sent Julian in after my pack of cards. I found other things to read, happier, duller stories that weren't believable and bored me. It was years before I found a book I loved. It was the book I borrowed from Helen, *The Yearling*. Long after I finished it it sat by my bed, and in a blue mood I would reach out and touch it, or drag it under the covers with me, or read the sad parts aloud. There's nothing better for sadness than a sad, hopeful book.

I folded my arms on the windowsill, waiting for Julian. I pressed my face against the screen. I loved the smell of screens, and the way they gently gave around your face and left their mark there. I loved the way the moths clung to them, showing their soft undersides, and the way the june bugs buzzed and rattled against them, their bodies hard as pebbles. I looked out into the bright darkness, straining to see through it, through the trees and into the woods and into the dogs themselves. They sounded more excited than ever, and I told myself it was only Julian walking towards them with his hoe raised. He was as good as a stranger to them in his pajamas. Why didn't he let them be? I imagined every move he made, and the way the moonlight slid down through the trees like long knives. "Come back, Papa. Come back," I whispered. I knew I would do anything to get him back. Jordan was right. We were held to this world by a thread, all of us, not just children, children least of all. The thread spun out from me to Julian, and with every step he took it grew thinner, and with every year he lived it grew weaker. He was old, my father. He was in his forties. People died in their sixties. He was more than halfway through. What would that be like to have an emptiness, a nothing, where once you had a father? There would be no garden. There would be no scent of shaving cream in the morning, and no one to polish my shoes. How would I ever stop missing him? How did people get up and live through the next day? It was a terrible terrible thought, and I was struck with grief and started to cry, and at that moment the dogs gave up their barking, leaving me more frightened than before.

I didn't hear her come into my room. She said my name, and I turned sharply, sucking in my breath. "It's me. I brought you something warm, some warm milk," said Harriet. She held out the cup, and I took it. "It will help you sleep."

We stood by the window. "What's out there, Mother?"

"Your father says it's prowlers. I say it's the man in the moon that's got those dogs going. It's not a night for prowlers with all this moon."

"I wish they'd bark again."

She yawned. "Why?"

"I don't know why. Maybe he's in trouble."

"When there's trouble, that's when dogs bark. The trouble is over."

After she put me to bed they started up again. I hopped to the window and saw nothing, saw no one. I looked up to find the stars at least, but some were hidden by foliage and the rest were washed away by the moon. Suddenly I remembered something Jordan had said, that to believe in what you couldn't see required great faith. It was true. I knew so little about the world. I knew more about the sky than I did about the world, yet I believed that life was precious, that it was worth something, that it might make sense someday and even if it didn't I couldn't possibly go away empty-handed. I had never thought about things like this before, and it startled me.

Just then Julian appeared in the shadows under the catalpa tree. He tossed his hoe onto the grass and left it there, then he walked towards the house. It was unusual for him to treat a tool that way, and I called out, "What is it, Papa? Here I am, I'm at the window. What did you find?"

"Nothing." He looked disgusted. "I found nothing. Just a bunch of crazy dogs barking at a shed."

"A shed? At my old shed?"

"It's nobody's shed, Gussy. You used to play there. Anyway, tonight the dogs think they own it. They're running circles around it. I thought there might be an animal on the roof, but there's no sign of anything, not even a squirrel's nest. It's maddening."

"Did you look inside it?"

"The door's shut. Nothing could be inside it."

"Someone could, maybe. The latch is broken. They could be locked in." He hesitated, and I offered, "I'll go with you."

"You won't," he said quickly. "You'll stay right where you are. Go back to bed now. Go to sleep."

He turned and walked into the woods. "Papa! your hoe," I cried, but he didn't come back for it. I fell on my bed, exhausted, and though I never expected to I must have slept, because the next thing I heard was his step in the hall. "Papa?" He opened my door and stuck his head in. "There was somebody in there, wasn't there?"

He nodded. "It was Helen's mother."

"Jordan. I knew it. Is she all right? Can we do something for her? Oh, Papa, I'm sorry."

"Sorry?"

"Yes."

"Yes, I imagine you are. As far as doing something for her—well, there are pills to make people sleep."

"I don't mean that. I mean Wallace. I mean Wallace's ghost." Then I remembered, "You don't believe in ghosts, do you?"

"I believe other people believe in them." He smiled weakly. "I believe in them as long as they're useful."

"Useful?"

"They're a way of keeping someone alive, and there's

often a good reason for that. Some people simply aren't ready for the death of someone they love—or someone they don't love, for that matter—and most probably, if that person were cut away from them completely, they would get sick and some of them would die. Your friend, Helen, doesn't have her father's ghost to hold on to. I imagine she never has had it, and this is one reason she has lupus. Though if you ever told Sal Beveridge that, I'd be laughed out of town."

"I won't tell him."

"Thank you. What worries me about Helen's mother is that if we take away her ghost before she's finished with him, she'll almost certainly collapse in some way. Yet at this point he seems to be killing her on her feet. Torturing her, at least. It's not very pretty either way."

"Can I tell you something, Papa?"

"Tell me something."

"I love Jordan, but I'm afraid of her. She forgets I'm not her age, that I'm Helen's age, that I'm Helen's friend."

"Can I tell you something, Gussy? Sometimes you forget you're Helen's friend. I don't know why you do, but you do, and it hurts her feelings. She can't show you that, because her feelings have been hurt too much in her life and she's learned how to make everyone around her think she's okay when she's not. I'm not guessing at this, I know it because she tells me."

"She tells you?"

"I'm her doctor. And I'm a father. Not just somebody's father, but your father. I suspect that's why she can talk to me, and talk is good medicine for Helen."

We said good night, then I called him back into my room. "Papa? Please can we not tell Mother about what happened? I promise I won't tell her if you won't."

He sighed. "How can I not tell her, Gussy? She's been awake half the night and she'll ask."

"Say it was a raccoon in there. Or say what you said when you came back the first time. You said it was nothing, remember? If I hadn't sent you back there it would have been nothing."

He nodded sadly. I knew he hated these predicaments.

"Please, Papa. It's not her fault, and she'll get better." I meant Jordan.

He closed his eyes. He leaned his head against the door. "All right. I'll tell her it was nothing. If she doesn't believe that, I'll tell her to ask you."

We said good night again. My sleep was full of strange dreams. In all of them I was a widow, though at the same time a child. I woke up once before dawn and looked out over the garden and saw that the stars had come back, and as I watched, one dropped right over the river, right over Helen's house, and it didn't grieve me at all but left me somehow hopeful. For if one light goes out, it goes out with a fury and a beauty it never knew in its patient, waiting life when it was a white pinpoint lost against a billion others. I had never known that star until it fell. That, I thought, is the way I love Helen.

# Chapter Nine

If you followed our river south, past the toppled chimneys and yawning root cellars of Murdoch, past the small factory towns of Black Lick and Abyssinia, one bright with soot and the other bristling with the blond heads of the brooms made there and ferried downriver in open crates—always a disconcerting sight, like a boatload of imprisoned children—you would find yourself on a high plain surrounded by short, thick mountains, and back in those mountains you'd find lake after lake in a long beaded line, threaded by the river. Each lake kept a town alive, and the larger lakes supported two, one at the head and one at the foot, a comfortable distance from each other.

The largest of the towns—and it was not large—was called Husband. It sat south of the middle of the chain of lakes, and it had a small winter industry as well as the summer commerce of fishing and boating. A short rope tow climbed the face of one of the nearby mountains, and every now and then, in a good snow year, a handful of outsiders would make their way to Husband and slap on their skis and pay their dollar to be dragged uphill for fun. I did it once and only once and hated it, but I was not there to ski, I was there to see what was left of the house my mother was born in. She left Husband when she was ten and hadn't been back since, but the house, which sat at the corner near the hardware store which bore her grandfather's name, seemed unchanged. It was a simple, square house with a gable roof and shuttered windows and a front porch supported by four wooden columns. It was pea green with gray trim, and the paint had been kept up, as had everything else about the house and yard. According to Harriet, nothing looked one bit different. Even the plum tree standing alone in the snow was neither taller nor shorter. It was all just as she remembered it.

My father suggested we walk up and ring the doorbell, but she was horrified. "Julian, please."

"Why not? They can only say no."

"We don't belong here," she whispered vehemently.

"Mother, you lived here," I said.

"I can't help it. Now I live somewhere else."

We don't belong to our own past? How could that be? If I ever grow up and come back and stand like this in front of my house on Flat Street, I thought, nothing will stop me from ringing that bell.

I was wrong of course. Though it's always easier if a place has been torn down or added to or in whatever way made unrecognizable. The first second is harder, but after that it's easier. Hardest of all is to walk inside and see your old place at the table, see the chair by the window and the book open to the page you started and never finished when you were ten, because you were interrupted by something, a very concrete something whose memory draws you one fathom deeper into a past from which you cannot extricate yourself, to which you do not belong.

On the way home that snowy winter day, Harriet gazed mournfully out the window, sighing and shifting restlessly until we were free of the mountains at last, then she thanked me and my father for coming with her and said she never needed to make that trip again.

She never did, and the next time I went that way I went without her. I went with Helen and her family, shortly after my father found Jordan Walsh in the shed. It was a very early morning in July, already hot and humid, not a good day for a long drive. Harriet got up at dawn with Julian and made us all breakfast, then woke me up to eat it—waffles with strawberry syrup and whipped cream, a queen's breakfast. I said good-bye to my father. He kissed me and said he would miss me and that I was brave, then he went off to the hospital. I sat and finished my breakfast, and Harriet sat with me, drinking a cup of tea.

"You're all packed?"

I nodded.

"You've got your stuff from the bathroom?"

"Yup."

"How about a barrette?"

"I don't need a barrette."

"Are you kidding? A long drive with the windows down? You'll need a barrette."

I suddenly wished it was a convertible. I asked if she'd ever ridden in a convertible, and to my surprise she said yes, once, a long time ago, before I was born.

"With Papa?"

"No. I didn't know Papa then. I rode with the mayor of Husband in the Independence Day Parade."

"Just you and the mayor!"

"Just the two of us."

"How come? Did you know the mayor?"

She laughed. "He was your great-grandfather."

A mayor! I thought. Then all at once I knew it wasn't true. "He owned a hardware store," I said, not lifting my eyes from my sticky, empty plate. "He wasn't the mayor."

"He was the mayor," said Harriet, "and the dogcatcher and the tax collector and one third of the fire department, and he owned the hardware store too. You weren't born out of the sky, Augusta, you were born from me and I was born from other people, most of them good, hardworking people, and they were all born from someone else, some good, some not so good, but none of them black marks on the face of this earth, and none, not one, born to be forgotten. They are all we have, these people. Every day we walk around with them inside us. You've got every one of mine and your father's, and if that doesn't suit you, there's not one thing you can do to change it. Choose your friends all you want, but we're the ones who know you, don't forget that. Now," she said, looking away from me at the clock on the wall, "do you have enough money?"

I said I did, I had the five-dollar bill she'd given me.

The doorbell rang, and we both jumped at the unfamiliar sound. It was a little after seven o'clock. As I got up to answer it my mother lightly caught my wrist, pulling me to her but not too close. "You're part of a family," she said. "This is a good thing." She let me go.

Helen was shifting back and forth on the doorstep, whispering, "Come on, come on." She was wearing long white pants and a white T-shirt. On her head was a faded straw hat. Her face was pale, and her long arms were bare and pale against the vivid green of the grass. Behind her the daylilies were in bloom, their burgeoning reds, oranges and yellows making the garden a living, fiery place.

I caught her with her hand out, about to ring the bell a

second time. I startled her, and she did a funny thing, she pressed her thumb against my nose and made a high ringing sound in her throat, like the bell.

"Helen!" I laughed.

She looked over my shoulder. "This is where you live?"

I led her inside, into the kitchen. Harriet turned around at the sink, her hands red and dripping soapy water. "So this is Helen."

"You know Helen."

"I don't know Helen. How could I know her? You keep her to yourself."

"You've met her."

"If I've met her I don't remember it. I can't keep track of your friends. I'll bet she's grown a yard since then."

"I've seen you at school," said Helen. "It was a long time ago. I've seen a picture of you, too."

"Picture? Hand me that towel, Augusta. What picture?"

"In Dr. Cotton's office, next to the rubber plant. It's an old picture. Gussy's in it and she's only a baby. You don't look very different at all. You look about the same."

"For heaven's sake, that's years old!" cried Harriet.

Helen smiled, and my mother smiled back.

"I'll get my stuff," I said. "You want to see the rest of the house?"

"You get ready," said Harriet. "I'll take her around."

When I came back they'd moved only as far as the sitting room. My friend was leaning over the record player and my mother was standing behind her, wearing the straw hat.

"It's the needle," said Helen.

"What needle?" asked Harriet.

"You know, the needle that makes the noise come out of the records. A record player won't work without a needle."

"I never heard of this needle."

"It's small. It's tiny."

"No one ever talked about a needle before, all the time it's been broken. What makes you so sure it's a needle? My husband said it could be in the plug."

"It can't be in the plug. The turntable goes around. It's not an electrical problem."

"So a fuse."

"No, that's electrical."

"What's not electrical?"

"The needle."

"Show me," said Harriet. She bent down, one hand securing the hat.

"You see where it's supposed to be?"

Their heads touched and came away abruptly. "I don't. I don't see a thing. But I don't see well. I'm not— I only have—" She pointed to her right eye.

"It's gray," said Helen carefully.

"It's glass."

"Your other one's green. I was supposed to have green eyes like that."

I came into the room dragging a small overnight bag. "Is this a grip?"

Harriet straightened up. "A grip?"

"I asked Joan what to bring and she said, Just fill a grip."

"That's a grip. That's a small grip," said Helen. She made a face. "Harry's bringing his golf clubs."

"Your friend fixed the record player," said Harriet. "She fixed it in a minute and your father hasn't been able to fix it as long as it's been broken. He thought it was in the plug, ha!"

I didn't say what we both knew, that even the simplest machines got the best of my father. Once I'd seen him take apart a lamp that needed only a new light bulb.

"It's the needle," I said.

Her mouth opened. "You knew it was the needle?"

"Sure," I lied. I looked out the window. Just then somebody sat on the horn of the taxi, scaring a flock of small brown birds out of the garden. They were scruffy-looking sparrows; we called them hand-me-down birds. They flew in a ragged clump to the neighbor's cherry tree and were lost in the summer branches.

Harriet went into the kitchen and came out with a paper bag of sandwiches and a bottle of lime juice. "I think your mother likes this," she told Helen.

"Likes it? She loves it."

"You go ahead, Augusta. I want your friend to write down the name of the place you'll be staying tonight."

"It's like an oven out there," Helen warned me.

I took a deep breath and walked out into the hot white heat of that simmering day. The air was thick and heavy, the sky the color of paste. Good-bye, cave of my own house! Good-bye, room! Good-bye, bed! Hello, lumpy cot in the attic of some motel! Halfway down the path the sweat stood out along my arms; it prickled the back of my neck. I trudged to the taxi, where Harry and Joan were wrestling the golf clubs into the trunk to make room in the backseat for me and my small grip. Harry whistled hello and Joan said, "Hey hi, slowpoke." Her face was red, and the sweat dripped off her chin.

Jordan sat in the front seat, facing away from me with her elbow out the open window of the taxi. She turned as I came through the gate. Her eyes looked large and watery, like the eyes of a deer. She reached her arm out to me and said, "Hello, you." She got out and gave me a hug, then we stood leaning against the taxi, my bag between my feet.

"Don't we get to see your ma?"

"She's with Helen. They're coming."

"Helen looks well, doesn't she?"

"She looks white."

"She's meant to look white. Your father's orders. Lupus loves the sun."

I heard Joan say, "Reach, Harry. That's not reaching. That's the opposite of reach."

What's the opposite of reach? I wondered.

"Did she remember Helen?"

"No."

"Well, how could she I suppose."

"I remember you. You had your hair up. I think I was six years old."

"I had my hair up?"

"In a twist."

"I never wore my hair like that, did I?"

"Yes you did, this one time. I remember you had a long neck."

Helen and Harriet came out of the house. "Look at that," I said, "they're laughing. Do you remember me at all, Jordan?"

"Yes I do."

"You really do?"

"Yes."

She didn't offer anything more, and I didn't ask.

Somewhere down the street a car started up. It was the car with the terrible paint job, with the eggplant-colored doors. The two big dogs sat in the backseat, and as it passed I thought I saw Jordan shudder.

"I've been sleeping for days," she said quietly. "I don't remember much of what happened in the weeks before that, but I never do. The miracle is that the body and mind survive a time like that. And the spirit," she added. "Dear spirit." She turned her face away and wiped her cheeks. "Gosh, it's an emotional day."

Helen came running up. "She bought us lime juice, Jordan!"

"I see she did."

"What happened?" asked Harriet. She turned to me. "What happened to her?"

"She's crying."

"She cut her hair."

"She's been crying all morning," said Helen.

"It's only a little after seven," Jordan managed to smile.

"It's nerves," said Harriet. "I don't envy you this day. Do this. This is what I do if I can't stop. Pinch your nose." She showed Jordan. "Pinch it hard and hold on to it and don't let go until you get to the lake."

"Or until it falls off," said Helen.

"When did you ever cry so much?" I asked my mother.

"Pff. The little you know, Augusta." She handed me the bag of sandwiches. "Now, scoot. Get settled. The day's not getting any cooler. See if you can help that lady in the back. What's she doing? Is that your boy with her?"

"That's my brother, Harry," said Helen.

"That's our boy," said Jordan. "Harry!" she called. He came around the side of the taxi. "There's someone here I want you to meet."

He cleared his throat. "Can I bring Joan?" His voice was getting deeper and deeper, and today I noticed a clump of fine white hairs on his chin.

"Joan can bring herself," said Joan. She lowered the trunk and pounded on it a few times until it clicked shut, then she joined us, wiping her hand on her blue jeans. "I am a prize perspirer," she explained. "This body just loves to perspire. Back in Georgia I once won a contest. I won this baseball cap in fact." She shook my mother's hand. "I am so pleased to meet you. I am pleased to meet anyone who calls themself the mother of Augusta Cotton. Pleased is not even the word. It goes a whole lot deeper than that. If I knew I'd get a daughter like her, I'd have a daughter."

Harriet looked bewildered. "Are you married?" she asked politely.

"No, I am not."

"Are you married?" Harry asked my mother.

Jordan answered for her, "Of course she's married, Harry. This is Gussy's mother. She's married to Gussy's father, who is Helen's doctor, Dr. Cotton."

"Oh." He blinked. "Are you married?"

Jordan thought a minute. "Am I married?"

"I believe you are," said Joan.

"I don't think you are," I said.

"Augusta!" said Harriet. "No one asked for your two cents."

"They don't have to ask. It's not like that."

"Gussy's used to us," Jordan said quickly. "Everybody's two cents is welcome. What do you think, Harriet? Am I married?"

"You mean legally?"

"No. I don't think Harry's concerned about the law."

"Because legally you're a widow, you're free." She looked at the ground and looked up again. "How do you feel? Do you feel married? If you feel married I would say you're married. If you don't I would say you're not."

"What if I feel both?"

"So you're human. Everyone feels both. Sometimes one way, sometimes the other. Sometimes more, sometimes less. I've seen people ruined by being married. I almost was. An ax over my head, I thought. The thing didn't match my idea of it, and it turned me sour. Maybe I should not say this in front of my daughter, but it's the truth of life. Who wants an ax over their head? Not me. So move the head, I say. To myself I said, Harriet, you live here. You've made a family. You have a daughter and your husband is a good friend. Who wants to be lonely? No one. Who wants to be out in the cold? No one. But who's got the temperament to stick like glue or be stuck to? No one. Some saint maybe. We're talking human error. That's what a marriage is. Something practical. Something loose. I don't mean running around chasing other people, loose. That's just being lonely."

"Sugar, take this handkerchief." Jordan was crying again, and Joan pulled a crumpled handkerchief out of her pocket. "It doesn't look like much. It doesn't even look fresh."

"It looks like Harriet's idea of a marriage," said Jordan, and blew her nose. "I'm all right now. I'll be all right. We're staying at the Marilyn Motel. Helen, find a piece of paper and write that down, and the telephone number. Oh dear, I don't even know if they have a telephone."

"They do," said Helen, "and we already did it."

"I want to write it," said Harry.

Jordan rummaged around on the floor of the taxi, looking for the telephone number. "I don't care who writes it, just write it so it can be read."

"I *said*, it's done."

"I'm doing it," said Harry.

Helen glared at him. "You don't listen, do you? With ears that big you'd think you'd listen, but you don't."

"They aren't big."

"They are too, big. I don't know where you got ears like that. They look like dried-up old cow pies."

"Helen, that's just plain cruel," said Joan. "I'm of a mind to leave you both here on the sidewalk."

"No one's got ears like that," said Helen.

"Joan does," I said. "She used to. She says he got them from her."

"Well, he didn't," said Jordan, emerging from the taxi. "Here's that telephone number."

"I never said such a thing," said Joan.

Harriet looked more and more distraught. "This is why I never had two. I was afraid they might fight."

"Might!" laughed Joan. "These two regularly act like idiots. All children do. We wouldn't recognize them if they didn't."

Helen and I squeezed into the backseat. It was piled high with everyone else's idea of a small grip. There were more small grips in the trunk, as well as the golf clubs.

"You've got enough stuff for a week," said Harriet.

"He brought everything he owns," said Jordan. "He's not our best decision maker, are you, boy?"

Harry sat in the front seat, in the middle. He was slowly penciling a message. He showed it to Joan. "Motel has a 't'," she said, "and phone has a 'p-h'." He made the corrections and handed it to Harriet.

"He's not really dopey," Helen explained. "He was in an accident. He has to learn how to read and write and do everything all over again."

"I can drive too. I am quite a driver."

Harriet looked worried, and Joan said quickly, "Not this trip, mister."

"I'm teaching him history and how to cook," said Helen. "Jordan's teaching him—"

"How to weep and cry," said Joan. "How to let go of Lady Grief, aren't you, Jordie? Come on now, where's that old rag I gave you? Harry, find your mama's handkerchief. Doesn't it feel good to cry?"

"Pinch your nose," said my mother. "Like this. Pinch it hard and keep it pinched. You'll get there." She patted Jordan's shoulder. "Have a safe trip all of you."

Joan started the car, and we all looked ahead of us as if we were already on the road. "Call me tonight," said Harriet. "Call collect—but for heaven's sake don't tell your father I said to!" She reached through the window and squeezed my hand. "That's for the lump in my throat."

"I'll miss you."

"I'll miss you too. I hate for you to go."

"Come with us. Say yes!"

"Go on," she laughed. "Go."

"I'll be back tomorrow night. I'll be right back!" I threw my arms out and she leaned in and I hugged her neck. She watched us to the corner, waving one arm as she always did, side to side in slow motion, as if she were washing an invisible window.

We turned left on Second Street, crossed the river and headed south on Murdoch Way. Between our road and the river sat the sanatorium, high on its hill, invisible if you didn't know just where to look. In a month the ground around it would be covered with bright red and orange wildflowers, penstemon and Indian paintbrush. I would be twelve years old. Eleven would be over. Thirteen would be next. There was no stopping it, was there? There was really no way to leap over it or duck under it or dodge around it as I had once hoped. Helen and I would never be old children together. We would grow and change like everyone else. We would say to each other, Remember . . . ? Remember . . . ? the way adults did, and whatever we'd forgotten we would make up. What was lost would be lost again every time we invented it, until the pearls of our lives were hidden under so many layers of story, that only through great effort and great love would we ever be able to bring them back. It was astonishing how quickly we became someone else—in our bodies, yes, but in our spirits most of all. Dear spirit, Jordan had said. Who are you, spirit? I wondered. Do you have a name? Do you belong to me? How will I know you?

The road was poorly kept up now that Murdoch was gone, and the taxi swayed back and forth as Joan tried to avoid the worst of the potholes. In the middle of nowhere we passed a small coffee shop on the edge of a field filled entirely with lavender flowers. It was painted turquoise, an old peeling turquoise, and there was an old turquoise truck, washed and waxed, with new whitewall tires, parked in front of it. There was no sign that said open or closed, but there were two people inside, a man and a woman, and as we passed we saw that they were thin and old, and though it was eight o'clock in the morning they were wearing fine clothes. She had on a green dress and a green feather hat, and he wore a black shirt with a pair of white suspenders. They were moving slowly in a circle under an overhead fan, she with her head on his shoulder and he with his cheek on her hair.

"They're dancing!" I said.

"How can you tell?" asked Helen.

"Haven't you ever seen people dance?"

"Look at that," said Joan, "they *are* dancing!"

"They're Negroes," said Harry, "and we're not."

"That's right, sugar."

"Why not?"

"Why are you a boy and Helen's a girl?"

"I forget."

"Well, when you remember, it's the same reason."

Jordan said, "I don't think I've ever seen that coffee shop before. Have you, Helen?"

"No. Maybe I was too young."

"When is a person too young to see a coffee shop?" asked Joan. "It's been there for about a million years. I used to drive out here every week and eat a dusty road, then I'd climb all the way up to the top of that hill and walk around the sanatorium until I was good and hungry again, then I'd come down here and eat another one. Do you kids know what a dusty road is?" We didn't. "It's an ice cream sundae with malted milk on top."

"What's it like up there?" asked Jordan. "I've never been up there."

Joan didn't answer, and I didn't say a word.

"I see. I have places like that too," she laughed.

Past Murdoch the road ran along the river and was joined by another, poorer road that carried us up into the mountains at last. It was almost noontime when we drove into Husband. We stopped in a park and spread our blanket under a pine tree and ate my mother's sandwiches and drank lime juice straight from the bottle. Jordan took off her shoes and lay down on her back with her hands under her head, and Joan lay next to her. It was cool under the pine tree, cool in these mountains. We were all sleepy from the morning's heat and excitement. I fell asleep quickly, and woke with Helen beside me, her head on my arm. She was breathing lightly and evenly, a light, fleeting sleep.

We got back in the car and Helen said, "This is where Harriet was born, you know."

"Harriet?" said Jordan. "Gussy's mother Harriet?"

She nodded.

"Did she ask you to call her Harriet?"

"No."

"Then what's the rule, Helen?"

"Call her Mrs. Cotton."

"Was she truly born here?" asked Joan. "What a funny place to be born, in a town called Husband."

"I was born in Children," said Harry.

Jordan laughed. "You were born in Childs. You and Helen were both born in Childs."

"Jordan, tell us that story," said Helen.

"What story?"

"About the swan and the girl and the war."

"That's my story," said Joan. "It's a story about you. It's the story of Helen of Troy. She was a girl, a beautiful girl who lived a long long time ago."

"Back in the B.C.'s?" I asked.

"Yes, in the B.C.'s. Now, for some reason her daddy was a swan and her mama was a goose, but she was so beautiful everyone was all the time trying to catch her and carry her off somewhere. Finally one boy did. His name was Paris."

"I bet he took her to France," I said.

"If she was a swan," asked Helen, "or half a goose and half a swan, why couldn't she just fly away?"

"There's a question," said Joan. "Jordie, you answer that question."

Jordan thought a moment. "She hatched out of an egg, Helen, but she didn't look like her mother or her father or any kind of bird at all. She looked like you do now, like a girl. When she looked at herself—"

"Which was always," said Joan. "She was always admiring herself in the mirror, or in one of those tall windows whenever she walked down the street."

"When she looked at herself," Jordan went on, "she saw arms and legs and a stomach and wavy hair, she didn't see wings. They were tucked up under her shoulder blades and she forgot they were there."

"They had tall windows?" I asked. "Back in the B.C.'s?"

Joan laughed. "I don't believe so, sugar. I made that up."

"Well, make up the rest of the story," said Helen. "What happened after Paris? Where did he take me?"

"That's where we get the 'of Troy.' He took you to Troy. There was a long war with a horse in it and Greek people inside the horse. You were a heroine, and that was the end of it."

"Did I do anything? Did I fight anyone?"

"No, you didn't fight anyone. You didn't do a thing. You didn't lift a finger. You were locked up in a tower for ten years, taking your meals on a tray. What could you do? It wasn't your war. You didn't launch a thousand ships, they did. The war was never your fault. What you did, if you did anything, was believe in your own good looks. Well, you couldn't throw them away. Why would you want to?"

"Why was I a heroine? What made me a heroine?"

"For not hanging yourself. A weaker person would have hung herself, or thrown herself off the tower. For believing in yourself, you were a heroine. For sticking it out, for seeing it through. For not letting all the mess on the ground depress you, all those messed-up horses and soldiers and people so deadly serious about winning, but nobody serious about living. Not one person but you, serious about staying alive."

"Harry's serious about staying alive," said Helen softly. "Jordan is too. So are you, Joan."

Joan reached over the backseat. "I like you, Helen Walsh, Helen of Walsh. I like you, do you know that?"

In the early afternoon we passed through Purchase. It was one long street of houses leaning into a lake. The lake was dotted with motorboats, and people swimming and fishing and waterskiing and diving off rafts. Childs was the next town, then Fourth Lake, Redoubt and Deep River. We stopped for gas in Deep River, and Jordan got out to buy us each a ginger ale.

"I need licorice," said Joan. "See if they have black licorice, Jordie."

An old man pumped the gas while a young boy washed the windshield. The old man said, "If you roll up them windows he'll wash them too. Not many folks drive all the way out to this puny place in a taxi."

I couldn't take my eyes off the boy. He was a little older than Helen and I, about Harry's age. He was quick and muscular the way soldiers are, but he was too young to be a soldier, and his hair was too long. It was dark and straight, covering his ears on the sides and longer in the back. It was clean, as was everything about him. Even his white T-shirt was almost clean.

Helen was watching him too. He made his way around the taxi, taking his time with each window. I had never seen anyone, not even my mother, wash a window with such care, and I wanted to find the courage to tell him that. But as he approached my side I knew I never would, that I wouldn't know where to begin, and if I did find the words he would probably laugh at me, that's what I knew about boys. Though he seemed different. He was shy, even with a body that gave off confidence. When Joan asked him a simple question, he didn't respond, not out of any rudeness or lack of attention, but out of what seemed like shyness. He smiled at her and kept on working. When it was time for my window I decided I was relieved to have that wall of glass to roll between us. I pretended it was a one-way mirror, and I watched him unself-consciously.

Between Deep River and Angel's Landing the road became dirt and narrow, overgrown with banks of sumac and poison ivy. Every now and then it was possible to look down through the pines and see a lake. Angel's Landing was a solemn town with three churches, one jail and a school. There was a speed bump in front of the school and a flagpole in front of the jail. Each church had its own clock, and they each told a different time.

On the way out of town we passed a store with a sign that said SUNDRIES, and Joan asked, "Do we need anything? Do they serve food at our motel?"

"They used to serve breakfast," said Jordan.

"Breakfast! One bag of licorice between now and breakfast, that's an awful long time to wait. I'll get us some milk and a bag of bread and some salami and hard cheese and something sweet. What else?"

"Nothing with nuts in it," said Helen.

"A barrette if they have one," I said.

Joan went in and came out again carrying a bag of groceries. Helen had to squeeze closer to me to make room for it in the backseat. It was more comfortable if I put my arm around her shoulder, and as we started off again I whispered, "Is this okay?"

She nodded, but her eyes were glued to the floor of the taxi.

"What's the matter?"

She spelled out on my leg: I DON'T WANT TO GET THERE.

HOW LONG NOW?

5 MINUTES.

PRAY FOR FLAT TIRE.

NO!

NO?

BUS. REMEMBER?

BUS?

JFK.

I did remember. It seemed like years ago, and it hadn't even been one year. YES, I spelled back. NEVER FORGET.

"Helen, look," said Jordan suddenly. She pointed down through the trees. "There's Lake Will Hayes."

"There's people on it, Jordan."

"It's summertime," Joan reminded her.

"There never used to be anyone out here, even in the summer. They never came out the dirt road, they all stopped in Deep River."

There were, in fact, far fewer boats and people than we'd seen on the other lakes, even the smallest ones. This was where the road ended and the river began, and to travel this far to touch the water took an uncommon patience, a peculiar need for solitude. Many who came once never returned, but spent the next summer in the small, more accessible towns of Purchase or Redoubt. To live here through the winter, to call this home, I could not imagine. It was beautiful. From the moment I saw it I liked that lake. But it was not peaceful. It was too still, too untouched to be peaceful. I knew its stillness was not real, that it hid a secret—a boat? a man also? I had a strange desire to plunge into that lake, jump from the taxi and run down the road and throw myself in. And take what from it? A smooth stone? A handful of reeds? Some knowledge? A need for air? Oh Helen, I thought, this is where you lived, and the thought humbled me, and I looked at my friend with new eyes, unself-consciously, as I had the boy through the window.

Helen said, "Did you recognize him, Harry?"

The lake had disappeared again where the pines thickened. We could see the town of Cley ahead of us.

"Who do you mean?"

"At the gas station."

"The one who washed the windows, or the other one?"

"The one who washed the windows."

"I think I know."

"It was Frank Moss, wasn't it?"

"Yes," said Harry. "It was."

Jordan said, "I thought he looked familiar, that boy. He's quite a different boy without his brother."

"Where am I going?" asked Joan. "To the motel? To the lake? To your old house? Where?"

"To the lake," said Helen. "To the old house and the lake."

"You're sure that's where you want to go, sugar? First thing?"

"Yes."

"You're a brave child. Point the way."

The road divided, and we skirted town on the right fork. Cley was a small town, not much larger than Purchase. The houses were not as well kept up as they were in the other towns, and all the roofs were metal, a thing I'd never seen before. Helen's house was farther around the lake, one of the last houses on the road. We were all quiet in the car. I tried to think of something to ask or a way to ask all the things I wondered about, but nothing came.

Finally I said, "Who's Will Hayes?"

Joan said, "He's Bill Hayes's brother."

"Who's Bill Hayes?"

"He's related to Will."

"Come on, Joan. Who is he?"

"I don't know. He's just somebody, I guess. He got his name on a lake, that's all I know."

"By lying at the bottom of it," said Helen. "That's what

Wallace told us. You see that rock sticking out of the water?" She pointed, and I followed her arm about a quarter of a mile off the shore. "You can just see the top of it, and if the lake's high you can't even see that much. It's a big, flat rock, and no one can tell you why it's there. The lake's so deep it's black, and there shouldn't be a rock there, there shouldn't be anything there, but it's there. Will Hayes found it, and that's where he is, leaning up against it with his boots on at the bottom of the lake. He was fishing at night, right, Jordan?"

"I don't know this story."

"He was fishing at night a long time ago, when he was practically the only person who lived here, and he hit that rock and sank his boat and his boots filled up and he went right down to the bottom. Do you remember now?"

"No, I don't, Helen."

"But you believe me, right?"

"Of course I believe you."

"Wallace said he didn't do anything wrong, he didn't even know what happened. It was dark and the lake was high. I believe that he didn't do anything wrong, don't you, Jordan?"

"Who didn't, Helen?"

"The man. Will Hayes."

"I don't know Will Hayes, but it sounds like he didn't do anything wrong."

"There shouldn't have been a rock there."

"No, there shouldn't have."

"But there was."

"Yes, there was."

"If there wasn't, we'd still be living here, wouldn't we, Jordan? I wouldn't know Gussy and you wouldn't know Joan. Harry wouldn't be so skinny, he'd look more like

Frank Moss. Wallace would be driving the car too fast but we'd be used to it, and maybe you'd even be driving. I'd go to school in Deep River and Harry would go to the high school in Childs. We'd be different people, wouldn't we? Maybe I wouldn't have lupus. We'd be happy, wouldn't we? We'd all four of us be happy. I didn't think one thing could change so many things, did you ever think that, Jordan? I'd miss Gussy, but maybe I'd meet her somewhere later, when we were older. I'd miss Joan, I think. I'd miss school, I'd miss the cello. At the school in Deep River we'd never learn the cello. I miss it now. I wish I could play it again. I wish my hands didn't ache and the lupus would stop so I could play it. Sometimes I dream about it and it's a person and we're walking by the river, or we're walking by the lake, this lake, and we have our arms around each other and we're making noises that sound like singing. We go out in a boat and the oars look like long arms with hands at the end of them, and I'm rowing as hard as I can but the water's against us. I can't explain that part but sitting in the boat you can feel the bottom being pulled away, and then the sides melt down and the oars flop into the water like fish. But just before I wake up, the cello reaches out and holds me. I climb into it like a boat, like the little rowboat Wallace made for me, and I don't have to do a thing, it takes me back to the shore." Ahead of us the road turned sharply to the right. "Take a left here, Joan."

"Here where? This?"

A barely perceptible dirt track ran away from the main road, down towards the lake. It was grassy and flowered with disuse, and the simple bent heads of the black-eyed Susans and their soft brushing sound on the floor of the taxi as we drove over them reminded me of the airfield.

The track ended in a clearing, and beyond that lay the

lake. A small, unpainted house stood near the top of the clearing. It looked frail and temporary, its gray boards buckling from the frame. It stood on wooden posts—there was no cellar, and though it had once had a decent front porch, the front steps were rotted through and some of the porch boards as well. As Helen had promised me, the roof was made of layers of linoleum. The whole house was no larger than half my front yard on Flat Street.

Joan stopped the taxi, and Harry said, "How do we know the people won't come home?"

"We're the people," said Jordan. "Do you remember this house at all? You used to live here. We all lived here, you and me and Helen and Wallace."

"Not Joan."

"No, not Joan. We didn't know Joan then."

"It's just about falling down," said Helen. "It doesn't even look like a house."

"It's a house all right," said Joan, "though it may not be a home."

"It's just the way I remember it," said Jordan, "except it's a little more peaceful."

Across the lake we could make out the distant, blocky houses of Cley. By squinting I tried to make it a pretty town, but it wasn't. It was plain and boring. The lake was much larger than I had first thought, its deep water cuffed with whitecaps. Cley and Helen's house were at one end of it, and from there it stretched northward for several miles, the far side hidden by an irregular shoreline.

"I'm not staying here," said Harry, "I'm staying at the motel."

"We're all staying at the motel," said Joan.

"I'm not getting out."

"You don't have to, sweetheart. You can stay right here and fiddle with the radio."

She switched it on, and it buzzed with static. She pushed through the stations, finally settling for the ominous noise of an organ, overlaid with a preacher's drawl.

"That's New Chaldea," said Helen, "the religious station."

"I can tell that, sugar."

"The organ sounds like a sick cow," said Jordan. "Harry? What on earth is the matter?"

He was clutching his head and rocking from side to side, whimpering like a puppy. He kicked at the radio, and Joan turned it off. He wormed around until he was kneeling facing us. His short hair grazed the roof of the taxi, and his hands gripped the back of the seat. His face was ashen, and in it his eyes were bright, almost black, the tears streaming from them. "I knew it would happen," he sobbed. "I hated that boat, Helen. He yelled at me in the car. He yelled at me in the boat. I hated that boat. I couldn't find the right music. I was under the table and I couldn't watch. I was embarrassed."

"You were fine. I won a prize."

"What are you talking about?" asked Jordan. "Helen, what's he talking about?"

"He's talking about nothing. He's talking about the night before the accident, something that happened that made Wallace mad."

"Well, what is it?"

"I can't tell you, Jordan. Don't make me tell you. It doesn't matter. It was nothing. The next morning he took Harry out in the boat. You were gone somewhere. You took the car somewhere."

"To Polk's."

"To Polk's to get something."

"Milk."

"To get milk. You were gone and I wasn't even awake and Wallace made Harry go with him in the boat. I should have gone with him."

"No one should have gone with him."

"No one should have gone with him but especially not Harry."

"Especially not anyone. In a mood like that he shouldn't have gone."

"He went, didn't he?" Helen said fiercely. She dropped her head. "I hated that boat, too."

"We all hated it, Helen."

"Not the dinghy," said Harry. "Wallace had a dinghy."

"No, the big boat," said Helen.

"How big was it?" I asked.

"I don't know, big. The outboard was even bigger. It put the boat right out of balance so it was hard to steer and hard to slow down. It was the wrong motor for that boat. Everyone told him that, even the man who sold it to him. He got the motor and then we didn't have any money, so he got a cheap boat to put it on, right, Jordan?"

"Why couldn't he put the motor on the dinghy?" I asked.

"Because he sold the dinghy to get the motor."

"He never did think beyond the end of his nose," said Joan.

"You knew him?" I asked.

"You mean met him? I never met him. But I live with him every day, and you do too, Gus. People don't disappear, even if they're gone, you know that."

I did know that. I had known it most of my life.

Helen said suddenly, "That stupid, crippled car broke down and you never came home from Polk's! I woke up looking for you, Jordan. I went down to the lake and stood right there, right where Wallace always pulled up the boat. I looked out and there they were. I was still in my pajamas. He was driving fast, and Harry was up in the front hunched over, scared. He hated the front. I waved. Why did I wave? I don't know why but I did, and Wallace saw me and waved back and turned the boat without thinking or looking or listening to Harry, who shouted, and the boat hit the rock and flipped up and went crazy. The people fell out and the boat fell on top of them. I looked for you, Jordan, I looked for the car and you in it and somebody to tell me what to do. I don't know what happened after that except, and I never told anyone this, when I got in my little rowboat, the one he made for me, and I rowed out there to the rock and the boat and the people, the boat was almost underwater and the two people looked asleep in their life jackets with their faces in the water, and there were two of them not moving and I could only take one. My boat was so small, and I was only a little girl, and I could take one and it was Harry or Wallace. Not just two people. Harry or Wallace. I took him. His head was split open and I got in the water with him and pushed him to the boat and got in the boat and pulled him back to shore. Then you came, Jordan, and the other people did too, and they got Wallace, and the boat sank. Then we didn't live here anymore, and Harry went away to sleep in a crib and learn to knit. Wallace died, Gussy."

"I know that, Helen."

"He died out there in the water, right out there. He drowned."

Jordan said, "Helen," and started to cry. "Oh my little girl. Oh my Helen." They reached for each other and touched foreheads, and Jordan said, "He was dead when you got to him. He was already dead. He was hit by the boat. It came down right on top of him and he died. You made the right choice. You took Harry. If you'd taken Wallace he never would have woken up, and Harry would have drowned, and now we wouldn't have either one of them. We have our boy, Helen. Because of you we have him." She kissed her on the cheek. Harry leaned into his mother, and she kissed him on the shoulder.

Helen flopped back against the seat, and we all sat looking out the windows and the windshield Frank Moss had washed.

"I'm going for a walk," said Jordan.

"I'm not," said Harry.

Joan said, "You've been walking all summer, Jordie. Sit still a minute. Let him be here too, old Wallace. It's his place, too."

"I forget that," said Jordan. "I forget he loved it here. He loved the water, he loved the woods. Even this dear old shack of a house."

"That's right," said Joan. "Give him a home."

"He planted a garden one summer. Do you remember that, Helen?"

"No. I remember a tree he planted. It was some kind of fruit tree but it never had fruit."

"It was a plum tree," said Harry.

"It still is," I said, and pointed to the closest corner of the house. It wasn't much of a tree, but it was loaded down with green plums. The trunk was no thicker than my arm.

"Look at it," said Jordan. "I can't believe it made it. Isn't it something?"

"It's more than something," said Joan. "It's a living, thriving thing with a load to unload. Not yet. Those plums are nowhere near ripe yet, but we'll come back, won't we?" She looked at all of us, one by one.

It was late in the afternoon and already cooler than a summer night on Flat Street, but the light was still flat and white, with not one hint of the liquid, tarnished light of long summer evenings. We staggered from the taxi, eager to stretch our legs, our cramped muscles. Joan and Jordan went directly to the plum tree. Helen and I played a brief, spontaneous game of tag in the tall, itchy grass of the clearing. It was childlike and comforting at first, fueled by the pent-up energy of emotion and that long drive. Then we felt ourselves becoming more self-conscious, and though it saddened us, there was no choice but to stop and stand apart and say something neutral or disingenuous to dispel the attention we'd drawn to each other in our brief flight backwards.